Long Point/Wood End Lighthouse, Provincetown MA
(with Fillan's imaginary beach cabin)

Cover art: LK Hunsaker

Elucidate Publishing
PO Box 1262
Hermitage PA 16148

United States of America

Pieces of Light

Ella M. Kaye

~ One ~

Fillan tried to put his mind off the girl and think only about the trail he was hiking, but thoughts of Ireland streamed back into his soul as he looked out over the fauna of Cape Cod. And however he tried, the girl's face kept creeping back into the forefront. Had she come home yet? Had she bothered to notice he was away? He had left Ireland without word to her. It was fair, Fillan told himself, since she left him first. Months ago. She needed *something new* and time *to figure herself out*, she told him, with luggage in hand as she walked out his door. How he hated that phrase. Fillan knew he'd rolled his eyes when she said it, which helped nothing at all, of course, but he hated that phrase.

Time to figure yourself out. What was that, anyway? You were who you were, were you not? What was to figure out? How insipid did you have to be to not know, toward your mid twenties, who in the hell you were yet? Or at least think you knew. What twenty-something didn't think he had himself, or herself, all figured out?

An excuse, of course. She could have simply come straight out and said, "Fillan, you are boring me to tears and I have to leave you now." He could respect that.

Turning the corner of the wood plank raised path out along the Cape, he got a nice glimpse of the Atlantic through the trees and other fauna, and paused, leaning his forearms on the weathered-wood railing, and watched seagulls dip and rise and make all kinds of racket. Noisy, raucous birds. He liked them about as much as he liked the *figure yourself out* phrase. Scavengers. Bullies, of sorts. He liked small quieter birds. He especially liked ducks. Fillan had no particular reason for his duck interest, other than because they were water creatures, but also air creatures. He liked the mix. And they were calm, peaceful.

Fillan liked calm. It was boring, he supposed, to be so infatuated with calm and quiet. She was right, whether or not she had said outright he was boring. The hint was there. Far more than a hint was her objection to his work.

"Get a real job, Fillan, would you now? What kind of a job is teaching outdated dances to elderly women who are there only to enjoy cozying up to braw young men who are paid to be nice to them? 'Tis a boy's job," she'd said. "Get a man's job. It would be right good for you."

With a sigh and rolled eyes – and why not, since she couldn't see it – he continued his walk-jog along the boardwalk. This path was less busy than many he had taken since arriving in Massachusetts only a couple of weeks earlier. It was nice, he supposed, to see so many outside in the fresh air using the plentiful paths along or near to the coast. Still, when he'd thought of coming to this little point on the very top edge of what was nearly an island, Fillan hadn't expected so many people to be swarming. It didn't bother him, necessarily, but he had come to clear his head. And then again, maybe the mix of people in crowds would give him enough varied perspective to see things differently.

Maybe later he would go into the heart of Provincetown and wander the sidewalks and pay more attention to the vibrant mix of Americans crowding the place. He could stop into some of the shops, as well, to see what he could find that was not too touristy but reminiscent of Cape Cod to take back to his family at the end of the summer when real life would continue, when he'd have to make the choice to contact her again or not, to continue his "boy's job" or change his path. Granted, his dancing didn't pay well. It had taken him forever to earn plane fare to the States to jump on the opportunity to teach under a work exchange program. It was a vacation, by all rights, but he was still teaching, only American old ladies instead of Irish old ladies.

Well, but they weren't so much old. Many younger women were coming to ballroom dance recently. That show on the telly, Fillan supposed. He hadn't watched it. The idea of making a contest show out of ballroom dancing and hyping it up with lights and cheering and all sorts of flashing and colorful noise annoyed him. Fillan bet those dancers made good money, though, with their for-television "boy job," but then, they were getting hand-picked celebrity students, not regular people who sometimes didn't know their right foot from their left.

If it was bringing people into ballroom again, though, it couldn't be all bad. It wasn't like he would be fool enough to turn it down himself if it was offered. Fillan supposed the girl would change her tune quick as anything if he was teaching on telly rather than in a small studio. What would it take to be a well-paid pro? Not that it mattered in the slightest since he was only in the States for the two and nearly three months of his work exchange.

He would return at some point, as vacation only, so he could travel farther into the country rather than being held on its outskirts where the first of the colonists had landed. It was a good place to begin, to start again, so he told himself.

If he wanted to start again, that was. Maybe he did not. Maybe all he needed was the impetus to remain on his own path, in his own way, whatever the girl said, whatever his father said. Why should he not? Unlike the girl, he knew right well who he was and what he wanted. She could deal with him or she couldn't.

With a shrug, and a brush at a little flying creature to push it from his face – how did Americans deal with the billions of little pests without going crazy? – Fillan increased his fast walk, turning it into a full jog. She could deal with him, though, if he would only get a real job and step up only a rung or two more into adulthood. So she said. The thing was, he was happy with himself as he was. He was less happy since she had left him. There was truth to it, and she knew he would be sorry to not see her each night. He was sorry. He missed her plenty well. Still, would having her make up for the changes he would have to make to have her?

Could be it would.

How did he figure it out without trying it? If he tried it, how could he go back again if it didn't?

~ *Two* ~

"Alright, settle down." Emma barked it out in order to be heard over the group of fifth graders who spent more time watching the clock to see when they'd be able to escape than actually working on their projects. She'd expected the activity would be engaging, sculpting figures and objects to create a scene that depicted their lesson on the Revolutionary War rather than simply reading about it, or being lectured. Emma tried the hands on approach as often as possible so they were fully involved.

It often didn't work that way. Twice already, she had to confiscate a piece of clay that had been turned into something very inappropriate for a classroom and smash it back into a lump to tell the student to try again and to behave. One warning. She always gave them one warning to straighten up without repercussion. One was enough at this age. For most kids, it was.

Trying hard not to sigh at the newest "character" made by the one kid for whom all the warnings in the world did no good, Emma gave up. "Okay, put it away. We'll do it through a lecture instead." Ignoring the groans and objections and laughter, she repeated herself, louder, until the noise dwindled into the thuds of clay returning to the box and shoes scuffing back to their desks. She agreed to leave what was already made alone for those who had thrown themselves into the project.

One of the boys was still working, though, and Emma watched him add detail to a wall he'd built, a nice representation of a stone wall. An artistic boy. He was always doodling on the side of his notes. Walking over to him so she didn't have to call him out in front of the class, Emma told him it was nice and he could keep working on it through the lecture if he liked.

A timid grin and a nod answered and one of the girls asked if she could, too. The girl who was always at his side, always doing the talking for them both.

"If you stay quiet and don't interrupt me while I'm talking."

Finally, she got a brief break in the form of lunch hour. Emma supposed her students might not appreciate the fact that she often wanted out of the classroom every bit as much as they did. Sometimes more, so she expected.

A sad realization, since she'd been so excited when she graduated and got her teaching certificate and more so when she got her first job. Emma still loved the actual work of it. She loved trying to help young minds see things in new ways, and she loved trying to come up with creative ways to keep them engaged.

That, though, was becoming harder every year. The only time most of them seemed at all engaged was before the first bell and after the last bell when their heads were in their phones, or their friends' phones for those who didn't have them. She'd had thoughts of gathering their numbers and texting their lessons. Of course, that wasn't an option, and they'd just delete it and move along.

And it was hard to criticize them for it when, as she walked into the teachers' lounge, most of her colleagues were on their phones as they ate, as were their parents while they waited to pick them up after school.

While she waited for her leftover pasta to heat up, Emma perused the flyer board for any pertinent information she'd yet to see. A different one caught her eye. Ballroom dance classes. No partner needed. Could she get the school to pay for the classes if she turned around and taught it to her fifth graders? She supposed not since she wasn't a PE teacher. And how many fifth graders would want to learn ballroom dance? Most were too hooked to their booty shaking vulgar lyric stuff she'd never allow, not at that age. Ballroom dance would be good for them. For posture. For grace. Health. She needed it for her own health, for her stamina. And maybe to help with her patience level that was dropping by the day.

The thought of doing it just for herself pulled at Emma, even if Mark had laughed at her once and said she was too entirely uncoordinated for dance. She didn't think she was. His opinion no longer mattered. And the idea of having something of her own other than work for a change pulled at her hard. Why shouldn't she? If she could arrange for someone to watch Patty that long...

With a sigh, Emma expected the fight of that would make it not worth the hassle.

Still, she thought about it through the rest of the day, through ten- to twelve-year-olds giggling when they were supposed to be studying together, through drumming lessons into their heads while knowing they'd forget most of it during summer break.

It was nearly summer break, thankfully. Emma should be able to insist on time off for herself at least twice a week just for the summer while Patty was at her therapy center. Much of that time, Emma would be teaching summer classes and tutoring, but if she took on fewer tutoring students and convince her brother to pick Patty up twice a week to take her back to their parent's house, she could fit it in. He made his own hours as a financial consultant. He could do that much.

When the final bell rang, Emma sighed a huge inaudible breath of relief and told them all to have a good night and to study... Her voice trailed off. She'd lost them. They wouldn't hear if it she said it, so she didn't bother.

Could she choose which ballroom dances she wanted to learn? Maybe not the Latin dances. She would love to learn them, but she didn't want to get stuck doing sensual dances with some stranger who also ended up there without a partner, especially if she got stuck with another woman, which she figured was entirely possible. How many men went to ballroom classes on their own? And of those who would, how many would she want to Latin dance with? A light shudder ran through her system. Maybe she'd get a video instead and teach herself on nights she didn't have Patty. That would be hard to do without any partner, though.

Nearly to the exit door, Emma grimaced at the ring of her phone. She knew without checking that it was Mark, and there was no way she could find the patience today to talk to him, so she let it go to voicemail. It would make him more crabby when he did finally reach her, but Emma just could not care any bit less at the moment. Her divorce said she did not have to care, and everything was final, had been final for months, so she did not have to speak to him, either.

Her jaw gritted enough it started to make her teeth hurt, and

Emma told herself she had to find a way to unwind. Turning back, she went to the break room to write down the phone number and address of the dance school. Maybe she would. Maybe she'd even do the sexy Latin dances with some hot single guy and... No, there would be no point in that. Her hands were far too full already.

~ Three ~

Fillan tried hard not to roll his eyes at the woman. Did she honestly have that much trouble following directions? Was it that hard to understand slow, slow, quick, quick, rock left turn? He swore some of them acted stupid just for the extra attention. Ten minutes of class left. He generally was in no hurry to leave for the day, to figure out what to do with the rest of his day. He was off kilter for some unknown reason.

"Once more and then by yourself." Fillan repeated the steps as he showed them to his class. His part of the class. The guy in charge didn't like him much, he had to figure, since he got most of the complainers. Or so it seemed. Or maybe he was too sensitive to being the outsider or the new guy. Cheney joked about it often enough, and made fun of his accent often enough. Otherwise, it tended to get him some nice attention when he was out and about and most of the women in his class liked it just fine. Fillan wasn't built the way Cheney was, with his four extra inches of height and thin dancer's figure, and he hadn't been teaching there for years. Right. He understood both. And yet, he had come across the ocean for the job, and he had different techniques and a more natural flow that Cheney did not have.

There was also the fact that Fillan liked women and they could very well see it. His girl had said more than once that he liked women far too much. Could be true; Fillan knew she could very well be right. Still, he treated them well and he'd told her as much.

"Aye, well, ye call it, do you? Ye let them right walk all over you, is my definition."

He'd argued, to no avail. Fillan could never win an argument with the girl. Could be that was proof enough she was right.

Pulling himself back into where he was, he raised an eyebrow at the woman in front, a leader-type, always in front, but with no coordination to speak of. "Your other left foot, hon." He tried to make a joke of it.

"I get all confused when you face us because I'm doing what you're doing and that foot is the one you're using."

"Yes, the male part is opposite the female part, as it must needs be so we do not step on each others' toes. Right?"

"But I'm following you to learn the steps."

"Right, then." He turned to do the steps the same way she was supposed to be doing them, as the way he called them out. The mirrors told him it wasn't his feet she was watching.

The mirrors also threw the reflection of a woman walking in the door, a young woman, compared to most of his students. She looked unsure, hesitant. Could be she was looking for aerobics or yoga and needed directions to the right classroom.

Cheney told his class to carry on and went to see what she needed. After a minute of discussion, he brought her in and motioned for her to have a seat on a chair against the wall. Any time Fillan glanced over, the girl was watching the class with interest, her eyes following the steps of the Foxtrot.

"Join us, if you like." Cheney gave her a smile and waved her over to his group. And of course he would put the girl in his own group. She was built like a dancer, young, as in nearly Fillan's age of twenty-five, as he guessed, dressed in a long thin skirt and thin tee with barely any sleeves to it. She shook her head at his offer and her light brown hair swayed gently across her shoulders, but she gave in when he encouraged her and took a spot at the back of the group, Cheney's group, which was meant to be for the more advanced...

"I think we lost his attention. Hey Fillan, we're still here." The leader woman, a fifty-some year old who flirted with him at least once per class, laughed and traded grins with another, her cohort, the one who always thought she was funnier than she was.

He made himself focus on the Foxtrot, on his group, while hoping the new girl wouldn't notice she'd had too much of his attention. If she joined, she would be added to Cheney's group. Fillan had no doubt of it. That was a good thing, perhaps, considering she had too much of his own attention already.

Emma felt like an intruder. They'd already started, had already learned the basic Foxtrot steps and had been working at it. Jumping in like that when she'd only stopped to ask about lessons threw her off, or she really was as uncoordinated as Mark said.

The man who came over to welcome her said she was doing fine, just to pick up what she could for now and not worry. Easy for him to say since he was a pro. She saw the glances, not only from the group he'd put her in, but from the group next to them. Had she done something out of bounds? She shouldn't have come. A stupid idea, really, just to stop on the way home and decide to ask, last minute, spur of the moment, what it entailed so she could think about it more over the weekend.

Emma was glad it was Friday, although too often she wasn't. Even working most of the day, she was more free on weekdays than on weekends when she had her niece full time, which would too soon be all week instead. Emma's parents had Patty on weekday mornings and took her to her center after lunch, and then Robert, her brother, picked her up from the center to have dinner with his family and took her back home an hour before bedtime. Emma had her on weekends.

That would soon change. Her parents were having too much trouble handling both Patty and her mother, and Emma and Robert agreed it was too much at their ages. Helen, their middle child, was now a full time job. Her liver was shutting down. She was frail. And she refused to try to find a donor for a transplant, said she had no strength for it and someone else should have it.

Robert had three children already, a full house. Emma had a room for Patty already set up. Automatically, that meant Patty would soon be hers nearly full time, which meant what time she had to herself would soon be nearly non-existent.

Emma blushed at the thought. She shouldn't let herself think about it. She really shouldn't. She had no energy to get down. It was what it was and there was no point letting herself wish things were different.

But this, the Foxtrot, was actually kind of fun. More than kind of fun. She was picking it up, just the basic steps, nothing to make it look like more than putting the slow, slow, quick, quick steps in the right places at the right time, but at least she was doing that already. Emma could easily see herself doing this twice a week.

Maybe she would. She could make it work. She was used to making things work no matter what happened around her. At least this was for her, not for anyone else.

Some of the other students talked to her after class ended, told her she should come back, that it was nice to see younger folks learning how to dance real instead of … well, she wouldn't repeat what a couple of them said even to herself. She expected it by now. Older women, middle aged, often were quite outspoken. She could even see herself getting more that way over time. Not that she didn't already speak out when she needed. More than once that got her in trouble in the current atmosphere of "always be nice and never scold, ever, no matter what" that was far too carried away for her own taste.

When they did games of any kind in her classroom, they had winners and losers. Emma believed in that. It was part of life. Sometimes you won, and sometimes you didn't, and you had to know how to get over it and move on when you didn't and how to be a good sport when you did. She knew darn well about that lesson and she was glad she'd had enough experience with it throughout childhood to be able to deal with it when it mattered more. How else would she have been able to deal with Mark walking out on her when she most needed him? Emma wanted her students to be prepared, also, for real life. But she had to do it carefully.

With a sigh, she pushed work right back out of her thoughts and answered the basic questions from the others in the class: what did she do for a living, was she married… and she skirted around the children question by changing the subject and asking how long they'd all been going to class.

As she headed toward the door and agreed to check her schedule and see if she could make room for a couple of classes a week, Emma found herself suddenly eye to eye with the other instructor, the younger one, with the accent. She got caught up for a moment in his curly blond hair that he'd slicked back somewhat, to tame the curls, she supposed, his hazel eyes, the round face, and the friendly smile.

He offered a hand. "Fillan Reilly. I am new here. Have you come before?"

"No. I'm ... Emma Turner. Nice to meet you."

"So we are both new then."

"You don't look new." Emma shook her head. Stupid thing to say. "I mean, you don't look new to teaching."

"I have been teaching for years already, only not here. My fault. I was not clear. Are ye signing up, then?"

"I think so."

"Then I will see ye on Monday. Enjoy your weekend." With a nod and a touch of a grin, he grabbed a bag beside the door and walked out.

Monday. Emma hadn't planned on Mondays. She would have to rearrange some things, move one of her tutoring students to another night or later in the evening. Or she should not sign up. Another complication was the last thing in the world she needed right now.

Still, she was doing this for herself, for the enjoyment of it. She could make it work.

~ Four ~

Not good, Fillan. Very much not good. You are there to teach and no more. No fraternizing.

He'd made himself walk away from her. He had done that much. His first thought was to ring the girl and tell her he had walked away from a beautiful woman interested in ballroom dance without a hint of flirting. Except she had asked him, made him promise, not to call until he heard from her first. And telling her he had wanted to flirt with a beautiful woman interested in ballroom wouldn't be wise. He had learned that much. He was capable of learning.

Push it aside, Fillan. You don't even know where she is. And do you even want to know anymore? Why should you want to know? It was her choice to be anywhere else.

The girl with the light brown hair – wasn't that an American song? – could make him stop wondering where she was perhaps. Perhaps not. And not if she was a student. Although she wasn't his student, he expected. What were the rules as far as fraternizing? He'd never bothered with the thought. He was there to clear his head, not to get entangled.

Not to mention he was only there for the summer. No love connections. *Love.* He laughed at himself. A possible look that could possibly be of maybe a wee bit of possible interest did not infer a possible love connection. *Get a grip on yourself, Fillan.*

Closing his car door behind him, he considered what he would do with his night. A local pub? Find someone to talk with who would understand him? He was unsure why some Americans found it so hard to understand his accent while others understood quite well enough. Or they acted as if they did. Maybe they didn't, to be honest. Maybe much of it was the same as when he had trouble hearing anyone who spoke far too softly and acted as if he heard them so as not to have to ask for repetition thirty times in a conversation. He hated to have to ask for repetition. And generally, he didn't care anywhere near enough to bother.

He didn't particularly want to go to a pub unless he could find one a wee bit more quiet than he'd found so far. Some nights, the noise was good with him, distracting, interesting even. Being as off as he was today, however, Fillan did not want loud. Were there such things as quiet pubs on Cape Cad? He guessed there must be. He had no small interest in hopping to them all to find one, though.

In another week, after the girl with light brown hair, Emma, she had called herself, had been to a couple of classes, maybe he would ask if she knew of one. Of course it would sound as if he was hitting on her, but then if he meant it innocent and could claim it was innocent, he would have both legs to stand on if something came of it.

Why then, she might ask, didn't he ask one of the men instead? That would be a good question, Fillan, and how would you answer?

Aye well, if she were to ask, it would mean she was too wary of him to invite her to go with him or to meet him there, and otherwise, could be she would take it as being hit on and try to take him up on it. Could get himself in a right mess asking her, but it would hardly be the first time he'd gotten himself into a mess. He was good at it. And he was getting better all the time at getting out of it with not a horrible amount of trouble. That was something he might want to learn to do better, since he saw no promise of not getting himself into messes in the first place. He could put it down as more practice before he went back home.

The first thing Emma did when she walked in her door was to take off her shoes. The second thing she did was to turn on her stereo to practice the steps she'd just learned. Friday. Her free night. In the morning, she would go pick Patty up. Tonight, she had no students to tutor and no plans other than taking a long hot bath and then vegging out with whatever old movie she could find, a big bowl of chips and her homemade spinach dip in her lap, and then shutting it all down to read in bed and sleep through the night, with any luck.

When she signed up, she said they would put her in the class with the beginners, which meant in Fillan Reilly's side of the room, and her heart jumped at the thought. At least it did until Cheney, the one who had come over to greet her first, overheard and assured them Emma could keep up with his students just fine, so they moved her.

It was probably just as well.

Slow, slow, quick, quick, rock, left, turn...

Not so hard, even to Bob Seger's *Against the Wind* instead of whatever music they'd been using, something without lyrics. Bob Seger was Emma's go-to for unwinding music. She had everything he'd ever recorded.

About jumping out of her skin when her phone rang, Emma sighed and turned her music down before she answered.

"You need to come pick Patty up."

Emma rolled her eyes at her brother's way of beginning a conversation. "Hello to you, too. And it's still your day, Rob. I'll be there in the morning. I just got home."

"She's refusing to come with me. She's been out of control since I picked her up from school and I hardly got her back to Mom's. None of us can get through to her. Helen is in tears because Patty won't even speak to her. I need you, Em."

A long, deep breath took hold and Emma shook her head, but of course she told Rob she'd be right over. Maybe she could calm Patty and get her to bed early. She wanted some time to herself before bed.

Emma took the time to change into more comfortable clothes, even if she maybe shouldn't have, and she grabbed a chocolate bar from the cabinet to hold her until she could eat. On the way, she knew she'd have to pick her niece up and take her home with her. With most kids, you could just tell them I'll be back in the morning to pick you up, but Patty didn't grasp the time concept. If Emma walked out, Patty wouldn't know if she'd be gone for the night or for several nights. Emma would have to take her home.

Walking up to the door, she heard her niece yelling, well, screaming, and tried not to see the neighbor in the next yard staring at the house with a hand on her hip.

"Thank goodness. Maybe you can make her stop." The woman called over top of the hedges between the yards. "She's been yelling like that for half an hour. I come out to work in my yard for relaxation, not to hear that. Third time this week. Something needs to be done.”

“Get some earplugs.” Emma didn’t care how rude it sounded. She went up and walked in without bothering to knock and found Patty in the middle of the living room floor kicking her heels, her hands over her ears and eyes on her feet, screaming. Rob was nearby waiting it out. Helen was in front of her daughter trying to talk over her, trying to take her hands down.

“Helen.” Emma went to interfere. “*Stop* touching her.”

“She’s my daughter. Don’t...”

“She *doesn’t* like it. Move back. Patty. Hey, it’s okay.” Pushing between Helen and Patty, Emma ducked her head so her niece could see her, but she kept her hands to herself. “Look at me, sweetie. Look. I’m here. It’s okay. You’re fine. Tell me what’s wrong.”

“She doesn’t talk. You know she doesn’t talk.” Helen tried to move in again.

“Please, go to bed. You’re too tired to deal with it. Go ahead. I got it.” With a glance at Rob as a sign to get their sister out of the way, Emma took a deep breath and started counting slowly. By the time she got to twenty, Patty had lowered her voice. At thirty, she’d switched from occasional groans instead. At forty, she was silent. Emma kept going to fifty and slowed at the end.

Silence.

“I tried that. Robby tried it. Why doesn’t it work for us?”

Emma looked up at her mom who was nearly in tears. “I don’t know. It’s okay.”

“I can’t handle her anymore. Your father hasn’t been well this week and I’ve tried to take care of him, but she...”

“Not well?” Emma looked at her father.

“Only a spring cold. Nothing to bother about. You’re doing fine.” He rubbed his wife’s hand. “Don’t worry yourself.”

Rob came back in and gave Emma a look. They both knew. It was time to take Patty out of there. It was too much for them. “Okay.” Resignation surged through her system. “Sweetie.” She lowered her face again, trying to catch Patty’s eyes. “It’s okay. Do you want to come home with me tonight?”

The girl jumped up fast, knocking her head into Emma’s nose.

Ignoring the pain, she followed Patty to her room where the girl grabbed her overnight bag and ran back out to the door.

"Don't open that door." Emma nearly panicked at the thought of her running outside by herself, but Patty stopped at the door and stared at it.

"Sorry. Hope you didn't have a date tonight."

She rolled her eyes at her brother. "You're kidding, right?"

"I've tried to leave your Friday nights free, Em, so you can if you want."

"For what purpose? We both know…" She looked at her niece and shrugged. "I'll call her school and let them know she's staying with me now."

"She has to be with her mother while she still can be." Her mom came to her. "Emma, Helen needs her so. It's the only bit of happiness she still has."

"I know. I'll pick her up from school and bring her over for an hour or so."

"An hour a day? That's not enough for Helen."

"Mom, I'm sorry, but it upsets her. Her mother upsets her. She's smart and she knows what's going on. That's why she's getting worse. We have to think of her needs first."

"But…"

"Helen's giving me custody of her daughter because she knows I'll put her first. And I will. Helen … made her choices, and I'm sorry, but Patty comes first." With a kiss to her mom's head and a quick hug for her dad, Emma told Rob they'd have to work out different arrangements, that maybe he could do weekend days for her… "Oh. I um… can you do Monday and Friday pickups? Just for an hour? I'll come get her from your place…"

"For your tutoring sessions?"

Tutoring. Hell, Emma had forgotten that. She had kids coming after school Monday through Thursday. They couldn't come with Patty there. "Okay, can you make that three hours Monday and Friday? I'll have to rearrange some things."

"Something else you have going on?"

"Yes, but, I may have to cancel…" A huge pit hit her gut. Emma did not want to give up dance already.

"How about I take Monday and Friday night, and Saturdays, and you take the rest? I don't want you to have no life of your own, Em. That gives you nearly half a weekend."

Half a weekend. She nodded. It would have to work.

~ *Five* ~

Emma greeted the few women she remembered from Friday. She nearly hadn't come after the long weekend with Patty walking circles around her couch much of the time as she wound down from her episode Friday night and waking up several times each night, and then her Saturday tutoring students being far more focused on end of the year events than on preparing for their finals at the end of the week.

And, it had been a heck of a struggle to get Patty to go in when Emma drove her to her school, which was more a therapy center, but they preferred to be called school. Emma didn't care what they called it. She was so very grateful to the young ABA tutor who'd come to help her niece settle down and get her to her classroom. Then they told her that once she was Patty's legal guardian, new forms would have to be filled out and she'd have to see if her insurance would cover the care and it may not...

Emma would think about that later. For now, she had an hour to do what she wanted, for herself, not for bills or for her family, just for herself. Cheney greeted everyone, told Emma he was glad to see she'd come back, and pulled her up to the front to put in between two more advanced students she could watch to help her catch up. She didn't want to be in front. She wanted to be in back and have more space to mess up with less attention, farther away from the other instructor who'd caught her eyes and given her a friendly nod.

It was too hard to concentrate between being so tired and feeling guilty about dumping Patty on her brother after school since the girl had been so upset before school, and Emma got frustrated too fast. Cheney was pandering to her and she hated being pandered to, so it only made everything worse.

She told herself not to feel guilty. It was Rob's turn and he could deal with it. She'd already given up far more than he had to help with their sister's child. And Patty adored him, for some odd reason Emma couldn't understand. Maybe she could. She used to adore her big brother back before things became such a huge mess. She hoped she could someday again, when things settled.

Not that she saw them being settled for some time, if ever. Chances were good things would never feel settled. Patty would likely be a never-ending project since she was showing little sign of improvement and she was eleven already.

Emma derided herself for the thought. That sweet little girl was not a project. She was ... a sweet little girl, although not too actually little anymore. It had been easier when she was still small enough to pick up and carry around or move when she needed to be moved. Now that she was nearly as tall as Emma, and strong, it was a whole different ball game.

Still, Emma adored the girl. She was a sweet girl. She only needed someone who understood, or at least tried to understand. And Emma did try. She'd been studying, researching, searching for any way to try to help her function better. Patty's main ABA tutor had given her plenty of pointers, much of which worked, some of which didn't, or didn't yet. They said to give it time, it took time to reshape learned behaviors. Much of the problem was that her parents would not do things the way Emma told them they needed to be done, so Patty had different rules in different houses, and that was just not working.

Rob blamed Patty's mother for her brain differences. He said it was the chemicals in her system when Patty was conceived and likely after that, as well. Maybe he was right, although nothing she found said he was, but it didn't matter by now. What mattered was that their sister could no longer even care for herself, much less for her daughter, and it was coming to the point where her parents wouldn't be able to care for Helen, either.

Emma tried, again, to push the thought away that she might have to take her sister in as well as her sister's child. Why not, her brother said? She lived alone now, in a three bedroom house. It made the most sense. Except Emma had to work and she didn't want to bring a caregiver into her home to invade what privacy she did still have. She'd already given up her marriage. How much more should she have to give up?

But she couldn't concentrate. Too much fatigue, too much frustration. Exercise was supposed to ease frustration, but it was doing the opposite since she'd been stuck in the front of the class and Cheney kept talking down to her like she was a child, and that was the last thing she needed.

So she walked out. Maybe she'd go walk along the shore for an hour before her first student of the afternoon came over. He was the most reluctant of her tutoring kids and his mother stayed because she was worried about "talk" in reference to leaving a ten-year-old boy with an adult female teacher, especially a divorced female teacher. Sadly, Emma understood well enough. Better to have the woman stay, even while she had her head stuck in her phone and chuckled at whatever she watched with earphones, distracting them both...

"Wait up. It is Emma, right?"

In the hallway, she turned to find the other instructor at the classroom door. "Yes. Sorry if I disrupted things."

"You are not enjoying the class?" He let the door close and moved slowly closer.

"I'm... It wasn't a good day to try. I can't follow well enough..."

"You have had ballroom experience?"

"No."

"Why did they not put ye over on my side, then?" His head tilted slightly, accentuating his beautiful soft lilting accent. "Cheney teaches the more advanced students. I most often have the beginners."

"They did, or they started to, but he overheard and said I could follow well enough, but I can't, really, and it's too stressful, right up front, and I just can't right now."

His eyes rolled. "I am sorry he put you in that spot. If ye come back in, ye can come on over to my group and stay all the way in the back, if ye would like."

Fillan could see her debating. "You have paid already for the month, am I right?"

"Yes, but..."

"It would be a shame not to give it another try then. I promise I will be gentle with you." He grinned and her shoulders softened, so he risked offering a hand. "Come and try again, Emma. You looked to be enjoying it on Friday."

"Yes, but..."

"You are doing this for yourself or to try to impress some bloke at a wedding you have to attend?"

"Oh, no, just because. I've ... been told I'm uncoordinated, but I think I'm not..."

"Absolutely, you are not, but it does no good for me to tell you as much. You will have to come in and find out for yourself."

Her chest rose and fell in a large sigh and she moved toward him. "Okay. If you won't call me to the front."

"You can put yourself anywhere you like and only do as much as you want. It is up to you, Emma, since you are paying me to teach you." Fillan wasn't sure what the look she gave him meant, but she did follow him back into class. He saw Cheney's look, as well, and understood it, but he didn't care at all. Casually, he motioned Emma to join his group and went back to the front to apologize and to thank the student who stepped up to lead for a few minutes.

Whoever had told the girl she was uncoordinated was a right arsehole. She was not. Fillan had to remind himself to pay no more attention to her than to the others, since she was a good dancer. He understood why Cheney thought she should be in the more advanced group, but Cheney didn't understand human nature well, from what Fillan had seen so far. You don't push someone already unsure. You ease them in, slowly. It was one thing Fillan was good at, and he didn't mind admitting it to himself.

After class, as always, he talked with his group while those who brought different shoes for dancing changed back into their street shoes and others mingled with each other. He was glad to see a couple of women talking with Emma, encouraging her, and he shifted himself casually over to join the conversation.

She looked at him, directly. "Thank you."

"You enjoyed the class?"

"Very much."

"Good, and then you will be back on Friday?"

"If I can." She took a sideways step toward the door, telling the other women goodbye, and gave Fillan a light nod.

Unable to help himself, he said he'd walk out with her since he had an hour before his next class and he wanted fresh air. At the door, he held it and caught a light scent of something floral. Rose? Perhaps. She thanked him again.

"Your schedule is full, then?"

She glanced over as they walked. "Yes."

"And what do you do, if I can ask?"

"I teach fifth grade."

"Ah, a teacher? And you still have energy to dance?" He grinned, teasing.

"Some days. Teaching is more mental energy than physical, so I usually still have that left."

"And it is a good tension relief. Dancing."

"That's my hope."

Fillan stopped walking. "Emma."

Luckily, she stopped, as well.

"Whoever told you that you were uncoordinated ... not that I have the right to say as much, but he, or she, must have felt the need of something to prove for whatever reason, because they are wrong. You are a nice dancer and if you enjoy it, you should continue."

She turned her gaze to the ground, silent.

"Have I said too much?" Fillan heard the softness in his voice. It was unintentional. But this girl had too much on her mind, too much tension. It showed all over her.

"No." She raised her eyes to his. "Thank you for saying so."

"You are welcome. Are you... I am quite sure I am overstepping now, but if you have time for a cup of tea, I would be glad to treat you. In thanks for coming back to class. It made me look good, if you don't know."

"Oh. I don't have. Really, I have to run, but thank you."

"You have plans on a Monday night? Big date?"

"No. Yes. I have plans, not a date. Nothing so interesting. I'll be back, though. Friday, I mean. Bye."

Fillan stayed where he was, watching her hurry to her car, a nice car, not fancy, but nice, newer model. She was making decent money, then, as a teacher. Or she was married. No date didn't mean no husband or boyfriend. Neither did no ring.

~ Six ~

"What do you want me to do, Helen?" Emma sat at the edge of the little wooden chair beside her sister's bed and held her hand. "She's upset. She can tell you're sick and it bothers her to see it."

"But she's my baby, Em. I need to see her. You don't understand. You don't have children. You should by now. You should have told Mark yes and had your own. So don't tell me how I should or shouldn't feel about my own baby refusing to come in and see me."

Only her sister's desperation kept Emma from telling her why she said no to Mark, and from going off on her about it. Her desperation, and her paleness, the bags and dark circles under her eyes. Helen was nothing more than skin and bones. It hurt Emma to see it. How could she expect Patty to be able to deal with it? "I'll try again. You're sure you can't come out to the kitchen? She'd feel better..."

"Last three times I tried, I fell on my face. Look." Helen raised a skinny arm to reveal a large dark bruise on her forearm.

Emma had to grit her teeth to check her emotions. "Won't you at least try to find a donor, go see if they can..?"

"No."

"Helen..."

"No. I'm not going to die in a hospital. I want to be home."

"But, maybe they..."

"They can save it for someone who has a better chance. A kid or something."

"What about your kid? She doesn't deserve for you to try?" Emma felt bad when her sister cried. "I'm sorry. I just... I'm not ready to lose you."

Pushing herself up, Helen wrapped her frail arms around Emma's shoulders. "It's okay, Em. I'll be at peace finally. It's okay. Really."

Fine and dandy that she would be at peace, Emma wanted to say. What about the rest of them? What about their parents, her daughter? How at peace were they supposed to be about losing a normally vivid and lively family member, the one with the biggest smile, the biggest heart? The one who made them all the most angry but also brought them all back together? The one who was okay with leaving them at only thirty years old. How were they supposed to accept her acceptance because *she* would be at peace?

The blaze of anger at her sister, and the betrayal Emma couldn't help feeling about what she'd done to herself, helped get her emotions back in check, as she had to do before she went to talk to Patty. Wiping her eyes, she told Helen she would go see if her daughter would come in just for a few minutes, but she wouldn't promise anything.

Patty was sitting at the kitchen table while her grandma cooked and talked to her, with no response other than a lot of hard, heavy circles colored on the paper in front of her. They always kept paper and crayons on the table, and Emma did the same. And Patty always drew circles. Only circles. Nothing else.

"Hey, sweetie." Emma sat next to her. "How pretty that is. I love the colors you used." She didn't get any reaction but hadn't expected one. "Can you come with me a minute? Your mom wants to see you. Just for a minute or two?" No response except for the circle drawing getting faster. "I know it's hard, honey, but just for a minute?"

Her mom looked over at them both, twisting a tea towel in her hands. Emma knew she expected an outburst. It was highly possible. Still, she had to try. Standing, Emma touched the back of her head lightly. "Come on, sweetie. If you come with me, we'll run through and get ice cream on the way home. What do you think?"

At that, Patty stood. Her mom said she should have dinner before ice cream, but Emma couldn't wouldn't worry about little details like that. She could only do so much. "Good girl. Thank you. I'll stay with you. Okay?" Slowly, Emma made her way back to Helen's room. "Someone here to see you."

Helen cried again as her daughter stood in the doorway shaking her hand at her side, her gaze on the floor. "Hi, Baby. How are you doing over at Aunt Emma's? Are you having a nice time?"

Patty's hand shook harder.

"We're going to go get ice cream in a minute. Sweetie, it's okay. Come in a little farther."

Patty stepped backward.

"Okay, no, it's fine. Stay right here if you want."

"Em..." Helen implored her. "Baby, please. Come see me a minute. Patty, come see me."

"Helen." Emma noticed the rocking movement that preceded an outburst and moved between them. "It's fine, sweetie. Let's go get ice cream now. Okay? Ready?" When Patty turned to head to the door, Emma gave her sister a quick apology and said they'd try again tomorrow and hurried to catch up.

Finally getting Patty settled in bed, Emma breathed a sigh of relief and checked her watch. After eleven. No wonder she was so tired. Grabbing a bag of chips and a glass of wine, she plopped onto her couch and listened to the silence, a different kind of silence than when her niece was awake and not talking. Her doctors said she could; she simply didn't. She used to. Emma remembered her excited baby squeals. She remembered the smiles. But both had faded out by the time she was five into the unemotional gaze that never quite caught anyone's eyes.

Emma was in college in Leominster when Patty was diagnosed. Since her sister had followed her boyfriend of the time to the cape, just for him to walk out on her, Emma spent many weekends driving the two hours each way to help calm Helen and try to figure out how to deal with the diagnosis.

After marrying her college sweetheart, Emma moved with him to Boston for his job, barely got her foot in the door of a nice private school where she loved working, and then the rest of the hammer fell. Helen's liver and heart were both failing, and still, she refused to stay in recovery long enough to recover. She kept saying it was too late, no matter how much Emma told her it wasn't. Rob, the always sensible oldest of the siblings, kept saying Helen simply wasn't strong enough to deal with it, her child's disorder on top of her own, and she gave up on purpose.

With a deep breath, Emma got back up to put the chips away and to search her cabinets for something else. She didn't want anything, though. Nothing she could eat would change the situation. All she could do was find ways to escape short term that wouldn't make things worse.

It was bedtime, but she needed to unwind, so Emma warmed a cup of day-old coffee and put an old Carey Grant movie on.

An old fashioned romance was what she needed. Someone who wouldn't leave. Someone who could deal with Patty at least as well as she did, or close to it. Or at least understand when she couldn't go out, couldn't talk on the phone for hours, couldn't go anywhere she couldn't be reached. Just that. That would have to be enough.

If it was possible to even find that.

~ Seven ~

Emma nearly didn't go to dance class on Friday, although she'd worked hard enough to move her schedule around to be able to do so, and she told Fillan Reilly she would be there. She was tired, nearly dead on her feet, and she still had to pick Patty up by seven and get her settled in to hopefully sleep sometime before midnight. Throughout the week, her niece had woken less often during the night, luckily, but the constant waking up every night after not getting to bed until one pm or so since Emma absolutely needed her quiet time after her niece gave in, was hitting her full force by now.

One week of school left and she couldn't wait for it to be done for the year so she could sleep in instead of forcing Patty to get up and ready and to get her to school on time for Emma to get to school on time. She would let the girl sleep in just as long as she wanted. In one more week.

They had just started by the time she got to her class and she gave them a quick apology and fell in at the back of the room.

The quick step. They were working on the quick step. Emma shook her head, since she was far too tired for that, but she gave it a good try. When she felt like she might fall over in exhaustion, she gave up and took a chair along the side to watch.

"Let's take five minutes to catch our breath." Their instructor didn't seem to at all need a break, or to be out of breath whatsoever, but the group thanked him in between panting and bending over to act like they were exhausted. He came over and sat next to her, his head tilted. "You look tired tonight."

"I am. Too much for this. Is it okay if I just watch a bit? I'll practice at home."

He gave her a grin. "You do not need permission. This is not elementary school. Do as ye wish."

"I guess I am used to the teacher being in charge."

He laughed. "Aye, well, Emma Turner, I am only in charge as much as ye decide to allow." With a wink, he got up.

Emma decided that might have been the smoothest come on line she'd ever heard in her life.

Back in front of the class, Fillan glanced over at her and called the group back. "How about we take a wee break from the Quick Step and refresh our memories on the Two Step. Grab a partner; whoever is beside ye will do if you did not bring one. Or if you would rather and do not need the breather, follow along with Cheney's class for the moment."

There were quite a few more women in the class than men, but a few of the women appeared to be couples and readily grabbed each others' hands. An even number. Just as well Emma was happy sitting and watching. Since both groups had to share the same music, being in the same room, Fillan had them half time to the quick beat, in a large couples circle. He walked around them correcting hand positions, and moved up in front of Emma with a light bow and an outstretched hand. "Can ye manage this one tonight?"

She knew how to two-step. Who didn't know how to two-step? And it was simple, slow. Although she had every idea in the world he'd done it only to dance with her, Emma gave in. Why not? She was there to dance, not to watch. When else would she have the chance? And how long had it been since she'd danced with a man? At her wedding? As far as she remembered, it had been that long, and Mark did not like to dance.

Emma eased into it well enough and didn't bother to tell him she already knew what she was doing, since listening to his voice was soothing, and he was soothing.

He was soothing. Friendly. Open. With a near constant smile. Much like her sister had been before. Emma had always loved Helen's friendly openness. Helen. Would Patty actually go in to see... Not tonight. Emma wasn't taking her tonight. Rob was taking her tomorrow because it was his day with Patty. Maybe he'd have better luck. Or he wouldn't and she'd have a meltdown and he would call Emma for another rescue.

"Are ye alright?"

She raised her eyes to Fillan's and nodded.

"I will release you and go back to the quick step if you prefer."

"Oh, I'm... like I said, tired tonight."

"Teaching always wears ye down so?" He said it with an extra syllable, as in dow-oon.

"The last couple of weeks are always the hardest, even worse than the beginning of the year and the week before Christmas break."

"Ah, they have be'er things on their wee minds than readin', writin', and 'rithmetic by now, yes?" He grinned.

"Apparently."

"You have only two weeks left?"

"One. Thank goodness."

"And then ye will have more time?"

"Um, yes and no." She knew why he was asking. If he thought he was being sly, he was very much mistaken, since Emma could easily see his thoughts. She was glad he didn't push the point.

As they approached where she'd been sitting, he took her out of the group, released her hand, and gave her a quick thank you for the dance. "Alright, back to the quick step now that ye have had a breather."

Fillan was glad she joined in toward the end, even with the quick step. She stayed on the outskirts of the group but where she could see him and kept her focus on his feet. He switched between partners, working directly with each of his students, adjusting their hand positions, straightening their shoulders, raising their chins. When he set fingers under Emma's chin to raise it, she caught his eyes, only a moment, but in that brief moment, Fillan saw a question or ... something in the gaze that made him not want to release her to move back to the front of the class.

He did, though, after a bit of a nod to acknowledge her look and encouragement to say she was doing well. Fillan believed in encouragement, in lifting up rather than tearing down. Cheney was more likely to criticize what they weren't doing well enough. And yes, of course you had to tell them when what they were doing wasn't right. It was part of the job. But it could be done better, and always with an uplift of what they were doing well, also.

Something he learned from his mother. She had been quick to

praise and slow to criticize and Fillan adored her to the end of the world. His father, although he admired and respected the man, always made him nervous. When he did speak, it was quite likely to be to tell Fillan what he was not doing well enough. He had yet to sort out whether the man thought he did nothing worthy of praise or whether praise wasn't in his range of necessary speech.

Purposely timing it so he walked out just behind her, Fillan said goodbye to the older women who had play-fussed at him about making them try to move their feet in ways they hadn't been moved in a lot of years and caught up with Emma.

She looked over at him but kept walking, not so fast this time.

"I have two hours before my next class since the other has been cancelled for lack of interest. Do you have time for tea before you are off to wherever you are going next?"

Emma stopped and looked him directly in the eye. "Why?"

For a few seconds, he was tongue-tied, but he shrugged it off. "I thought it might be obvious by now." Fillan waited for a response that didn't come. "Alright, then, let me try it this way. Emma Turner, I would very much like to sit and have tea with you and get to know you better. Of course you have not said whether you are attached already, but I had a feeling you would have said if you were. And aye, I am your teacher. In your line of work, that would be against every rule in the book. However, this is an adult class and there are no regulations saying we cannot ... hang out a bit. Right?"

"Hang out?"

"In full disclosure, I am here only for the summer and I amnae looking for more than a bit of pleasant company."

She nodded and dropped her gaze. "I have an hour and..." She looked at her watch. "About ten minutes. For tea, if you want. I drink coffee, though. I'm not a fan of tea."

He grinned with a slight bow. An hour wasn't much time, but Fillan accepted and they walked down the street to a little place she knew. A small, quiet place. And she chose a small table out of the way after ordering and waiting on their drinks.

Fillan held her chair, glad she thanked him for it rather than berating him, and sat across from her. "I would be right, then, that you do not have a husband or boyfriend to mind that you are here with me?"

"I don't have either. I'm divorced and I don't have the energy to start that again."

"Divorced? At your age?" He caught her raised eyebrows and apologized. "I do not mean to be rude. But you are young for that already."

"I started young, right out of college. It only lasted three years and ended five months ago."

"I am sorry to hear it."

Emma shrugged. "You know what? I'm going to grab a muffin to go with this. Do you want anything?" She got up as he declined and Fillan watched her, noticing a bruise on her forearm as she paid and returned with a large dark brown muffin, and a fork. "I hope it's not rude to eat in front of you."

"Not at all, Emma. Is it chocolate?"

"Yes, with chocolate chips. I'm addicted to these."

He grinned. "It does not show on you."

"Thank you. I'm rarely off my feet."

"And yet, you added a dance class to that?"

"For fun. And something different."

"I am glad you did." He raised his tea mug in a salute and returned a nod to a guy who looked over, checking him out.

"A student?"

"No, I do not know him. I seem to have that look."

Emma smiled. "Well." She bit a piece of the muffin off with a fork and swallowed it. "You move like a dancer, so it's not surprising."

"It is a myth, ye realize? That most male dancers lean to other males rather than females. Most of us do not." Fillan leaned forward across the table. "As a warning, I am very much enamored with beautiful women, in case ye were wondering at all. I believe I might be in the minority here with that."

She laughed, a beautiful laugh. "No, I can tell. But thanks for the warning. And you could be. Provincetown is very artsy and fairly well known for its diverse population."

"Is that why you are here? Trying to avoid men who are enamored with beautiful girls?"

"No. I'm here because my sister moved here a while back and then my parents did. I can't say my parents like the place a lot, but I do. Actually, I'm from the Boston area. That's where I lived before my divorce." With a swallow of her coffee, her expression shifted from humor back to too much sadness. "So, do you have a girl back in … the UK somewhere, right?"

"Ireland. Southern Ireland, not part of the UK."

"The Republic of Ireland." She nodded with another bite of muffin. "It's beautiful, right? I've heard it is."

"It is very green, plenty rocky, plenty cold and rainy, and hilly, but yes, beautiful, as well, if ye like that sort of thing."

She smiled. "What part of the country do you live in?"

"County Galway in Connacht." A test, which was rude of him, he supposed…

"So you're used to living by the ocean."

"Technically, I live along Galway Bay, but yes. And your geography is better than most here I have met."

"I'm a teacher."

"Right, then." He grinned.

"But I'm also interested in going to the Aran Islands someday. For the history."

"I have thought as much myself."

She frowned for a second. "But, it's right off Galway, isn't it? You haven't been?"

"I am afraid I have not. When I wander, I go east to the Wicklow Mountains or more east into Scotland or Wales. If you come that way at some point, though, you will have to let me know and I will jump on over to meet you. If you would like."

"Well, it wouldn't be for probably a good long time yet, so I won't hold you to that." She graced him with a bit of a grin before they lapsed into enough silence she could eat some of her muffin and look around at the other patrons, mostly disinterested in them, the way it looked. "Wicklow Mountains." Her head shook softly and she took a good swallow of her coffee. "That, I don't know. Where is it?

Does it have some kind of prominence?"

"East Ireland, near to Dublin and part within County Dublin. It is our largest mountain chain."

"What do you do there?"

"Hike. Climb hills. Enjoy the scenery. Boring, aye?"

"No. That sounds nice. I can just imagine the views."

"Do you hike?"

"No, not really. I used to go out on some of the trails around here when I had more time, but that's really just walking. I've thought now and then about doing some of the Appalachian trail, just because. Not something I'd do alone, though."

"If I had time while I was here, I would gladly do it with you."

She nodded lightly and took another bite, with a glance at the people coming in the door, still disinterested upon seeing them. "So what brought you here for the summer?"

"A work exchange. As of now, there is some poor bloke freezing his arse off in Connemara teaching American variety ballroom dance to stubborn Irish lasses while I take in the warmth and sun of the Cape."

"Is it that much colder there?"

"It is well noticeable."

She nodded. "I guess I better remember to dress warm if I ever get that direction." The sadness encompassed her face again, mainly in the eyes. "You didn't answer about whether you have a girl back home. You have someone back there freezing without you there to help keep her warm?"

"That, Emma, is a hard question to answer."

"Is it? It shouldn't be. Meaning you have one but you're not sure how serious it is?"

"Meaning..." Fillan rubbed his chin. "I did have, but by now I am not sure."

"Because you left for a couple of months?"

"No, because..." He figured he might as well just say it. "I wasnae entertaining enough. She went out to find some adventure, so she called it. My idea of adventure is hill-walking on my own paths rather than those premade, and taking photos of anything I see of interest. I like to be up and out early. She is more a nightlife and pub scene girl who likes to sleep in late. Yet, we did well for a couple of years or more. Suddenly, I became a right bore, never mind I was the same as when we met, and she up and walked off, with a maybe she will be back to grace me with her presence and maybe she will not."

"So you're hoping she'll come back."

"For quite some time, it was my hope. As of now, I cannot say for sure." At her nod, and when she again checked to see who was coming in as though watching for someone, or watching out for someone, Fillan decided to turn the conversation. "May I ask what made you leave your husband after only three years?"

Emma took a good bite of the muffin and looked out the window as she chewed. After a sip of coffee to wash it down, she gave him a soft shrug. "I didn't leave him. He left me. Pretty much the same reason. We had different needs, meaning I didn't give him what he wanted, and when he gave me the ultimatum to do that or to sign the papers when he sent them, I signed the papers. He didn't expect that; he expected me to cave, but some things matter too much to give in."

"Good for you for standing your ground."

"I suppose."

"You are not sure you should have?"

"Yes, I'm sure I should have, but that didn't make it easy. We'd been together for years before we were married, most of our college years."

"Emma." Fillan couldn't help but asking, so he reached across the table and took her hand, turning it gently to reveal the bruise, a very large bruise. "Are you safe?"

"Oh. Yes. That's ... I hit it on the doorway a couple of days ago. I don't see him anymore and he never did anything like that."

"Must have been a hard hit. And ye did it yourself?"

"I bruise easily." She reclaimed her arm and checked her watch. "I'm going to have to go soon. Thank you, though. For asking."

Fillan knew there was more to it, but she didn't know him well and he didn't want to get too pushy and push her away. "Thank you for having tea with me. Maybe we can again?"

"I'd like that, when I have time. After this coming week, it'll be somewhat easier."

"What do you do with your summers off that ye are still so busy?"

"Summer classes. Tutoring. And ... I take care of my niece a lot, so..." She checked her watch again. "It's that time." Emma swallowed the last of her coffee and took the cup and fork over to the dirty dishes stand, dumping the muffin paper and napkin.

Fillan walked her back to her car, waited as she opened her door, and took her hand to plant a light kiss on her fingers. "I will see ye Monday, then. Unless you have time tomorrow to meet somewhere. Do ye like to swim in the ocean?"

"I do, but I can't. It'll have to be Monday. See you then, and thanks for asking me for tea and for putting up with coffee on my breath instead."

He chuckled. "To be honest, I have not been close enough to smell your breath, but I would not mind it."

With a light tilt of her head, Emma leaned in to kiss his cheek and told him to have a good weekend. No, he didn't at all mind her coffee breath.

~ *Eight* ~

Already? Emma looked over at the red numbers on her alarm clock. "It's only five-thirty, Patty." On a Sunday morning yet. "Go back to sleep."

The girl started to fidget where she sat on the other side of Emma's double bed.

"Okay. You win." As always. At least she'd only been up four times during the night instead of five or six as was more usual. It wasn't good for her to jump back and forth. She liked a regular routine. Emma knew she should tell Rob that when school ended in a week's time, she would just keep Patty full time. Except that time would come soon enough. It was in Helen's will that Patty went to her. Even so, she shouldn't wait. Her mother said Patty should stay with Rob on weekends to allow Emma to find another man first, one who would take turns getting up with the restless girl.

Where her mom thought she would find this Prince Charming was beyond her. She could imagine that conversation: *Hey, I want you to marry me and move in with us and help raise my severely autistic niece and be even just decent to me despite all the changes you'll have to make in your life and despite the fact we'll never have a free weekend and in return ... uh ... I uh...* Emma rolled her eyes. Right. That would happen.

Starting to ask what Patty wanted for breakfast as she rubbed her eyes and dumped last night's coffee out to make fresh, Emma didn't bother. It was a pointless question. Scrambled eggs with just a touch of white American cheese – she wouldn't touch yellow cheese – and a banana, peeled just a touch to make it easier for her to do the rest herself, but not too far or she wouldn't touch it. And a third a glass of orange juice with absolutely no pulp and only after she was done eating. It was the same every morning she was there, which would soon enough be every morning. Rob could deal with it twice a week for now.

Sitting with her coffee as Patty ate her breakfast in silence, Emma wondered if she would have better luck getting her to visit with her mom than Rob had the day before when she went straight to her grandparents' kitchen and stayed right there until he said it was time to leave. Emma was going to have to get Patty into her mom's room to spend actual time with her. Soon. The doctors were giving Helen five or six months, as though they knew. It was all a guessing game. By now, Emma thought it might be a relief to not have to force Patty to see her mom. In many ways, it would also be a relief when Emma didn't have to go see her sister every day just to see her in pain and suffering when she could do nothing about it.

A selfish thought. Patty needed to stay connected to her mom as long as possible, not that they were ever terribly connected. Helen was always so into herself, even without the autism that kept Patty so far within herself. Emma wasn't sure Helen had ever truly connected to anyone...

Was her sister autistic, also? Low end? In her research, Emma read that a lot of girls, just like with ADHD, went undiagnosed because they learned to compensate well and silence in girls was far more accepted than silence in boys. An unfair assumption. Still, the more Emma thought about it, the more she realized it very easily could have been genetic, coming from Helen. Where before then? How would she know if it ran in the female line and it wasn't diagnosed? Would she carry the strain also? A scary thought.

Either way, she had to get Patty to talk more to her mom, or rather, to be close enough to her mom that Helen could talk to her.

Maybe Emma would skip doing summer classes this year. She had good reason. Other women got maternity leave. This could be her version of it. They could hang out on the beach since Patty liked the beach as long as she didn't get wet.

And she hated doing summer class. The kids hated to be there, although in almost every case it was their own laziness that put them there, and they were disrespectful and disinterested. The ones who were there not through their own fault, she paid the most attention to – the ones who didn't function well under the strict schedule and guidelines, the lecture teaching method. If she had only those kids, she'd gladly take it on. They only needed someone who understood. Helen had been the same. Emma got her through her classes all the way up to graduation by teaching her after school the way Helen was able to learn.

For what, exactly? After all of that and her sister had given up on herself. The alcohol and drugs were killing her, as Emma kept warning her they would.

With the banana and eggs gone, she moved the glass of orange juice in front of her niece. "What do you want to do today, sweetie? How about a walk on the beach?" No answer and no squirming. A good thing. "Okay, so when we wash up from breakfast, I'll put your cartoons on while I try to wake up, and then we can take a walk on the beach and then stop to see your mom before we come home for lunch. After lunch, I have to grade papers, though, so you'll have to do some art or play while I work. Just a heads up." Or maybe Rob would take her for the afternoon, after church, this once since it was the end of the school year and Emma was swamped with stuff to do.

Rob had stopped trying to take the girl to church with them long ago because every time they did the group reading, Patty threw a conniption. Once the hour was decent enough, she would call and see if she could drop her off after they visited Helen.

She considered calling Fillan to ask if he wanted to walk on the beach with them if he had nothing better to do, but she wasn't ready yet to deal with the Patty conversation, and chances were good that the girl would throw a fit if he got too close to either her or Patty, so she decided against it.

With a deep breath and another check of the time to be sure Rob would be out of church, Emma hit his number.

"Everything okay?"

She grinned with a shake of the head. "Fine. Just wondered about your plans for the day. I have a ton of grading to do and, well, if you have any time you could take Patty today, it would be really helpful. We're heading out to the beach in a bit, but I could drop her off at some point..." Realizing she was almost holding her breath, Emma made herself stop talking and breathe.

"How about we meet you at the beach once we've changed from church and had some lunch? The kids have been wanting to go, anyway. If she doesn't throw a fit, she can come to dinner with us and I'll take her to see her mom afterward, before bringing her back to you. Sound okay?"

Emma felt like hugging her brother. She wouldn't get her hopes up since it was possible Patty wouldn't let her leave. Still, it could work and maybe she would have half a day or so to herself. In which case, she would take her papers and find a café along the beach to work and have coffee and enjoy being out.

Or, she would stall on going out and get some of the grading done while her niece was absorbed in *Tom and Jerry*. Deciding on that option, Emma refilled her coffee for the second time, grabbed a piece of toast and spread a touch of jelly on it, and sat at the little living room table to keep an eye on Patty while she worked.

~ Nine ~

Propping his legs out in front of him, close enough to the water to let it roll up and caress his feet but far enough to keep his khaki shorts dry, Fillan let his lungs fill and released it slowly. Ocean air. The Atlantic. The same ocean that caressed Ireland at such a far distance. It felt less a distance when he sat out on the sand of Cape Cod and let the water come in to touch him. And recede again.

Although he was enjoying his time in the States, his native land pulled at him every night when he went home alone to his ramshackle tiny rented cottage. One bedroom, such as it was, a bath, and a small space for sitting at one side of the main room with a cook top and tiny oven on the other. At least there was electric. And a toilet that flushed. When he'd arrived at the place after renting it online, he hadn't been sure from the outside.

Maybe he would try to video chat with his sister, send her a message and see if she had time. Except his laptop was still acting up and he still didn't have much interest in annoying himself enough to try to fix it. Time to take it to someone who could, he guessed, but he had better uses for that money, or at least more fun uses for it. Probably another virus created by some kid sitting in his parents' basement trying to get back at everyone who did actually have a life outside the computer and real friends. Fillan would like to pop the kid in the nose for causing him trouble when he'd done nothing to ask for it, at least not to that kid. Or adult. Whichever.

Stop feeling sorry for yourself, Fillan. One of your worst faults.

He stood and brushed sand off the back of his trousers and wandered along the beach front. A mostly abandoned part of the beach, which was why his cabin rent was so low and so rundown. It worked well enough for his purposes.

To be honest, he wasn't sure anymore what his purpose had been. Change of scenery, he'd told himself. New shores, different faces. But he could have found that in a new part of Ireland, or taken the ferry over to Scotland and wandered a bit. It had been some time since he had.

Anyway, he was there for the summer and he would make the best of it around the classes he'd signed on to do to help fund the trip. Other than seeing the girl, he no longer looked forward to them. Only homesickness, he told himself, and long weekends too much on his own...

Fillan stopped in his tracks. Since when had he switched from thinking of *her* as 'the girl' to giving Emma that title? Very much not good, Fillan. Back off, impertinent fool. A couple of months and then home again. You can jolly well behave yourself for that long, you can.

A good lecture from his sister would do it. She would let him know straight he had to behave with the girl.

He jumped when his phone rang. No one called him on a Sunday. No one called him much at all other than work. Answering with hesitation, he was ready to jump on whoever thought they could call on a Sunday to try to sell him something.

"Fillan? Hi, it's Emma."

His heart nearly stopped. "Emma, I was just now thinking of you." Fillan rolled his eyes at himself. A stupid thing to admit.

"I'm flattered. Are you busy?"

"No, I am bored all to hell, to be honest. Thought about going into town, but not so much in the mood to be hit on and ... well, full disclosure, I am sitting around feeling too sorry for myself, which I should not admit."

She chuckled. "Don't worry. I do the same often enough. So, I got a reprieve today and I'm on my own, just hanging out at the beach. If you want someone to be bored with, I'm available until seven o'clock. Any time before..."

"Where are you on the beach? Which beach?"

"First Pilgrim's Park beside Wood End lighthouse. But I can meet you somewhere else."

"No, that is good. I will be there in just a bit."

"I'll meet you at the start of the breakwater."

"Sounds good. Emma? Thank you for calling." Fillan thought again he shouldn't have said it. It sounded desperate. But she'd chuckled about him feeling sorry for himself, so maybe she understood well enough. He needed company, and if she called him as soon as she got time to herself, maybe she did, too. A nice hang-out buddy. He hadn't done that often with a girl, not since he was grown, but he used to. He'd had a few girl friends he enjoyed just hanging with back home. He wouldn't mind doing that again, especially with one who loved dancing.

Jumping onto Route 6 to circle around to 6A, Fillan felt himself get far too excited by the thought of seeing her, out on the beach where they could walk alone. It wasn't far from the dunes at the east end to the point at the west end of Provincetown, but it felt like it took forever with visitor traffic. From what he'd heard, the town went from about 3,000 people during non-tourist months to over 50,000 during tourist season. A hard thing to fathom, except that there were always people everywhere.

At the park, Fillan saw her car and backed in behind it. She was sitting in the sand facing the water, beside the long row of large rocks. Her hair was down and the barely-there breeze swished it over her back and bare shoulders. She was in a dress, with wide shoulder straps and a pale yellow and gray floral patterned skirt lying over the sand. At that moment, Fillan thought she could be the most beautiful thing he had seen in his entire twenty-five years. Or he was far too homesick and she helped him not to be so much.

She smiled when she saw him and stood. The dress went only to her knees, not quite to her knees, and the breeze flipped it open where it wrapped around in front to show gray shorts underneath. Not a dress. Two pieces with a skirt over top. Possibly the sexiest thing he had seen a girl wear, or again, he had been away from his own girl too long.

"That was fast."

Fillan returned the smile and, touching her fingertips, leaned in to kiss the side of her head. "I was not far away."

"You were already out, or you live close?"

"West side by the dunes. I didnae fancy myself, only came as I was. I hope that is alright." He gestured at his navy T-shirt and tan shorts.

"For the beach? Pretty much anything is."

"You look nice, Emma. For sitting around the beach. And I mean, you are dressed well for it. Do you have other plans?"

"No. I'm pretty likely to run into students or parents, so I tend to dress decent wherever I go. Too much?"

"Perfect. So what did you want to do?"

She shrugged. "No plans. Up to you pretty much."

He looked out over the walkway of rocks. "Have ye ever walked along it?"

"Often. It's the easiest way to get to the lighthouse. Of course by easy, I mean it's about a mile and a half on the breakwater and then about the same distance through sand, so it's a hike, but..."

"You like to walk. I remember as much. Can we go?"

She gave him a nod and grabbed a little bag at her feet. "Water and a couple of fresh plums. Do you like plums?"

"I have no idea. Were you expecting a date who canceled?"

"No. I was here with my niece, but my brother picked her up for the day, so... You've never had a plum?"

"I have not, but I am willing to try."

She grinned. "At the lighthouse. You might want it by then."

"Good enough. Mind if I grab my camera? My family is expecting to see what I have been doing while I am away."

"Of course. You should get some nice shots out there."

Emma was somewhat surprised when he came back with an actual camera on a strap, not a small one, but a nice one with a long lens attachment. "You're a professional photographer?"

"Nae, only a hobbyist, but I may have to get a new card for it soon. There has been far more to see than I had expected."

"I'd love to see what you've taken, if you don't mind. I mean, if it's personal..."

"I donae mind at all. At the lighthouse when we stop to rest our feet and eat plums?"

"Sounds good." She tried not to laugh when he claimed her hands as though offering to help steady her. She was an old pro at walking the uneven boulders of the breakwater, and she'd worn lightweight tennis shoes instead of sandals since she'd learned fast to wear stable footwear when she had Patty. Fillan was every bit as good at navigating the rough terrain. They talked about his photography and the wildlife he loved to capture, up in the rugged hills of Ireland's east coast and along the west shore full of ancient stones and tall cliffs.

"Ye should come and see it sometime. I will take you to a festival, as well, and teach you to dance to the pipers. If you can quick step, ye can learn basic step dancing, as well."

"Not that I did well with the quick step."

"It is hard when ye are tired, but you were getting the hang of it. What do you think? Would you consider visiting Ireland at some point? Other than the Arans, that is?"

"Bagpipes? I have to say I'm not a big fan of that."

He laughed. "Yea, and I would guess you are referring to the highland pipes, which is what ye nearly always see in photos and such. I prefer the uilleann pipes. They are smaller and held under the arm rather than in front of the body, making them lower pitched and easier on the ears. Highland pipes are Scottish. Uilleann pipes are Irish."

"I've never heard of uilleann pipes. Spell that for me."

Fillan couldn't help but grin at her need for the spelling. "We will have to look it up so you can hear the difference, if I can get my laptop to work well enough. Look." He released her hand and pointed to a couple of black and white birds sitting along the rocks, then raised his camera and took a few shots in between playing with the settings. He showed her one of the photos.

"Beautiful. You can even see the red around their beaks. What are they? Do you know?"

He raised his eyebrows. "Atlantic puffin. We have many along our coast."

"I've seen them before, but more often in colder months."

"Not surprising. As I said, it is colder in Ireland and they prefer that." He crouched to take photos of the boulders by themselves and with the water, moving around to get different angles. And he stood. "If I stop too often and it gets annoying, you can say so. I am used to hearing it."

"You're fine. I'm not in a hurry."

Fillan gave her a soft grin and reclaimed her hand, maybe not for the purpose of steadying her on the rocks this time. It was possible the first time he took her hand wasn't actually for that, either.

When they reached the sand, Emma took her shoes off, and as he did the same, she pulled out two thermoses of water to hand him the one she'd packed for herself. She kept the pink one with unicorns that Patty always used.

"Cute bottle." His eyes sparkled when he grinned.

"My niece's. I figured you'd rather have my purple one than this one."

"I would have used it." He took a swallow and leaned in close. "Wha'ever others might think, I have no trouble with my masculinity."

Emma choked on her water and he laughed, apologizing through laughing and asking if she was alright. "Okay, then. Good to know. Ready to walk more?" His grin was far, far too charming, added to the round face and round green eyes with long lashes, and the curly blond hair topping it all.

By the time they reached the lighthouse, Emma was ready to sit. She headed over to the sand along the water and sat barely out of reach of the waves coming in sharply, foaming at their tips. She suspected a storm could be moving in, although the sky was still plenty blue and only lightly cloudy, enough to break the hot sun now and then.

Fillan lowered beside her, sitting close. "It is peaceful out here." He looked up at the gulls. "Other than those, that is."

"You don't like seagulls?"

"They are pests, and ye can ask any fisherman who will tell you the same."

"Why?"

"For one, their shite will destroy a boat's equipment. They carry parasites. They are aggressive. And they are loud."

"I never thought about it, since they're everywhere."

"Right. They are everywhere."

"So, you like to fish along with hiking in your mountains?" Emma pulled the plums out of the insulated bag inside her bag and handed him one.

"I cannot say I like it so much as it is expected. Not the way ye are thinking, I would guess."

"Expected?"

"It is the family business. My father owns a fishing company. I have worked for him, or under him, for years now. Part time. He thinks it is time I make it a career. Before I locked myself into that, I wanted to get away and clear my head and consider if I should."

"But you're a teacher."

"They think I should have a real job by now. Could be they are right."

"Real job? Like teaching isn't a real job?"

"Well, the teaching you do, yea of course it is. And they do not mind so much that I teach dance, only that I not do something more along with it. Something ye can support a family on, Fillan, my father oft says. Never mind the fact I donae have anyone more than myself to support, with no near plans of that, and so I amnae sure why he is so concerned."

No near plans of it. Meaning he wasn't too awful serious about his girl back home. Emma bit into her plum and looked up at the seagulls circling, waiting for something they could grab. He was right, really. They were pests. To her, they were just part of life, part of the Cape. *A real job.* It was a little reminiscent of the way her ex had felt about her teaching, that it wasn't doing much good, anyway, since it was only memorizing stuff for tests. Not really true. She tried to teach them why learning mattered, and how to learn what they needed to know. She tried to stretch their brains, and their imaginations.

With a sigh, she shrugged. "If it matters, I think teaching of any kind is very much a real job. Maybe not high paying, but important. It's something you do for the love, right?"

"Right, but yours is a real job far more than mine."

"That's not true." Emma shifted to face him. "It's not true. Dance, the arts, they matter. If we would incorporate more of it, all of it, including dance, into our daily schedule, kids would enjoy school so much more and I think they'd learn a whole lot more. Creativity is such a big part of the learning process and we've lost so much of that with our standardized tests and learning facts just to pass tests that they forget over the summer, anyway. I think they wouldn't if we merged in creative elements and made it all work together, like it does in real life. Who goes through any day without something creative? Music, books, dancing in your living room to your favorite song, or singing with it, or sewing or crafts, even television with stories and those games everyone plays where you create your own stories…" She paused at his look.

"Sorry. I get really carried away on the subject, but I keep trying to push it into my curriculum and it's hard to do when I have to be sure they're ready for their tests so the school looks good and tests highly enough for accreditation that's supposed to be proving we're teaching them enough, never mind the students are getting lost in the mix and it's not about them anymore, really. You look around Provincetown and it's filled with art and music and life of all kinds, and then there's the classroom…"

Emma stopped and looked out over the water. "Anyway, no, mine isn't more important. Not at all. Your job matters. It sure matters to me after I've had a rough week and need the release."

"I am glad it does."

"It does." She caught his eyes.

"Thank you." The softer voice and the emotion in his eyes gave away a vulnerability she hadn't seen before. He came to clear his head. In some ways, Emma supposed he was in a similar place to her own. He was about to be tied down to a job, a harsher job, and he was partly resigned and partly still fighting the thought.

As she was. About Patty.

"So? Are you going to try it or just play with it?" She glanced at the plum in his hand.

"I was … too taken by your thoughts. Here goes, then." Fillan took a good bite of it and Emma followed suit.

"Hm." He nodded as he swallowed. "I could get used to these."

"You don't have plums in Ireland?"

"Aye, we do have, but they do not look the same and they are not so common, I think."

"Different varieties for your colder climate, maybe?"

"And the wind. Wind is always a factor in crops. It is odd to me to have so many non-windy days here. It feels stifling at times."

"Really? I love wind. Everyone else will run inside when it picks up before a storm, and I'll look like an idiot standing out on my porch, head tilted back, just enjoying the wind on my face."

"A beautiful thing to see, that would be." He smiled and then looked out over the water, silently, as they finished the fruit and washed it down.

"We should start back." Emma hated to say it.

"I thought you were not in a hurry today."

"No, well, I have until seven, but if we stay too long, high tide will come in and we'll have to walk the long way around to get back."

"How long is the long way?"

"Maybe twice as far? I'm not sure, but a good bit longer."

"I am up for it if you are."

"Another time." She checked her watch. It would put her too close to seven if they stayed longer and then took the long way back. Another time, though, when she wasn't on call later and when she wasn't so tired, Emma would love to bring him back out and take the long way home.

~ *Ten* ~

"Look." Emma took Fillan's arm and pointed out at the ocean. "Seals?"

"Yes. Babies. It's been a while since I've seen them."

Adjusting his camera, he took several shots of the seals, and then moved farther away and turned the camera on her as she watched, childlike, so relaxed and unwound, although still tired. The longer they were out, the more tired she looked.

"Oh, don't get me. I'm a mess." She smoothed hair from her face that blew right back in.

He angled himself so the lighthouse was in the photo, as well, at a distance, but visible.

"Fillan. Really."

He caught a shot of her giving him a scornful look. "Alright. Alright. I could not help myself. My family will want to see my hangout buddy as well, you realize."

"Why would they?"

Taking her side again, he repeated her action with her hair, smoothing it away from her face. "They are curious that way. Did your parents not want to know who ye hung around with?"

"Not since I was old enough they couldn't say no. Although, they didn't worry much about it before then, either."

"They did not care?"

"They weren't worried. I was the typical, or atypical, girl who listened to her parents and did what I was told and studied when I said I was studying. I didn't give them reason to worry about it."

"Do me a favor, will ye, Emma? If you were to meet my parents, donae tell them as much. They will be right jealous of your parents, since I was far more a handful."

She chuckled. "I just bet you were. But my sister gave them enough trouble, your parents wouldn't need to be at all jealous."

"She is the wild one of the family?"

"Yes, she was." Her expression changed and Emma started

walking again. "At this point, I would probably have to claim that title. Not that I am, really, but just because, well..."

"Because of your divorce?"

"Right. I can't tell you how much I've heard that I gave up too easily, that I should have fought for it. I just... I didn't. He sent the paperwork and I signed it and that was that."

"Why should you fight for someone you have to fight for?"

She stopped and caught his eyes. "I don't know. Why are you waiting around to see if someone who walked out on you might come back?"

His stomach twisted. She had a point. But her family had a point, as well. Some things... Some things were worth fighting for, even if you had to fight for it.

"Sorry. It's not my place. I guess I just think you deserve to be treated better. So did I. I didn't have enough reason to fight for it, but maybe you do." With that, she walked again, off the sand and back onto the rocks, still carrying her shoes.

Her phone rang and she stopped walking, seeming afraid to even look at it. Finally, she checked the number, sighed, and answered. "What's wrong? ... Did you try..? ... I can't run over for a few minutes right now... No, I'm out on the breakwater. It'll take me a half hour if I hurry and... I'm not by myself. I'm with a friend. ... Rob, take her to Mom's. I'll be there when I can get there. ... I'll head back, but call me if you get... Okay. I'm sorry, but... I know. Call me back." Hanging up, Emma rolled her neck. "I have to head back."

"All alright?"

"Just ... family stuff."

"So, I suppose asking you for dinner is not going to work?"

She touched his eyes.

"Casual, I mean. Along the shore somewhere. If..."

"I um, I'll have to see."

He gave her a light nod. "I will take that." Fillan brushed the sand off his feet and put his shoes back on. She kept hers in her hand. He wanted to ask more, but her brush-off said she didn't want to say more. They walked silently and he took a few more photos without stopping to spend much time doing it. Her pace was quicker than on the way out. The tension returned to her face.

"Emma." Nearly back to the park, Fillan took her hand to stop her. "I listen well if you need to talk."

"There's no need to bother you with it. Did you get good pictures today?"

"My favorites are the one I took of you... and we did not sit to look at photos as we ate our plums as we talked of doing."

"Another time. I should..." She reached for her phone and frowned. "Let me give him a call."

"Your ex? Do you have a child you have not spoken of?"

"Oh. No. I don't... One reason he's an ex is because I wouldn't. It's ... my brother. We take turns taking care of our niece because her mom isn't well. Anyway, give me just a minute to check in to see if I need to hurry away."

Fillan nodded and moved farther from her in the guise of taking photos, which he was. He crouched to get another side shot of the water against the boulders from nearly a straight line out and found a starfish in a small puddle of water held by rock crevices. After getting a couple of pictures of it, he started to ease it back into the water so it could go on its way.

Emma crouched at his side. Very close to his side. "Reprieve. I have until seven still. You found a starfish. Still alive."

"I am glad you do not have to rush off. And I was about to move him back into the water but thought you might want to see him first."

She grinned. "You're incredibly sweet, you know."

"Sweet. Aye, great." He rolled his eyes. "Is that another way to say boring or unmasculine?"

"Not close to either one. Why would you..." Emma tilted her head slightly, as though she'd just figured something out. "Your girl back home thinks you're boring and not masculine enough?"

"She hasnae said it straight out, but given comments about other men who catch her eye..."

"Well, as a woman who had that tough, in charge kind of guy, I could tell her she should be lucky she has your interest instead. Show me how to use this." She reached for his camera.

"Why?" Fillan never let anyone play with his camera. Never.

"So I can get a photo of you moving the starfish back into the water, to add to your vacation journal."

"I do not need a photo of myself..."

"I want it. And it's fair, since you took some of me. I could get it with my phone, but the quality won't be as good. Can you set it for me so I only have to click the button?"

With a grin, Fillan set it to auto and handed it to her. "Just press it half way and let it set itself."

"That's not what you do."

"No, I do not tend to use the auto setting, but otherwise, it takes some time to learn the right exposures for the right light and distance. Auto should work well enough for your subject."

"Fine. For now."

Grabbing the back of his shirt when he leaned way over to gently set the starfish back into the water, Emma laughed when he told her not to drop his camera. "You about fell in and you're more worried about the camera?"

"Of course." Fillan steadied himself and got up. "I would dry and be right as rain again, but this..." He claimed it from her. "This would not be. I have too many good photos on here to risk losing them. Let me see what you have just put on it."

"Don't you dare delete them. Send them to me first, at least."

He tilted his head with raised eyebrows. "We will see." Setting it so he could go back through the pictures, Fillan held it where she could see, with his arm up against hers. He groaned now and then, but Emma loved how they turned out. So youthful and charming, with his hair tousled about in the breeze and from leaning over, and so sweet with the way he so carefully handled the little creature.

"Send them to me. Please."

He caught her eyes. "Ye will have to give me an address to use, then. And you know, Emma Turner, if ye do so, I will save it to use when I am home again, as well."

"Good. Then you can send me pictures you take in Ireland, too, since I'm unlikely to ever get there."

He smiled, but whatever he was about to say was interrupted by some guy coming up to them, followed by a woman with a notebook in hand.

"Sorry to bother you." A tall man, at least three to four inches taller than Fillan, offered his hand. "Eli Forrester. This is my wife Delaney. Was that a sea star you just put back in the water?"

"It was." Fillan set a hand on Emma's back. "Why? Is it not legal to move a starfish back into the water?"

The man laughed. "Well, I sure hope it is, or my wife is going to be in so much trouble."

The dark-haired woman, also tall at nearly Fillan's height, gave her husband a lightly chastising look. "Never mind him. He still gives me trouble about yelling at him the day we met for kicking one." She was soft-voiced and Emma had to focus on hearing her over the noise of the seagulls and the water moving in and out against the rocks.

"In my defense, I didn't look at what it was and didn't know it was alive. Anyway, Delaney is a travel writer with some kind of odd affinity for sea creatures. She grew up in Jersey. Explains it, maybe." He laughed again when she gave him that look. "She's doing a feature on Provincetown and it's always nice to get a local point of view. We're finding it hard to find real locals, though, at least any willing to chat with us." He focused on Fillan. "You don't sound local, either."

"He's not. I am." Emma noticed tension in Fillan, for the first time since she'd known him, so she tried to draw the focus away. "I've lived here for a few years now. I'm originally from west of Boston, if that counts as local."

"Good enough, yes?" He asked his wife.

"Of course. If you have some time, just a few minutes."

"What did you want to know?"

"Nothing terribly particular, only basics of how you feel about the area and tourism and favorite spots, especially places most tourists don't tend to know about. Real life here, basically."

"We'd love to treat you to coffee and dessert or something if you could meet us somewhere." Eli took over again, obviously used to doing the talking. "Or out here is good, too. Your choice. It's easiest to just kind of sit around and chat as though we know each other, even if we don't."

Again feeling Fillan's wariness, Emma suggested a little coffee shop just down the street where she was already thinking of taking him. She asked if he minded, and he shrugged.

The girl who was almost always there working greeting Emma with a friendly smile and asked if she wanted her usual. Catching Fillan alone for a second while Eli and Delaney found a table, she told him she was going to wash her hands and asked if he was okay with talking. If not, she'd bow out and they could go elsewhere.

"He is one of the in-control types. Ye are sure you want to talk with him?"

"I don't think he is. Did you see her looks? She adores him; you can see it. I think he's just really friendly, and obviously from the west somewhere, not from here."

"Alright, then, but if he starts any macho crap..."

Emma squeezed his lower arm. "Then we'll leave. I'll be right back."

When she returned, Fillan was leaned back against his chair, an avoidant pose, and Eli was joking with his wife. She looked amused, honestly amused, in between looking around the place and taking notes. Emma pulled her chair closer to Fillan's and touched his arm. "If I get a muffin, are you going to share it?"

"No, but you enjoy it." He looked up at the girl who set a chocolate muffin in front of her, with another in front of Delaney. "I took a chance that ye might want it."

Fillan thought about telling her if she wanted no more than to hang out, she might want to stop touching him so often, stop smiling at him the way she did. He mainly listened as Emma talked with the couple from Indiana, sharing coastal stories with the woman who had lived on the coast until she moved with her husband. She was expecting although it wasn't obvious until she smoothed the flowing top down over her stomach. Her husband looked fully overjoyed by the thought. A nice way to feel, Fillan supposed. Still, he was glad it was that guy and not himself.

Emma had said not having kids was one reason her husband had left. Shame she lived an ocean away, since she was looking too terribly much like a woman he could actually stay with. She was far more compatible than ... than his girl back home, as Emma called her. Why did he still have any interest in the girl who walked away? A good question, and it had lingered in his mind since she asked.

The more time he spent with his new *buddy*, the less time he spent thinking about the girl.

And Emma did seem to be right about this guy, Eli from Indiana, a construction worker. He deferred to his wife often, in between keeping up the conversation. His wife was quiet, speaking softly when she bothered, but she was picking up everything, writing much of what Emma talked about, to include her job and having family in the area. Emma told them she was single, not divorced. Fillan found that meaningful, as though the marriage hadn't even happened and she didn't want to acknowledge him.

The writer girl asked where he was from and what he was doing in the States. To his surprise, she was truly interested in the fact that he taught dance and with gentle prompting from her husband, she admitted she had taught herself some Flamenco and some more contemporary dance through videos.

"Why not take classes?"

She deferred to her husband who said she wasn't a big fan of social situations, which was why he did most of the talking. The girl did joke back to say he did most of the talking because he liked to talk, especially to strangers, to which he laughed and admitted she was right.

Emma was far too enamored with the guy. Otherwise, it turned into a nice conversation, with dance added, and Emma told them that's how she met Fillan, with a smile. Finally, the couple left, after giving Emma contact information in case she wanted to be notified when the article would be published.

"Can I take you to dinner, or did the muffin fill you too much?"

Again, she touched his arm. "Is everything okay? You're awfully quiet."

"It is all fine."

"No, it's not. What's wrong? If you didn't want to talk with them, I would have..."

"No, Emma. They were nice enough. It is ... the way you speak of your home. And..."

"Why?"

"You love being here, yes?"

"I do. It wasn't my choice, but it's nice. At least other than winter months, it's nice. It feels far more like home than where I was raised, and much more than Boston did. Why?"

He pushed his chair back. "Can we go?"

"Sure. Where?"

"I donae know. Out. Outside somewhere."

She grasped his hand. "What did I do?"

Fillan felt himself gape. What did she do? Why would she even think..? "You did nothing." He checked his watch. Only an hour and barely more until she had to leave. Getting up, he held her chair and then the door.

Beside their cars, she gave him a soft shrug. "Maybe I should go on home."

His stomach lurched. "You do not want to have dinner quick first?"

"I think maybe you'd rather..."

"I would rather not have to rush through dinner, but otherwise, there is nothing wrong."

"Then why are so quiet all of a sudden?"

"I am..." *Hell, Fillan, just tell the girl. Might as well admit the truth.* "I am only wishing you were not so entrenched here. Nothing more, Emma."

She stared a moment, searching for a hint he wasn't telling the truth, maybe, or at least the whole truth. "Why?"

"It does not matter. As you said, we are only hanging out for the summer and ... that guy, Eli, is more your type, I would assume, and so it..."

"No, he's not." She stepped closer. "That's what's bothering you?"

"You found him attractive, yes? Not that I could blame you..."

"Why would it matter if I did?"

"Because he is fully opposite of me."

Catching what he meant, Emma studied him, silent, with cars zooming past on the street beside them, people laughing on the sidewalk behind them. "You have a girl back home. And I..."

"I think you are right, Emma. Why should I care anymore whether or not she might want to come back to me? She left. Months ago. I have been a right fool to worry about it this long."

"Fillan..."

He closed the distance between them. Still, she waited, watching him, without backing away.

"My life is so complicated right now." It was a near whisper against his skin. "I know that sounds like a line, or a cop-out, but really, it's not. This... I can't expect to have many days like this, with this much time free. I keep waiting for my phone to ring..."

He touched her face. "Right, and I have only until mid-August to be here."

She nodded. Slightly. But her breathing increased. Her chest rose and fell faster.

"Where would you like to go to eat that will not take long?"

Emma was partly thankful he drew back rather than kissing her, but so much of her wished he'd gone ahead and done it. Right there on the sidewalk. But he was only there for the summer, and she didn't have enough freedom.

Suggesting a buffet nearly next door to her mom's house so she wouldn't have to leave too early, she again led in their separate cars. He thought she was attracted to someone else's husband? No, she enjoyed his friendliness, his openness, but he was not her type. Fillan... Fillan was more her type than ... maybe anyone else she'd ever met. She couldn't tell him that. Emma couldn't encourage him. She couldn't leave, just move away from her family for him the way Delaney had for Eli. Patty was hers. Soon, she would be legally hers. And from Fillan's comments during the baby conversation, he had absolutely no interest in children. He'd said he wouldn't even teach them.

That could be a drawback. Big time. If he were going to be there longer than the summer.

They didn't talk much while they ate, other than him teasing about having only soup and salad, to which she said she had to balance out that muffin somehow since he wouldn't share it with her. He said her dancing would balance it well enough.

Except she admitted not having had any time to practice between class.

"Maybe we should have been doing that today." He grinned, his old charm and demeanor returning.

"It would have been hard on the rocks or the sand, I think."

"The parking lot would have worked, along with the car stereo."

"Right, because I'm going to do that in a public parking lot?"

"Why not?"

"Tripping over my feet in class is one thing, since everyone else is doing it, too. In public where people would stare is different." She took a swallow of her iced tea. "Would you? In public like that?"

"I would. Why not?"

Emma wasn't sure how to answer. Under the right circumstances, maybe she would, too. "Well, with you being a pro and everything, it makes a difference."

"So when you get more comfortable with it? Then you would dance in the parking lot with me?"

"Maybe. And I hate to say it, but I really have to go."

In the parking lot, Fillan told her to hold on, and went to open his door, turning on the radio. Loud. "You have a few minutes until seven. Foxtrot? I will not ask you to do the quick step in public yet."

"Fillan..."

"You have this one down. I want to know if you were serious."

"You're questioning my honesty?"

"No, Emma. You seemed not sure if you could. I want to show you that you can."

Against her better judgment, she let him guide her to the open area behind their cars, took his hand, set the other behind the shoulder, and followed his lead. It was a song she didn't know, featuring a Celtic sound, but rock style. Fillan added in a couple of twirls and she laughed when she nearly tripped over her feet since it was so unexpected, but he caught her with a smile. He caught her easily, as though she was no heavier than one of the seagulls he didn't like, and moved them both back into the steps she'd learned. A few people stopped to watch, and when the song ended and he backed up to give her a bow with a smile, they applauded.

She returned the bow with a curtsy, thanked their small audience and told them how they could learn what she'd just done, specifically that Fillan was the teacher they wanted, and set a hand on his arm. "Okay. With that, I really have to go."

Fillan walked her to her car door, held it, and told her to have a nice rest of the day with thanks for sharing her day with him.

"You, too. I have to tell you..." She hesitated.

He stepped closer, enough she could smell something lightly spicy mixed with the ocean scent that seemed different than her own. "Tell me what, Emma?"

"It's been a very long time since I've had any reason to laugh. Thank you. I can't tell you how much I needed a day like this. Exactly like this. It was perfect." Emma swallowed hard to choke back the sudden emotion she didn't want to show him.

Fillan leaned in to touch her lips. Gently. A barely there *it's up to you* kiss.

Emma decided to allow it, but not push it, forcing herself to pull back rather than throwing her arms around his neck and making it deeper, longer. They'd known each other too short a time. And maybe he'd decided not to take the girl back if she tried, but it was a new decision and could easily change when he went home. Besides, there was Patty. Emma wasn't as free as he was.

She could not let herself go that far. Breaking the kiss, she slid fingers down his shoulder to his hand and gave it a light squeeze. "See you in class tomorrow." Getting into the car, she let him help close her door and he stood back to let her pull out before going to his own.

～ *Eleven* ～

Emma managed to get to class a bit early, and she walked straight into one of the women from Cheney's group hitting on Fillan. Trying to act like she wasn't paying attention, she sat close enough to hear the conversation, behind the woman's back.

"Yes, I can see that would be hard." Fillan glanced over at her as though asking for help.

"It is. Especially since their father gives them anything they want all weekend so when they come back to me, I can't do anything with them. Eight and twelve. Impossible ages. Emma Turner, the one you are paying special interest to, was my Davy's teacher last year, by the way. As a warning, you might want to stay away from that one. The stories he told of her... Well, I don't like to talk about people, but she's not particularly kind. I'd feel sorry for any child of hers. But, if you're looking for weekend company, I'm usually free. It has to be hard, too, being so far from home."

"Excuse me, if you would." Fillan backed away from her hand on his arm, but she followed.

"I know a lot of nice out-of-the-way places..."

Emma moved up beside him. "You must be Mrs. Grayson. Davy's mom."

"Oh." The woman at least had enough intelligence to be embarrassed. "Yes, but my name isn't Grayson. I changed it back when I divorced the cheating jerk."

"I understand. I don't think we ever met, did we? I don't remember you answering any of my requests to come in for a conference."

"No, I don't do conferences. They're a waste of time."

"I'm sorry to hear you feel that way. I think David could have benefited, since I had thoughts on how he could better control himself in the classroom rather than sleeping on his desk all morning and throwing spitballs at the girls all afternoon."

"My Davy wouldn't dare..."

"He did dare, and often. I am sure he did think I was mean for wanting him to be awake and non-interruptive. I wish we could have spoken. I'm guessing he's happier with his teacher this year?"

"That old bitty?" The woman flushed. "No, he..."

"You might consider a conference. I think it could help Davy rather a lot."

The woman tossed her head and pulled her shoulders back. "You might consider minding your own business."

"I would be glad to do so, if you wouldn't mind not spreading rumors behind my back. It's not my fault when parents don't teach them how to behave at home so I can teach them what they're supposed to be learning at school."

She huffed away and Emma seethed. No wonder the kid was so uncontrolled.

"I am sorry ye had to hear that. You handled her well." Fillan tilted his head, studying her. "Are you alright, Emma?"

"I'm... Yes. Hi, by the way. Guess that's what I get for coming early, right? So, apparently we're being talked about?"

He shrugged. "Not surprising. Does it bother you? Will it interfere with your job?"

"No. I'm allowed to have friends. Even if I am a mean teacher who should never have children of my own, poor things."

He laughed and looked over at the doorway with a nod to tell her she should look, too.

Almost afraid to do so, Emma grinned when she saw Delaney, the travel writer, and her husband Eli, and gave them a wave. Delaney looked awfully uncomfortable, almost as though Eli had dragged her there, but she'd said she danced ... and that she wasn't a fan of social situations.

Fillan touched Emma's back as they approached. Possessively. But he was friendly enough when he greeted them. "You need more for your story?"

"No, I think I've talked her into trying ballroom with me." Eli kept watch over his wife. "At least we're going to give it a go. The front desk said it was fine to try a class. I think they're hoping to be mentioned in her article."

"It is fine, mention or no. We are working on the waltz today." He gave Emma a quick nod, told them to fit in anywhere they liked, and took his place up front.

Fillan gritted his teeth when Cheney came over and took Emma in his arms, cutting in on the older gentlemen she'd been dancing with, to "correct" her position. It hadn't needed correcting. He did it only because Fillan took her out of his group, and he likely heard the rumors. Within a couple of minutes, Emma pulled away from him and returned to the older guy. Cheney threw Fillan a gloating smile and went back to his own students.

The Indiana couple did far better than he expected. She kept her eyes on her husband and looked tense, but her movements were good. His were okay for a construction worker, Fillan supposed. When he walked around his group to comment on foot position or head tilt or arms, he complimented them for being fast learners, told the guy to hold his shoulders straighter, and paused by Emma to tell her how nice her position was, making himself not touch her only because he wanted to touch her.

She threw him a smile, a smile that went well beyond *thanks for the compliment.*

The man she was dancing with released her. "Dance with your young man a while. I'm taking a breather."

Fillan saw heads turn at the comment, but he dipped his head toward Emma and took her in his arms. Such an elegant dancer. The waltz was her dance. He soon realized the rest of the group had cleared away and stopped to watch them. Emma noticed, also, but she just gave him a grin and let him lead her into more advanced steps: the underarm turn, the natural turn, and the side whisk, teaching his class with her help. She picked them all up fast, and he went back to the underarm turn and told his group to give it a try.

At the end of class, he stepped back, gave her a light bow, and raised her hand to kiss her fingers. Fillan knew by now there would be no denying the rumors, but if she didn't care, neither did he.

"Can I take you to dinner, Emma?" He asked as soon as everyone except the Indiana couple were out of ear shot.

"I'm sorry, I can't. And I have to run."

"Right then, tomorrow?"

"I..." She checked her watch. "I'm late already. Sorry, I really have to go. I'll call you, okay?" Emma squeezed his hand, told the other couple goodbye and she hoped they'd be back Friday, and started away.

Cheney stepped in front of her. "I think you are far too advanced for the beginner's group. Starting Friday, you should move to mine."

Fillan started to interfere, but Emma threw her shoulders back and faced him head on. "Thank you, but no, and don't do that again. I'm where I want to be, and my position was fine without your help. If it's not, Fillan will let me know." Leaving Cheney slack-jawed, she turned back a second. "Was there anything wrong with my position?"

"Not a thing." He tried not to laugh. "And yes, I would have told you if there was. Good night, Emma."

She gave him a half hug, thanked him for the dance, and swerved around Cheney out the door.

"You are only supposed to be teaching dance here."

"That is what I am teaching. Did you see me do more than that?"

"I've heard you're seeing her outside class."

"And if I am?"

"She's married, Reilly. There is a code of conduct..."

"No, she is divorced. For months now. Do not worry about my conduct, Cheney. Worry about your own, because if you harass her again, I will report you for it. Let her be." Turning from the arrogant jerk, he apologized to the Indiana couple and talked with them about whether they wanted to come back. They had only a few more days in town, but they agreed to come Friday.

Emma would be glad, he expected.

"She threw a huge fit when I picked her up today."

Emma shrugged with her hands at her brother's greeting, such as it was. "Hi to you, too. And I'm sorry, but it happens."

"She kept swirling that bracelet you gave her with the beads. They think it means she was asking for you. Em, you can't pick her up after school on Mondays? I had enough trouble yesterday when you couldn't get there..."

"Rob, that was the agreement, right?"

"She's upset right now with moving away from her mother. You don't think it would be better to keep things more constant than that? She expects you after school, not me. It throws her off."

"Where is she now?"

"With the boys in the kitchen. She won't touch her food. I told them to sit with her and see if she'd get something in."

Emma sighed and headed that direction.

"Em. Please. I can't do this. She's getting worse. She knows Helen isn't well. It's why she's avoiding her and she needs you."

Getting worse. Yes, Emma had that same feeling. Patty's moods and stimming episodes and outbursts were getting worse. It was too much change too fast. He was right. But she'd have to give up class if she couldn't have those two hours. "I'll pick her up this week and we'll go from there."

Finding Patty rocking back and forth on the kitchen chair, Emma greeted her nephews, asked where their mom and sister were – cheerleading practice, of course – and sat next to Patty. "Hi, sweetie. How was your day? Okay? You're not hungry tonight?"

Leo, her oldest nephew, a ridiculously responsible and sweet 14-year-old, said she hadn't even touched it, even with him trying to make it into a game.

"Thank you for trying." Emma gave him a grin, wishing she had more time to spend with the boys without always being so focused on her niece, and touched Patty's head. "Ready to go home? Maybe we can find something there you want. You're coming to my house. Remember?" Emma pulled her bangs out of her eyes.

"She needs a haircut."

At Rob's voice, or the haircut word, Patty rocked harder, twisting her hair ends.

"Not tonight, sweetie. We're not doing that tonight. Come on. Let's go home and find *Tom and Jerry*."

At that, Patty got up so fast, she nearly knocked the chair over and Emma threw a goodbye to everyone to follow her out the door as Rob shoved Patty's bag at her.

A haircut. She did need a haircut, but Emma was putting it off. She'd tried before to do it herself so Patty wouldn't have to deal with a beauty shop, but she'd done it badly. Emma didn't want to mess it up again, and yet taking her in to the beauty shop was a nightmare. Maybe if she could arrange to take her when almost no one else was there, when there wouldn't be a blow dryer in use, if she warned them not to get closer than necessary...

With another deep breath, Emma figured it would wait another week, at least until after the school year.

~ Twelve ~

Emma ran her bath halfway full, with plenty of lavender Epsom salt added, slipped out of her robe, and immersed herself in the hot water, hoping like everything Patty would not wake up again in the next hour. She'd been up three times already, and Emma was so flustered by now that even at two o'clock in the morning, she couldn't sleep.

Two more school days left. One and a half, really, since they were out early on Friday. She had to call Fillan and let him know she wouldn't be at dance. Emma had to pick the girl up herself. Rob was right. Every day Patty saw her mother, she became more upset and harder to control, and yet Emma didn't have the heart to tell Helen she wouldn't take her. In which case, she had to do whatever else it took to keep Patty as calm as possible.

Fillan had called her last night, Tuesday night, to see if she had any time free. Emma nearly told him then about Patty, but something made her unable. For now, she wanted to just be herself with him, keep it simple and easy. Once she brought Patty into the conversation, the whole thing would change, and maybe it wasn't necessary. Emma hoped Helen would hang on through the summer. She wanted that much longer with her sister. By then, Fillan would return to Ireland and it wouldn't matter that she'd suddenly become a mother.

Mark had called her, also. Just to check in, he said, but Emma did not at all buy it. He wanted something. Possibly, he'd found someone else already and wanted to stop the alimony payments that paid her mortgage. That wasn't part of the deal, though. Their divorce decree said he owed it to her for three years, since he'd kept her from working on her master's degree for that long, the whole time they were married. He'd readily agreed. The only way out of it for him was if she married again before then.

That wasn't likely to happen.

She wanted to call Fillan and let his voice soothe her. Of course she wouldn't call him just after two in the morning. Instead, she put her ear buds in, tuned her MP3 player to Bob Seger, rested her head against her bath pillow, closed her eyes, and thought about Monday's class, waltzing with Fillan. Emma had actually done the waltz with a sweet, kind man who had looked as though he wouldn't have wanted to waltz with anyone else in the world at that moment.

It could be if his girl back home had popped in, he'd change his mind. And chances were good, Emma knew, that once back home, if she did contact him, he'd welcome her into his arms and do far more than just waltz.

The thought annoyed her and Emma tried to tell herself it only annoyed her because he deserved better, because she wanted him to have someone who wouldn't just walk out. It was one reason, but mostly, she was starting to feel as possessive with him as he'd acted during class.

And at lunch the other day with Eli. He'd asked if she was attracted to the construction worker.

Unsure whether to smile or cry, considering he was going back to Ireland soon and she'd never be able to take Patty on an airplane for however many hours it took to fly across the ocean, or at all, probably, Emma settled for a shake of her head and a deep breath. She'd enjoy hanging out with him for the summer and maybe he'd still want to talk online now and then after he left.

If not, her hands were going to be too full to worry much about it, anyway.

Five in the morning.

Fillan poured hot tea from the pot on the stove, added a good bit of cream, put a Van Morrison CD into his player on low, and went to sit on his front steps with the door open behind him. The sky was still mainly dark and a few of the brightest stars still glowed in the midst of the coming dawn. He shivered at a breeze off the ocean.

Ye have acclimated already, have you? Up before the sun and a shiver from the warm Massachusetts June air? He shook his head. Ireland would feel colder after his summer on the American coast. Not only per temperature, either.

He would miss Emma. Already, Fillan knew he would miss her like mad. *Ye are a right eejit, to have fallen so easily. With a girl who has accepted it is only a summer hangout, no less.*

Nothing he was going to do about it now. He had already made it clear he was interested if she was. *A pure eejit, Fillan Reilly, to leave so much in her hands.* He wore his heart too exposed, the girl had said. And what if he had? She would laugh at him about this one, if she ever knew. There was no reason she should ever know, if she ever decided to come back.

If he ever decided to allow her back. And chances of that were growing more slim with her distance, her obvious disinterest in trying to hold him. Still, it was hard to put off the times they'd had together over the years. Some glorious, passionate, crazy wild times. It wasn't something he could easily forget.

And yet she had grown up and away from him. Too often, she had brushed him off when he tried to take her in his arms wherever they were when a good song came on. *It isnae dignified, Fillan, and I amnae a mere girl anymore to give in to ye so easily.* She talked as though he had become a bore to her, but he was not the one who turned from what he had been, what they had been.

He sighed and watched the sky and reflecting ocean turn from dark blue-black to red-orange to orange-yellow to white-blue.

Emma had danced with him in her own town in the parking lot with people watching, and she'd laughed. Tuning into the song, Fillan decided to try to arrange dance lessons for Emma under the moon in private. With this album. A quick step to *Moondance* to see if she'd laugh again and then a waltz ... to *Crazy Love.*

Could be it was the last thing he should do, since he did not need that kind of turn on potential with his hangout buddy.

At the thought, Fillan took a swallow of his now lukewarm tea, went back into the cabin to stop the song, downed the rest of the mug contents as he went to his room, and put his jogging clothes on. A quick run along the cold water of the beach would cure what his thoughts had provoked. Then a shower and a video call to his sister, to bring him back to reality.

"I have to go." Fillan smiled at Emma's name on his phone, knowing Eugenia would have seen him do as much, and told his sister they would talk soon.

"Who is calling that you have to cut off your own sister?"

"I will tell you later, Genie. I do not want her to hang up. Bye for now." Before he disconnected the internet camera, Fillan answered his phone. "Good morning."

"Hi, I didn't wake you, did I?" Emma's sweet voice filtered through.

"No, I have been up for a bit now. Is everything alright to be calling first thing in the morning?" He knew Eugenia was still hearing the conversation since his laptop was being a pain in the arse and not hanging up as he told it to, but he would explain later.

"It feels late to me. I could have called at two a.m. while I was taking a bath, and I did think about it, but I did at least wait this long."

Fillan hoped the camera had stopped broadcasting, since his expression had to be...

"Still there?"

"I am. Er... why were you in the bath at two a.m.? Or maybe I do not want to know? You don't... You're not ... seeing someone? Because if you are, it was fully inappropriate of me to kiss you the other night."

She laughed. "I barely have time to see you. Actually, that's why I called. I was afraid you'd be busy during my lunch hour and I didn't want to... Well, I can't make class tomorrow night. Maybe we can..."

"Why?" At the silence, Fillan realized he'd sounded too blunt, but she had him a bit riled. "I meant to ask ... that is..."

"Are you alright? Did I call at a bad time?"

"No, I am still trying to process how you were thinking of calling me in the middle of the night while you were in the bath."

A slight pause came over the line. "I think you might be taking that for more than it was." Her voice was slightly lecturing, with a lightly amused tone.

"I would not be at all surprised by that." He paced outside into the sand. "Why were you up so early, Emma?"

"Couldn't sleep. It often helps me unwind so I can."

"Alright, that is one question down. Next, why are you unable to come to class?"

"Family issues. And don't fuss. I'm not happy about it, either."

Fuss? "I would not fuss at you about it. I am only hoping things are alright. It sounds as if they are not." Silence came from the other end. "Emma?"

"No, they're not so much. I have to get to work now. I just wanted you to know so you didn't wonder why I didn't show up."

"Thank you. I would have worried otherwise, to be honest."

"Is that right? You worry about any of your students who don't show for class?" She was teasing.

"No, Emma. Only you." He crouched to pick up a broken shell. "Call me when you can next. If you have any time today when I am not working, I would be glad to come meet you."

"I'm packed solid the next couple of days, but maybe Sunday at some point?"

"Yes, whenever you can." He hated to let her go since it sounded like she needed to talk, but he told her again to call whenever she could.

Family things, not going well, and not once did she ever talk about it when they were together. Fillan had to wonder if he was making her think she couldn't. It was one of the things the girl had said, that his immaturity made her not comfortable talking to him about anything that mattered. Did Emma think the same?

They referred to each other as hangout buddies, and by now, he wasn't sure who made that inference, but it didn't speak of intimacy. And yet, she was thinking of him while in the bath. In the middle of the night. Even if he was making it more than it had been, it was at least that.

Thirteen

Fillan glanced over at the door in between correcting arm positions and couldn't help but smile. She'd made it. Nearly fifteen minutes late, but she was there. Emma threw an apology for being late as she moved to the back of the group beside her new Indiana friends.

"It is fine. Glad you could get here. We are doing refresh day, going back over the dances we have learned. You are just in time for the quick step." He grinned at her grimace.

No matter how much she grimaced about it, though, she was good at it. Cheney was right; she could easily be in the more advanced group, but she wanted to be in his and that was good enough for him. Fillan walked around couples, some actual couples and some thrown together out of necessity. Emma was dancing with another woman this time, one he didn't think would ever manage to move her feet fast enough for the quick step since she could barely manage the foxtrot.

"You do this." The woman rolled her eyes at Fillan and stepped away from Emma.

"You will not learn it if I do it for you."

"No offense, sweetie, but I'd rather watch you do this one. I think it's beyond my scope." She wiped her forehead and moved to the chairs.

"May I?" He offered a hand.

"Anytime." Emma smiled and moved into the dance with him, now and then watching his feet until he reminded her to look up at him, chin up, shoulders straight.

Others in the group watched them while they worked at the dance, using them as guides. Some gave up and just watched. As the music ended, Emma tripped over her feet a bit, laughed at herself and half fell into him in a hug.

It took everything he had not to kiss her right then and there.

Remembering where he was, Fillan told her she was picking it up well, told everyone to take a couple of minutes for a water break and to catch their breath, and asked her quietly if she was free for the night.

"Two hours, including this. Best I could do and I had to fight for that."

"Can I take you for dinner after class, then? To celebrate the end of your school year, if you will. It was your last day?"

"It was, and you can if you'll let me return the favor at some point."

"Deal."

Emma saw the looks as they left class together, but she couldn't care in the slightest. She did wish she had time to go home and clean up, and said as much, but he was a true gentleman and assured her it didn't matter.

Somehow, it turned into a double date with the Indiana couple, more at their doing than hers or Fillan's, but it was fine. They wound up at Spiritus Pizza so they could sit outside and not offend anyone with their after-dance-class sweat.

It was nice, an easy conversation. Emma could easily see it becoming a routine, except for the fact that she was the only one staying in Provincetown and Indiana might as well be as far as Ireland, considering the amount of stress it would take to travel that far with her niece. The more Delaney talked about travel writing and the way she and Eli just took off whenever he could get time from work to see whatever they wanted to see so she could write about it, the more Emma wished she'd never married Mark, that instead, she'd done the same, just jumped into her car and...

"What are ye thinking so hard of?" Fillan touched her hair, smoothing it behind her ear.

It was a sensual touch and changed her thoughts to wishing she was able to do the same with him, run around and just be together, alone, unencumbered...

"Em?"

"Sorry. Actually, I was thinking it would be nice to pick up and go here and there now and then." She kept herself from saying she meant with him.

"You have never done so?"

"No. It was straight from high school to college, working summers to save money, and then, well ... Mark, who never had time to travel."

Eli asked about Mark and Emma gave them the basics about her ex being, or thinking he was, a big shot in the Boston financial world, similar to what her brother did which was why she'd started talking to him in the first place, and then turned it back to travel stories, letting them do most of the talking. The longer they were there, the closer Fillan nudged toward her until Emma finally leaned over and gave him a soft kiss.

She shrugged at his curious look. "It felt like you were trying to get closer, so..."

"And I thought I was not being obvious." He said it to Eli, who laughed and said he was being plenty obvious, enough he was about to start taking bets with Delaney on how long it would take Emma to tell him to back off. Maybe she should have asked him to back off, but she didn't feel much inclination to do it. With her kiss encouraging him, Fillan set an arm around her shoulder. It felt much nicer than pushing him away would have.

Watching the time, Emma sighed when she had only ten minutes left. Their new friends gave them hugs goodbye and promised to keep in touch. Fillan told them to drive safe on the way home and Emma wished Delaney continuing luck with her baby, that she'd love pictures if she wanted to share.

"I do not suppose you can argue to get another hour?" Fillan held her car door, standing very close.

"I can't. But thank you, for dinner, and for wanting me to fight for another hour."

"Do not thank me. It is fully selfish on my part." He stroked fingers along her face again. "Emma..."

"What are we doing here, Fillan?"

"I am trying to figure out the same. I know it is not fair to you, considering I have not even two months left in the States, but ... I am drawn to you more the more we are together, and even when we are not. Talk about fighting, I am fighting myself non-stop about whether I should be keeping distance, or..."

"You realize I do already know that? I know you're going home. I know I'm staying here. So, it's not like there's any question about what happens at the end of summer. The only question is..."

"What happens until then."

"Right."

"Well, Emma Turner, as far as I am concerned, it is up to you. And with that, I will let you go to wherever you need to be tonight. If you can find an hour or two over the weekend, call me, yes?"

"Do me a favor?"

"Of course, if I can."

"Stop using my last name. It's not really mine and I'm thinking about going in and changing it back."

"Just to have to change it again when you find a man who deserves your heart and ye marry him?"

"I don't expect that to happen for ... a long time to come." She felt her eyes moisten and looked away with a deep breath. At least not one that didn't live across the ocean. "So, anyway, yes, I will call you when I can get away. And thank you, for being so understanding. I keep thinking you'll just give up..."

He slid his fingers along her face and back behind her head. Holding her eyes all the way up to the point they were too close together to hold the gaze, Fillan gave her a warm, soft kiss. "I am not one to give up easily." With another sweet gaze, he backed away and let her get in her car.

It was about all she could do to drive away from him.

Ambling along the beach in front of his cabin, Fillan continuously thought about calling her to check in, to see if things were okay or if he could help. It was after ten p.m., though, and given as tired as she'd been, he was afraid of waking her.

She'd asked where it was going. And she'd kissed him at the restaurant, outside, where anyone could see. It sounded as though she might be fine with a summer ... romance, for lack of better terms. Emma was a strong girl; she fully knew herself and what she wanted.

She had no issues standing up for herself. Much like his ... his ex girlfriend, except gentler, less pushy, more accepting. A girl he could stay with.

Except he couldn't stay.

Grasping a water-smoothed stone, Fillan threw it out as far as he could make it go and listened for the plop he couldn't see in the night, in the dark covering the ocean. He was of a mind to go for a hard swim, but he was not quite fool enough to swim alone in the dark at a point of the beach where a good strong current could pull him under. Besides that, he wouldn't hear his phone from out there in the ocean, in case she called.

Instead, he went back to his cabin, catching strains of music coming from somewhere not too awful near, and turned his own music on to block it out.

~ *Fourteen* ~

"*Ouch*, Patty. Stop. It's Uncle Rob. You can go with Uncle Rob today, right?" Emma rubbed her arm just below where the bruise Fillan had asked her about had finally healed. "Come on, sweetie. Just for the day. I'll come get you tonight."

Patty pushed at her and Rob tried to take over, but she started squealing and Emma told him to back off.

"She's going to hurt you, Em. Let me deal with her."

"She doesn't like to be touched. You know that. Patty, come on. It's fine."

"Emma, you can't always give in to her. How will she learn?"

"Look, I'm the only one who can get her to calm down." Emma had to raise her voice over the squealing. "So don't tell me how to handle her."

"Fine. Then I guess you can take her to see her mom today. She doesn't want me when you always give in to her."

"She's not a toddler, Rob. She's autistic. She doesn't understand."

"Of course she does. She's only being stubborn."

Emma felt her eyes roll. "Just go. I have her. *Go* on." She nearly shoved her brother out the door and went to find Patty walking circles around her couch. "Okay, sweetie. Relax. He left. See? Look."

Patty slowed her circles and glanced up with her eyes, her head still down. The circles slowed and after three more laps, she stopped.

Emma had been considering calling Fillan to see if he had free time at any point during the day, although she seriously needed to do laundry and a bunch of cleaning, but now she couldn't do either. Patty hated the sound of the washer. She always covered her ears and curled into a ball when it was on. It wasn't loud, so Emma didn't know why she did that. The shower running was fine. Doing dishes in the sink was fine, but the washer was not, and neither was the vacuum or the broom which didn't make any noise.

"Okay, so what are we going to do today?" Talking to herself as always, Emma knew she'd have to take her to see her mom. While they were out, maybe Patty would let her run into the grocery store. And she had to do that. She was out of bananas and heaven forbid there wasn't a banana for breakfast in the morning.

"I have to go to the store. Okay? Do you want to go to the store with me?" The girl was going to have to learn to do that much if she was going to be at Emma's nearly full time. "Alright. Let me get my bag and we'll go." Hoping her silence meant Patty wouldn't throw a fit, Emma went to grab her handbag and returned to find Patty at the door. A huge sigh of relief surged through her system.

Fillan shook his head as he hung up. No, no matter how often they asked, he was not taking over the children's class on Saturdays. He had not agreed to do so. It was not in his contract. And he had no interest in dealing with little ones who mostly were there only because their parents dragged them against their will. He did not do children's classes back home. He'd gone out of his way to avoid it since most wee ones annoyed him to beyond his fairly tolerant limits. Fillan hadn't liked them much when he was one himself. He liked himself far better now that he was not one.

The girl had found that reprehensible. She'd said something had to be truly and ridiculously wrong with a person who didn't like children. Could be she had a point. Still, he was who he was. And more and more he saw no need to worry himself about where she was. Not all women wanted to marry and settle to have a brood of runny-nosed little banshees that made even leprechauns look well-behaved.

She'd said he must fairly be a leprechaun himself since he acted enough like one. Eh. Could be true enough he hadn't argued.

Getting out at the grocery store, Fillan thought he might treat himself with a big steak to throw on the barbecue grill that was planted in the sand in front of his rented beach cottage. It would be nice to share it with someone. Emma came to mind, but she was busy today, doing what, he didn't know. Grading papers? Did that happen after the official end of school? He'd no idea. Still, he'd think she could spare a bit of time out of her day. She had to eat, after all, no matter how busy she was. Maybe he should call and see if she could at least do that.

He could say it was an actual end of the school term celebration, without anyone else around, at his cottage, with a couple of steaks on the grill and the soda of her choice. He should offer her an adult drink, Fillan supposed, even if he couldn't have one himself. Did she drink wine or beer? He imagined her as a wine girl, but it was hard to tell. He could get both. Or ask. It would be far more wise to simply ask her which she'd rather have when and if she accepted his invitation.

As he entered the market, he shook his head about some little one throwing a holy conniption somewhere in a checkout lane, one who sounded far too old to act that way. Another reason he did not want his own. Why would you volunteer to put up with a child you did not know how to deal with properly? Fillan knew he was not equipped for it, and the poor soul dealing with that one was not either. At least he was smart enough to know better.

A woman's voice caught his attention. Trying to calm the child. A familiar voice. He didn't want to be one of those who stared at other people in a mess, but he knew the voice. She was apologizing to the cashier.

Emma. And a yelping girl of far too many years to act that way. The girl was nearly as tall as Emma herself and built sturdier. As she carried two bags on one arm, Emma took the girl's hand and tried to coax her to walk. A man behind her fussed at her, said she should teach her daughter how to act in public. She ignored it, but the louder he got, the more the girl ducked into herself, getting louder herself. Fillan headed toward them.

"Okay, *stop.*" Emma yelled behind her at the guy.

"You're telling *me* to stop? Try teaching her how to act..."

"She doesn't understand."

"She'd understand a good paddling, I bet. Have you tried that?"

Fillan went around from behind and stepped between them, facing the man. "Mind your own fucking business. Were you not taught any manners?"

"I'm not the one letting a nearly grownup kid scream in public. Try minding *your* own business."

Fillan nearly slugged him in the nose, but a store worker interfered, so he turned to Emma who cradled the girl's head in her arms, talking softly to her, calming the noise. Until another worker crowded in to ask if everything was okay and the girl got louder.

"Give her space. Please." Emma was nearly exasperated and she caught Fillan's eyes, but looked away.

The girl was not undisciplined. Something was not right with her. Fillan asked the worker to move back, said all was fine, and made a path for Emma to lead the girl out, taking the bags from her arm. Once outside, the girl stopped yelling and stopped walking and glanced around.

"We're done." Emma stroked her hair. "I'm sorry, sweetie, but we're done. We'll go home now."

Fillan followed at enough distance he wouldn't bother the girl and waited a few steps away while Emma got her in the car, in the back seat, with her belt hooked around her. She opened her own door before closing the one beside the girl, and turned to take the bags. "Thank you." She didn't quite look at him.

"You are welcome." He tilted his head to try to see her averted face. "You said you did not have children."

Her eyes touched his. "I don't. I have a niece, and I did say as much. I told you I take care of my niece."

"Right. That you did. I did not expect... I was thinking a young child, I suppose, and not much of it at that. What is wrong with her?"

Anger flooded her face. "Nothing is *wrong* with her. That man kept crowding in, kept clicking his fingernails on his cart right behind us and I asked him to back up. He just moved in closer and it scared her. She was doing fine. Sometimes she doesn't, but she was..."

"Emma." He took a chance and a step closer. "How do I ask without insulting you, which I am not trying to do?"

A deep breath raised and lowered her shoulders. "I'm sorry. I'm just... I hate that question because... because it's not her fault and she's doing nothing wrong. She just... She's autistic. Low functioning, or whatever they call it these days, and non verbal. She's eleven, but mostly she's more like three and that will likely never change. She hates the store, but I had to go, and she was supposed to be with my brother today but he can't handle her when she's upset, when he wants her to do something she doesn't want to do, and I usually can. Not always." Emma shoved a hand through her hair and looked in at where the girl was twirling the end of her hair around her finger non-stop.

"So, now you know and it's fine if you don't want to try to hang out anymore, because I have to be here if she needs me, no matter what else is going on. I understand, really..."

"Where are her parents?"

"Her parents." Emma snickered with a shake of her head. "The sperm donor ran off after she was born. She was two weeks old and it was too much for him. They weren't married, and he refused to have his name on her birth certificate since my sister refused to marry him, so I came to help until Helen, my sister, could manage on her own. Turns out it was too much for her, too. Our parents had to come down to take care of the baby and Helen went back to running around and usually coming home at night, not always. Anyway, she's ... not well and getting worse, and my parents are getting too old, so..." She shrugged and looked in at the girl again.

Autistic. Fillan knew almost nothing about it other than all of the awareness campaigns that only made him aware it was a thing but didn't give him any real idea what it was or what you did about it. The girl's mother wasn't well? And so it fell on Emma, whether she wanted it or not, from how it sounded. But she had other family, and he had to ask. "Your brother? You have mentioned him."

"Married with three half grown kids of his own. Busy. Always. I don't have kids and my marriage was apparently expendable, so here I am."

Expendable. She gave her marriage up for her sister's child who would always be like a toddler? Something inside told Fillan to walk away now. This... He had not bargained for this. And yet, too much more of him wanted the time with Emma he could get. So be it. She hadn't bargained for it, either, but there she was. "Alright, and so..."

"So really, I understand if you want to find someone else to hang out with this summer. I don't have much free time and that's not going to change..."

"Emma." Fillan stepped up next to her and took her hand. "I was only going to ask her name."

She stared a second. "Patty. Patricia, after the sperm donor Patrick, which I told her she shouldn't do when she did it, but anyway, it's Patty."

The horn blew and he jumped.

"Patty. No, ma'am. Sit back down and get that seatbelt on." Emma got into the back seat enough to wrestle the girl from where she was blowing the car's horn, and belted her up again. "Okay, we're going. Sit still." With a sigh as she closed the back door, she moved to her own. "Sorry. I have to get her home before she... Anyway, thank you, for what you did in there."

"I should have thrown a fist into his nose as I nearly did."

She chuckled. "No point getting yourself in trouble. I'll ... maybe see you in class. At this point, I'm not sure anymore what I can do."

"Bring her with you. Dance might be fun for her."

"Too much commotion. She can't. I tried years ago, thinking it might help, but she just couldn't deal with the noise and everything. The other kids were loud. That bothers her more than most anything, kids being noisy. I know there aren't kids in your class, but some of the adults are just as bad. Anyway, I thought I'd have more free time for a while and I probably don't, so don't feel guilty if you can't..."

"Em." Fillan stroked her hair and cupped his hand aside her head. "Look at me." He kissed her lightly and kept his face close to hers. "I am not walking away. I want to know how I can help you."

She fell in against him, snuggling close. Only for a couple of seconds. "I have to get her home."

"Can I come with you?"

"Oh, no, she... She's not good with strangers in the house." Emma leaned into her door to tell the girl they were going.

"Alright, I will let you get her home, but call me if I can do anything for you. Wha'ever time, Emma. Even two a.m. It is fine."

With a touch to his arm, she got in, talking to the girl, telling her everything was fine, and gave him a glance as she pulled away.

She hadn't trusted him enough to tell him. Fillan stood watching the car drive off for a bit, and then went back into the store.

As he tried to remember where he'd left his car, Fillan nearly jumped at his phone's ring. "What is wrong, Emma? Are you alright?"

"Nothing that serious. We're home fine. But I messed up big time and I just can't make myself go back to the store. I can call my brother, but..."

"What did you forget?"

"Bananas. If she doesn't have one in the morning, it'll be a major meltdown. If you're still at the store... Are you, by any chance? If not or if it's too much bother, I'll call Rob..."

"Tell me your address and how to get there."

He saw the questioning look from the same lad who had rung him up the first time, said he forgot something in case he couldn't tell, and wished him a lovely day. The lad rolled his eyes in return. Fillan nearly took his wish back, but he had no energy to bother.

Pulling in front of a house as small as his own place back in Ireland, but with other houses nearly identical pushed nearly right up against it on both sides and hardly any grass at all in the little space between house and sidewalk, Fillan frowned. Was it the right one? The number matched.

He made his way up to the door that needed new varnish over warped wood steps that needed stripped of peeling horrible gray paint, and knocked softly since the sign taped over the doorbell said not to ring. Starting to wonder again if it was the right place, he took a couple of steps backward and the door opened to a mighty ruckus inside and Emma's exasperated face.

"You're a saint. Truly." She shoved hair out of her face that had fallen, or been pulled from her ponytail that had been neat only moments before.

"Everything alright? Do y' need help at all?" He offered the plastic sack of bananas along with a box of chocolate chip muffins.

"Thank you. More than I can say." She pulled a ten dollar bill from her pocket.

"Put that right back in your pocket. Do y' need help?" He flinched at a loud bang.

"She's still upset. I have to go. I'm sorry..." At another bang, she looked back. "Patty, stop that *now.*"

"Can I come in? Sounds like it will not do harm at this point. Am I wrong?"

"I don't know. She'll stop."

Fillan stepped closer. "Let me try to help, Emma. What will it hurt?"

She hesitated ... and arms wrapped around her arm, yanking at her. "Patty, stop. Okay, I'm coming, sweetie. Look, I have your bananas." She started to pull them out but her arm was yanked harder. "Ouch, Patty. Stop. You're hurting me. That's not okay."

Fillan didn't wait longer for an invitation. He pressed into the house, brushing Emma's skin on the way, but it was enough to make the girl let go and back up, shaking her head hard as she looked at the floor.

"Fillan, she can't..." Emma went to her, stroked her head. "Okay, sweetie. Remember, you just saw him at the store. This is Fillan. Can you say hi? Just lift your head up for a moment to tell him hello. He's ... a friend. Okay? Calm down, sweetie. It's fine."

As the girl calmed, he carefully closed the door behind him and remained still otherwise.

"That a girl." Emma stroked Patty's hair and calmed her voice. "Thank you. Can Fillan come in and sit with us? We can share our ice cream with him since he brought your bananas. Okay?"

The girl glanced up at him, at his chin, and looked back at the floor.

"That's as good as you'll get as an acceptance." Emma gave him a tired, forced grin. "Come on in. Keep a little distance from her. She doesn't like to be crowded. You'll have to excuse how the place looks. I haven't had energy to do anything with it. No one ever comes here, so..."

"I did not come to see your house. I came to see you."

"And I'm as much a mess as my house. Or more. Sorry." She pulled her hair down only long enough to straighten it with her fingers and put it back up.

Carefully staying on the side away from Patty, when the girl wasn't looking, Fillan brushed Emma's face with his fingertips. "Stop worrying. And stop apologizing. You are fine as you are."

Emma felt every nerve in her body tense as though waiting for the explosion. Patty couldn't even stand to have Mark in the house. She'd never been able to stand it. Only her family, and Mark had never apparently been counted as that.

So far, though, she was acting like Fillan wasn't even there. She hoped he wouldn't take it personally, but ... he knew and not only hadn't he run, he had brought bananas and come inside her house and acted like the ridiculous mess didn't matter in the least.

"Do you want to have ice cream with us?"

He glanced at Patty. "Will she be okay with that?"

"I have no idea."

He gave her a charming grin and kissed the side of her face. "I am willing to risk it if you are." His eyes said he meant more than the ice cream.

To his credit, he took the chair farthest from Patty and didn't pull it all the way up to the table. So far, so good. She somewhat glanced over at him and otherwise stayed focused on her bowl.

"What do you ladies have planned for the rest of the day?"

Emma watched for signs of agitation in her niece as she brushed a strand of hair back from her own face, a piece she'd missed. "I'm not sure. I thought I was going to catch up on some of this housework today, but..." She glanced at Patty. Nothing.

"That will still be there tomorrow, yes? What would you say to a walk on the beach? Do you like the beach, Patty?"

Emma tensed, but still nothing. "She doesn't talk."

"So ye said, but she hears alright?"

"Yes. She hears very well. Too well, sometimes, since I can't vacuum or run the washer. How much she understands, I'm not sure, since she won't tell me."

Patty finished the ice cream and shoved the bowl at Emma, pointing at it.

"You've had enough, and don't bother to argue with me. You know you only have one bowl. How about we find *Tom and Jerry*?" Emma held her breath waiting to see if she'd have to jump up to stop another outburst, but the girl stood and went to the living room.

She resumed breathing, picked up her bowl, and told Fillan he could bring his into the living room. Her laundry basket of clothes waiting to be washed was still where she'd left it when Patty started to throw a fit, expecting Emma was going to turn the washer on, she supposed, and her bras were sitting on top so she could pull them out and throw them in a separate bag. With warmth creeping into her cheeks, she set her bowl down and grabbed the basket to push back into her room.

"Sorry." She barely looked at him on the way to turn on the *Tom and Jerry* DVD Emma was completely sick of by now.

"I have seen washing to be done before, even girls' things." His eyes sparkled with his teasing.

"The last week of school combined with, well, more hours than I expected... Really, I'm not this messy."

"I do not care if you are." He lowered into a chair on the opposite side of the couch where Patty always planted herself. "Relax. It is all good. And I think she likes me already."

Patty tilted her head slightly his direction, but put her attention right back on the television as the DVD started.

"You could be right. That would make things a lot easier." Emma nearly whispered it as she took the couch end away from Patty and close to Fillan.

When they finished their dessert, Emma took his bowl and went to the kitchen, glancing back a couple of times to be sure Patty wasn't going to throw a hissy about being in the room alone with him. Still okay so far. She took a deep breath to tell herself to relax as he said she should and set them in the sink. When she turned around, he was there, in the kitchen, and Emma moved close to him to where she could still see her niece.

"You have always had this much care of her?"

"No. She's... Her mom is not well and going downhill fast and Patty's getting worse because of it, more upset. Even her school is having trouble with her although she was doing well there. We've had to change her routine and that's the hardest thing for her. I'm the one she's most comfortable with besides my mom, but Mom's so busy now with Helen, my sister, she just can't..."

"There is no one else she is good with to help more?"

"Rob, my brother, and his family. Usually that works, but it's not right now. Fillan, I don't... I'm about to have her full time, and I can't ever leave her alone anymore than you can leave a toddler alone and... She's in school part of the day, and now that I'm not working, I'll have that, at least for the summer since I told them I just can't do summer school this year as I usually do, but of course you work during the day..."

Fillan wrapped a hand around her head, the other around her back, and pulled her in for a kiss. It was a nice long sweet somewhat deep but not intrusive kiss, and Emma nearly melted right there in his arms. She let her head rest against his shoulder and he caressed her back.

"I do not start work until one o'clock, so we have mornings if you want."

"I really expected..."

He moved back to catch her eyes. "Ye expected I would walk out on ye when I knew?"

"Yes. Everyone else has. My friends, even a couple I thought would always be there for me, they can't deal with the fact I can't just go out with them if they call. And Mark... He walked out because of Patty, because I had to be here and ... because I just couldn't think about having kids on top of this. I mean, if changing who picks her up after school makes her this upset, what would adding a baby to the house do? Can you imagine? And really, I'm just not... I'm not real sure I want that, anyway. I work with kids all year and Patty is exhausting. I love her like my own. I do, but it's hard and I just... Anyway, he wanted me to quit teaching and stay home to have his babies and I said no. Patty has to come first to someone since she never did to her mother and... That was petty. And it doesn't matter anymore since Helen only has a few months, if that. Someone has to put her first."

He kissed her again and then rested his forehead against hers. "It sounds like someone might need to put you first, as well, Emma."

"I'm... No, I'm..." Put her first? That would be a novel idea. "Oh,

Fillan, don't do this. Okay?"

"Do what?"

"I can't... You're only here for the summer and I can't..." How did she say it? How could she explain that if she let herself start counting on him when she knew darn well she couldn't, it would just make everything harder when he left? "I have to only think of this as ... a summer romance or hangout or such. I can't..."

"Yes, luv, I understand. But I can at least be here for you this summer, can I not?"

Emma wasn't sure how to answer.

"Go on and do what you want to do around here and I will sit with her. *Tom and Jerry* is one of my favorites."

"You are kidding?"

He chuckled. "Afraid I am not. Go ahead. I will call to you if she needs you."

~ Fifteen ~

Emma woke with a start. The first thing she saw was the small television turned almost too low to hear. The next thing she saw was Fillan, coming from the hallway, the hall that led to the bedrooms.

She jumped up and headed to find Patty.

He caught her shoulders. "She is back in bed. All is well. I was trying not to wake you."

"What? What time is it?"

"Just after four a.m. I am sorry. I fell asleep just after you did, so I imagine."

Fell asleep. With him in the house? With Patty... "I have to check on her." She brushed past him. What had she done? Brought a man she hardly knew into her home with her niece there, her non-verbal niece. She was insane. Emma had long ago read the statistics of how often mentally different children were assaulted because they couldn't tell, even worse than the rates for children as a whole, which were already appalling. And she fell asleep on the couch with a man in her house she hadn't known long? She'd truly lost it.

With her heart throbbing until her chest hurt, Emma went in quietly and touched Patty's head. She looked asleep. Calm. As peaceful as she ever did. She never looked fully peaceful as most children when they slept and Emma was always disturbed by that. Couldn't the girl even have a peaceful unworried sleep?

Her body started to unclench as she stroked Patty's hair. Such a beautiful child. Her child. She was. She needed to keep her full time and help her have a more normal life, as much as would ever be possible for her.

Was Emma ready for that?

With a sigh, she straightened and stretched her shoulders and went back out to ... to Fillan, sitting at the edge of the couch, his elbows propped on his knees. He raised his head and watched her move closer in the soft glow of the television. He'd stayed all night. Most all night. Just hanging out with them. No more. Letting Patty get used to him. Keeping distance. From Patty. And from her. She'd felt no threat, to either of them. And he was simply sitting there waiting for her to return. He wasn't a threat. She wasn't insane. But his expression said he knew she wasn't sure.

Emma sat next to him, maybe too close, but it was comforting. He was comforting, and comfortable. "Sorry. I ... was just startled. No one except my brother has been here since..."

"Since when?" Fillan shifted, turned more to face her, adding more distance. "Do you want to talk now that we can? She was paying attention to everything we said. I could see she was. I hope I was careful enough."

"You were wonderful with her, and yes, she does. Most don't realize it. They treat her like she's ... well, she is disabled in a way, but in some ways she's an incredibly normal kid and smart. She is smart. She understands things."

"Yes, but I think you are avoiding my question." He took her hand and caressed her fingers. "Since when, Emma?"

She hesitated. But what did it matter? "I moved in here right after my husband left. Six, almost seven months ago. It needs work, of course, but that helped me afford it and I'm handy, so when I have time... Anyway, three days after I got the papers in the mail while he was away on a business trip, I packed up, stayed with Rob until I found this, and that was that. Although, it was some time before that when we'd ... bothered to..." She shrugged. "He said if I didn't want to risk having children, there wasn't much point. Meaning I'm sure he had it from somewhere else."

"Nearly a year, then? Ye donae have to beat around the bush."

"Right. Nearly a year. Longer than that for the emotional support, which I needed far more than I needed the physical stuff. I was fine without that, so even though I suspected, I guess I didn't care too much. He kept insisting he should matter more than my family since he was my husband, after all, but he never once put me first, so I didn't think it was unreasonable to... Anyway, when Helen was diagnosed with liver failure on top of her heart problems – alcohol and drugs, way too much of both – he just kept saying it was her own doing and I shouldn't give up my own life because of it. I disagreed and that was pretty much that."

"I would say it was *pretty much that* long before that point if he did not care about being with you other than for children. I have a hard time imagining how he could feel that way, when you are..."

"When I am..?"

He ran fingers through the hair alongside her face. "Far too beautiful to treat as ... property, or such. Not that anyone should be treated that way, but..." His fingers slid down to her neck, around behind her neck. "It is hard to imagine how he could not want you only for you."

"Thank you."

"He is a good looking man, then?"

"Why do you ask?"

"I expect he must be far too full of himself, figuring he could be this lucky more than once."

Emma had to think about how to respond. Lucky? She'd always thought she was the lucky one, that he'd pay attention to her in the first place. "Mark ... is very together, very fussy about how he presents himself, always surrounded by women who are plenty interested in offering whatever he wants. Yes, good looking, but more because of how cocky he is about his looks than how he really looks. Does that make sense? He puts off that everyone should think he is attractive and smart and charming, and so they do. Really, he's hardly better than average. But don't try to convince him of that."

"You liked his cockiness?"

"I liked ... his confidence, when I didn't have much of my own. His interest made me more confident. Not the right way to choose someone, I'm sure, but that's the story."

"I cannot say much on that note."

"No? So, what drew you to your girl back home? She's pretty, right?"

"She is. And I will admit that was the big draw. It turned to more than that, but I cannot say I was looking for more than that at the time."

"You were together a long time. Two years? No wedding plans?" Emma knew she was stalling, just keeping him talking to try not to wonder if she should make him leave or ask him to stay.

"No, it never came up after the night we met when I mentioned I did not ever intend to marry. That worked for her, she said. If she changed her mind about it, she never said as much."

"If she had? Would you have given in?"

"That, I cannot say. Never bothered to wonder if I would, since it never became a conversation. Maybe that should tell me something, right? Should I not have thought about it if I had wanted it to be forever?"

"I don't know. Some couples never do, even after a lot of years."

He lowered his hand to claim hers. Softly. "Could you do so? Live with someone for years unmarried?"

"Oh. By now, probably, since I've been down that road already. Back then, no."

"Right. It would be harder to take the chance again, I would guess."

Would it? Maybe. But then, she'd come through it once and came out okay. She could again if needed. She didn't want to talk more about Mark, though. She wanted to know more about Fillan. "So, how did you meet?"

He looked at her as though he knew she was stalling, but he gave in. "We met at the birthday party my mates threw me for turning twenty-one. I spent much of it only talking with her and she went home with me that night. After a long weekend together, we went our separate ways. A year later, we met again accidentally and ... when she went home with me that night, she decided to stay. I am not sure I invited her to stay. She just stayed."

"So when you're back home and she walks through your door, you'll just let her stay if she decides."

"I think I might have to change the locks so she cannot just walk through the door again. You were right; I deserve better." He squeezed her fingers. "And so do you." With that, he stood. "I should go. Your neighbors will talk already. I am sorry. I did not mean to stay."

"I don't care." Emma heard herself say it and realized she actually meant it. She didn't care. She stood beside him. "They don't talk to me. They've never offered help. One of them even called the police when Patty was having one of her fits and wouldn't get in the car to go home because she didn't want to go home. Why should I care what any of them think?"

"Because you are a school teacher? It does not matter?" He closed the distance.

She swallowed hard. "Well, I'm single. You're not one of my students or co-workers, and you're far from too young or too old for me. I can't imagine why it should matter. I'm allowed to date. Not that this is..."

"Can I stay, then? I do mean here on the couch. You can go on to bed and get some sleep and I will listen for her. Sleep in, Emma. Things do not seem so hard when you're not so tired, from what I have found."

"Maybe true, but she'll be up in an hour or two and she'll want breakfast..."

"I can manage it."

"No, actually, you can't. It has to be the right thing and it has to be on the plate right and the dishes have to be set in the right places. They thought maybe she just had OCD when she was younger, and then they thought she was bipolar because of her sudden outbursts. It's all a guessing game. I do what I've figured out works best and leave the guessing to everyone else. But anyway, I have to get up with her soon, so..."

"So you should be off to bed." He leaned in and kissed her cheek. "Goodnight, Emma. I will be here if you need anything."

For a moment, a flicker of a thought of something she needed he could probably do, and probably fairly well, taunted her. He was ... well maintained, physically, and fairly cute and ... and only there for the summer, although she wasn't at all sure she cared about that, either.

With a light nod, she headed away. And stopped. He was settling onto the couch, with a throw pillow under his head. "Let me at least get you a real pillow and blanket. I'll be right back." She heard him say he didn't need it, but she couldn't have a guest stay without at least somewhat proper accommodations.

Returning, she handed him the only extra pillow she had, from her own bed. He stuck his nose against it and grinned. "It smells like you."

"Sorry. I might have a fresh pillow case. I'm behind on laundry, as you could see. Story of my life, really. Let me check..."

He grasped her hand. "Don't you dare change it. I like that it smells of you." Raising her hand to kiss her fingers, he inched closer. "Thank you. Do sleep well. I look forward to breakfast with you, and if you can, I'll take you both to lunch in return. Will that work for Patty?"

"Maybe, but you don't need to..." She stopped when he stepped closer. And she met his lips. *Four in the morning, Emma. You need to sleep. And you need to stop this right now.*

He stopped it instead. "You kiss nice. Go to sleep now." With a grin, he backed away and settled on the couch, his head on her pillow, the blanket only half tossed over half of him.

Again, she started away, paused, and went back. He looked up at her when she stood in front of him, trying hard to decide what she was trying to do, what she wanted. She was tired. Her brain was hazy. And still...

He moved the blanket, scrunched himself tight against the back of the couch, on his side, and motioned silently for her to join him. He was fully dressed. So was she.

Unable to resist the tender, strong, caring arms, Emma lay next to him, faced away from him. Her body fit his well. Her curves cuddled right in against his form. Her head tucked just under his, half on her pillow and half on his arm. Her eyes closed as he kissed her head, grasped her hand in front of her stomach, and held her in. Protectively.

She could get used to this. Just this.

~ Sixteen ~

Fillan had to get in touch with his sister. And soon. He was complicating things far too much.

And yet watching Emma and Patty as they sat across from him at the table outside Art House Café, one of the only places she could take Patty, she said, since they could sit outside but close to the building, Fillan wasn't sure he wanted to uncomplicate things.

Breakfast had gone smoothly. Emma was surprised Patty didn't throw a fit that he was still there when she got up. He tried to give the girl space without ignoring her and it seemed to be working. Patty watched people walk by as they ate their sandwiches, but if they looked over, she lowered her head and only crept it back up after several seconds and carefully. She also stared up often at the Pilgrim Monument that towered over the town.

Fillan sipped on his cola as Patty tapped her spoon against the table. "Can you give me a suggestion as to where I can take my laptop to be fixed?"

"What's wrong with it? Patty, do that quieter." Emma set her hand almost over her niece's as a sign of some kind which she understood. She kept tapping, but not so loud.

Trying to explain about the thing jumping to pages he didn't try to go to and not loading pages he did want to go to, Fillan grew annoyed with it again.

"Sounds like you have a nasty virus."

"Yes, but I do not want to spend as much as it cost in the first place to have it fixed. Ideas?"

"I can try."

He eyed her over his soda.

"Really. I'm pretty good with them. I've had to teach myself since I can't afford to leave mine for service for two weeks when I need it for grading and such. I fix the ones in the classroom most of the time. I can't promise anything, but I won't charge you for trying."

"I cannot take advantage..."

"Are you kidding? You're not. I'd be glad to return some of the ... well, the..."

"Tell you what. How about you both come out to my cabin this evening and I will make you a beautiful barbecue on the beach while you look at that dreaded machine. Sound fair? Is it more work than that?"

"I won't know until I look at it, but I can't. We go out a bit during the day and then back home by mid afternoon to regroup." She glanced at her niece.

Fillan scratched his chin. The stubble was rough since he hadn't brought his razor for his unexpected overnight stay. Or extra clothes. He'd tossed his shirt in Emma's dryer with some fabric spray she'd made herself that smelled of flowers (lavender, she said, which was what he kept smelling on her), so he was unwrinkled and smelled okay. Still, he needed a shower and fresh clothes. "In that case, I could head back to the cabin for a bit when you ... do your other thing, and I'll clean up and bring dinner, if you donae mind."

"Maybe. I'll have to see if it's going to work and how things go over ... there today."

"You can call and let me know if I should come back or not. So, what do we do next?" He got up. Patty looked to be getting antsy. Fillan didn't want her antsy.

She stood, also, and actually touched his eyes for a moment. A very short moment, but she did, and he couldn't help but smile. He nudged Emma's arm. "I think I might be able to get away with it. What do you think, Patty? Do you mind if I come hang out tonight?"

Patty gave him another fast glance, and started walking.

"Is that an okay?"

"I'm not sure yet."

"Where is she going?" He had yet to see her walk anywhere away from Emma's side.

"To the Pilgrim Monument. I have to take her every time we're out where she can see it. She won't go in, but she likes to look at it up close."

Emma kept an eye on where Patty sat on a bench and stared up at the monument. She wished she knew what the girl was thinking. Now and then, Emma had brought a sketch book and colored pencils to see if Patty would draw whatever was on her mind, but she only drew at home, at the kitchen table, and mainly only circles. There was something in the way she drew circles and walked in circles. Her ABA tutor suggested it could be a sign of looking for security, a safe place she could be away from things that bothered her. They were sure that since she drew connected circles that were round rather than oblong and misshapen, she could learn to write her letters, also, but Patty absolutely refused.

"I'm going to talk to Fillan, okay? He's right there where you can see us." When Patty didn't react, Emma figured she didn't mind, so, watching to be sure it was okay, she moved to where Fillan stood reading the plaque of the Mayflower Compact and slipped her hand onto his arm.

He set his hand over hers. "I have ancestors who came here in the early years."

"A fair amount of Irish came. It's not surprising you would have."

"And you? Are you of direct relation to the early settlers?"

"Not that I know of. But I sure heard about Mark's descendant." She pointed to the top right name. "At least he says it is. Makes him feel important, I guess, to believe his family has been here from the beginning."

"You do not believe it?"

She shrugged. "I don't know. It doesn't matter much to me. I tend to think it matters more what you do with *your* life than what your ancestors did with theirs. Maybe that's the wrong attitude. He says I feel that way because mine didn't do anything of importance. I don't know that they didn't. I haven't the faintest idea."

He turned to her, his gaze direct. "It sounds more and more like he was a right arsehole."

"Oh, no, he wasn't, really. At least I didn't think he was. I was happy enough for the most part. You're only hearing the worst of it because I'm..."

"You still hurt from him leaving when you needed him."

It was a question, although not phrased like one. Emma knew it was. She shrugged again. "Mostly ... I'm just tired and it would take too much energy to worry too much about it one way or the other. I can't change it, so I moved on. I'm good at that." Emma touched his face. "And I will again, at the end of summer. But it's nice to have this now, whatever it is." With a grin, she released him and went to ask Patty if she was ready to go.

~ Seventeen ~

Emma was glad Rob was there when she took Patty to visit her mom so she could sit with Helen a while, as she hadn't been able to do recently. The girl would not go into the house. She sat cross-legged on the front porch and would go no farther. Emma couldn't have left her out there alone, but she was fine with her uncle.

Helen hardly said more than that she wanted to see Patty, although Emma tried to talk to her about the end of the school year and about her dance classes she finally got around to doing, since her sister kept saying she should. She even mentioned Fillan, talking about him as a friend. Usually, that would fuel Helen's interest, but Helen only stared at the door.

"Can I get you anything?"

"My daughter."

With a sigh, Emma gave up trying to reach the sister she'd always known, the one who looked out for her when they were young, who pushed her to follow her dreams, to ignore anyone who said otherwise. The sister who used to love to talk about their days and everything under the sun. The sister who took Emma under her wing for the birds and bees discussion since their mother would never dream of talking about it. Helen said to forget what else she ever heard about sex, that all she really needed to know is that her body should only belong to a man who had her heart enough she was willing to give up a piece of herself to him, because that's what it did; sex with a man gave away a part of yourself that you'd never get back. Helen said she'd learned it the hard way and she did not want Emma to do the same.

Her sister was disappointed when Emma married Mark. She said she'd sold herself out. Why she hadn't listened, Emma wasn't sure, but Mark ... had said all the right things before marriage. Helen had made a joke about Mark BM and Mark AM, before marriage and after marriage, referring to a bodily function that at the time, Emma hadn't found funny.

She badly wanted that laughing, irreverent sister back.

"I'll go try again to see if she'll come in." Emma touched her sister's head. "Try to eat more, okay? Are you taking the vitamins I brought you?"

"No point."

"Oh, Helen. I'd really... You need to meet Fillan. I need your opinion."

"You didn't take it before."

"And I was wrong."

"You'll know what I'd think of him, Em. Consider it or don't. But do something for me." Helen raised a shaky hand to clench Emma's fingers. "Do what makes you happy. Doesn't matter how strange others think it is. Be happy, Emma. You deserve it. I love you, you know, more than anyone other than my baby of course."

"I love you, too. Try to get better. Please." Clenching her jaw to control her emotions, she went out to the front porch, took a deep breath, and sat beside Patty. Rob studied her face. He was already resigned, long ago. Emma couldn't be yet.

She couldn't.

"Sweetie, come with me, please." Emma took the girl's hand and stood, glad Patty stood with her. "We're going to go see your mom, okay?"

Patty pulled away, toward the steps.

"Please. Patty, only a few minutes? Rob, help me out."

"What do you want me to do? Pick her up?"

"No. Just..." Emma wasn't sure what he could do, but Helen would not try to get better if her daughter refused to see her. She *had* to go see her. "I'll get you ice cream on the way home. Okay? But only if you go in and see your mom. I know you understand me. Let's go. I'm not asking this time." She saw her brother's raised eyebrows, but it didn't matter. Helen needed her. She could do it this once. "Come on. Let's go."

With Rob behind the girl and Emma tugging her hand, they got her inside the house. She was jittery, playing with the bead bracelet on her wrist, but she was taking steps.

"That a girl. Thank you. Come on, sweetie. I know you miss your mom."

Patty stepped backward, but Rob was there and set a hand on her back, at which she jumped forward again and Emma used the forward motion to pull her in farther. Seeing how it worked, Rob again touched her back. It worked again. Emma wasn't sure how ethical it was to do it that way, but she got Patty into her mom's room.

Helen smiled, which Patty didn't see since her gaze was on the floor. "Hi, baby. I've missed you. Come sit with me."

With another touch to her back, Patty moved closer to the bed, shaking her wrist. Helen asked Rob to help her sit up, and then to stand. She was shaking almost as much as Patty's hand, but she touched her daughter's face. "Patricia, my baby. I'm so sorry for everything. I want you to know that, okay? I love you so much. You be good for Emma. You'll have fun with her. I know you will." A tear fell and Helen didn't bother with it.

Emma had to work hard to control her own. She was saying goodbye. If Emma had known Helen wanted Patty there to say goodbye... She still would have done it.

Helen kissed Patty's cheek and gave her a soft hug...

And Patty exploded, knocking her mother away from her onto the bed, as Rob kept her from falling too hard. Emma tried to soothe Patty, touching only her head, but she flailed and shoved Emma away, pushed out of the room, knocking furniture over as Emma's mother called for her to stop, which was fully ignored, until Rob grabbed Patty in a tight hug, which made her scream.

There was no choice. He had to do it. Emma realized her nose was bleeding and her mom fussed over her, bringing tissue and then a wet paper towel as the girl screamed while captured in her uncle's arms and Helen called to her from the bedroom.

Making her way to the kitchen to find ice to put on her nose, Emma stayed out of Patty's view until the blood stopped, since the sight of blood would freak her out more. The screaming persisted, but she could do nothing until she wouldn't make it worse. She braced one hand on the counter while the other pinched the ice against her nose. It had to stop. Someone would call the cops again if she didn't stop.

Checking her nose, Emma told her mom it was fine, kept a clean tissue on hand just in case, and moved where her niece could see her. "Sweetie, it's okay. Look at me. Calm down. It's okay. Uncle Rob is going to let go, but you can't swing at me. Okay? You'll hurt me and I know you don't want that. I'll tell him to let go, but calm down first. One, two, three..." Emma counted slowly and as soon as Patty looked calm enough, she nodded to her brother to let go.

He did, but carefully, ready to grab the girl again if needed.

Emma kept counting. By the time she got to fifty, Patty seemed okay and she stopped. Silence. Stillness.

She took a deep breath. "Okay, sweetie. That was my fault. It's alright. I won't make you do it again. Let's go home."

Patty shook her head hard and pantomimed bringing a spoon to her mouth.

"Ice cream first?"

She headed to the door.

Rob suggested she shouldn't be awarded for that, but Emma hushed him. Her mom said Rob should go with her, for her safety, to be sure Patty wouldn't swing at her again, but Emma insisted that Rob stay with Helen and that she and Patty would be fine.

The girl got in the backseat and did her own buckle. It was fine. They'd be fine. Emma stood beside her door for a moment, letting herself settle before getting behind the wheel. Her nose hurt and she checked to make sure the tissue was still stuck in her pocket just in case, but at least Helen got her contact. Short, but the best she was going to get, Emma expected. She would not force it again.

Fillan had every window and the door open in his cabin as he prepped dinner to take over to Emma's, in case she agreed. He'd showered and wrapped in only a towel to keep from sweating again before he had to get dressed, turning his music on for company. Loud. His neighbors weren't at all close. No one came to this part of the beach other than a stray jogger down by the water, so he wasn't likely to bother anyone.

His phone was on as loud as it went and was right by his side on the counter. If he didn't hear it, he'd see the light come on when she called.

Cutting up a variety of vegetables to go with the barbecued chicken he'd done on his grill before showering, he turned to grab a bowl and about jumped on top of his counter at the figure in his doorway. A girl. Smiling. Alone.

"Ye scared the holy crap out of me." He had to yell over his music.

"I knocked. Twice. Am I bothering you?" She glanced at his short towel.

Fillan went to turn the music down, which took him closer to the girl. "Is it too loud? Sorry. I did not realize anyone was close enough to hear it."

"No, I wouldn't have from my place. You often play music with your door wide open dressed in, well, not dressed?"

"When I think I am alone. How can I help you?"

She smiled with another scan. An open scan, appreciative. "We're staying down the beach in the row of cabins nearby. You've probably seen them." She looked to her right from the door. "There are quite a few of us here for the summer. We've been hosting parties at night now and then, just grilling some stuff and having some beers. I've seen you come and go alone and wondered if you wanted to come over and join us." She glanced down his body again.

"Thank you, but I have plans with my girlfriend." Could be Fillan shouldn't call Emma that, but he made his point.

Her smile faded and she shrugged softly. "Well, if you're ever home when we're out, feel free to come over. Bring your girlfriend if you want."

"Thank you again."

"Can I ask where you're from? That's a really nice accent."

Fillan had to make himself not comment on her drawn-out drawl that marked her as from the south somewhere. "Ireland. Galway area."

"Wow, that's cool. It's where Guinness comes from, right? It's my favorite brand. Do you go pick it up from the factory when you throw a party?"

"Guinness Storehouse is in Dublin." He could see that meant

nothing to her. "On the other side of the country."

"Oh. So it would take like a couple of days to get there, right?"

"Two and a half hours more or less."

"What? To the other side? You're in the middle somewhere, then?"

"No. Galway is on the west coast of Ireland. Dublin is on the east coast. It isnae a big country. It would take you near twice that long north to south."

"That's pretty cool. It took us over eighteen hours just to drive up from Tybee Island. So it's like the size of... Texas?"

He couldn't help but laugh. "Not near as big as Texas. More like Indiana."

"Wow, really? Guess it would be easy to travel around, then. Anyway, come over if you want. Whenever." She gave him a flirting smile. "Bye, um..."

"Fillan."

"Fillan. That's a cool name. I'm Deb." She smiled again and waved. "Bye, Fillan. Remember, it's an open invitation."

As she left, he rubbed a hand over his chin and went to close his door. A nice invitation with plenty of flirting. Probably, if not for Emma, he would have taken her up on it.

With a shake of the head, he went back to his stereo, but his thoughts wandered to Emma and Patty. He hoped their visit to Patty's mom went okay, since he knew Emma was not looking forward to it. He checked his watch. Nearly seven. Past dinner time. Had they eaten already? She said she'd call.

Instead of turning the music back up, Fillan called her. No sense packing the food to go if she didn't want him there.

She answered on the fifth ring, sounding breathless.

"Em? All alright?"

"No. Hi. Um, the visit did not go well and when we stopped for the ice cream I promised her, she had another meltdown because some stupid kid bumped into her and we're back home, barely, but she's... I'm sorry. I meant to call when I could."

"Have you had dinner?"

A pause, with some squealing in the background. "Um, no time to

even think about it. I have to go. I'm so sorry. I'll call later, okay?"
She hung up.

Fillan stared at the phone a second, then went to get dressed, threw the food into containers and into a couple of grocery bags, one for warm, one for cool, slipped into his shoes, shut his windows, and locked his door on the way out.

The drive felt like it took forever, even if it wasn't all that far, and he grabbed the bags and went to knock on her door. The squealing was still going on, louder, with Emma's voice telling her to calm down. He heard it through the open window as he saw a neighbor in the yard staring at the house and shaking her head.

Fillan couldn't help calling over to the busy-body. "So I am wondering: have you ever offered her a hand?"

"Not my place."

"Then it is not your place to be rude about what she is trying to deal with. Offer to help or mind your business." Fillan knocked again as the woman turned on her heels and went back into her house. No answer. He tried the doorbell and the squealing got louder, but Emma came to the door as though about to scream at someone herself.

She stared instead.

"Can I help?"

With a gaping breath, she opened the door enough to let him inside and threw her arms around him. "Have you ever just wanted to run away from home? As an adult, I mean?"

He rubbed her back. "I have done that this summer, so ... yes." Fillan felt her body gasp for air, trying to calm herself. "What can I do, Emma?"

"I don't know. I can't... She's... Helen insisted on seeing her and she didn't want to, and then she hugged her tight and that... She about broke my nose trying to get away and knocked furniture over and Rob had to hold her down and..."

Fillan released her enough to see her face and touched her nose gently. "Does it still hurt?"

"No, but be careful. If it bleeds again and she sees it..."

"Oh, Em. This is not alright. You need..."

"I can't take her back to her mom. And I can't tell Helen I won't.

I just don't..." She jerked back at a crash and rushed into the living room where Patty was jumping up and down looking at a potted plant shattered all over the floor, with dirt covering the light-colored carpet.

Fillan touched Emma's back. "Let me try. Right?" Without waiting for an answer, he slowly went toward the girl, stopping before he got too close. "Hey, Patty cake. Come on in here with me. I brought dinner. Are ye hungry a'tall?"

Her eyes flickered up and went back down to the floor, the dirt, but at least she switched from jumping to rocking her upper body.

Emma moved up to her. "It's okay. I'll clean it up. Come on, sweetie. Come on in here."

The girl took a swing and Fillan caught her arm before she caught Emma on the nose again. "Enough of this." He stepped between them. "Come now. Into the kitchen." By some miracle, Patty went with him. He hated to leave Emma alone with the mess, but he figured it was best for now just to get the girl calm. He sat her at the table in the place she'd used the night before and talked as he pulled out plates and food containers, keeping an eye on her to be sure she stayed.

Once everything was set up, he went back to find Emma ... crouching on the floor, with her hands over her face.

Fillan crouched next to her and ran a hand over her head. "Are you alright?"

"She's mad at me. I forced her to see her mom and she's mad. I don't even blame her, but Helen..."

"Okay, Emma. You know you can only do what you can do. You meant well and she will know as much."

"No, she won't. That's the problem. She doesn't know. I've always been the good guy for her and now I have to be both and... Where is she?" Emma jumped up.

Fillan grasped her hand. "Sitting at the table ready to eat. Come and join us."

She looked at the mess. "I have to get this cleaned up."

"It will wait. Emma." He slid his hands aside her head. "It is only a setback, right? She is calm now. Come and eat with us." Sliding his hands down softly to her neck, his thumbs in front of her ears, he gave her a light kiss.

Emma considered telling him he could not leave, could not go back to Ireland. Patty sat and ate as though nothing had happened, but Emma's stomach was in a knot. The chicken was wonderful and she told him as much. He touched her hand and said he'd leave the rest for when she was more in the mood to eat.

To fill the silence, she supposed, he told her he got a visit from his neighbor while he had his door open and only a small towel wrapped around his waist, that he nearly jumped onto the counter, it startled him so much.

"It would have been more fun for you to take her up on the invitation." Emma spoke into her plate since the idea of that girl who didn't even know him getting that much of a view made her suddenly jealous, and the last thing she needed to be was jealous.

"Only if you could have come with me." He picked up her hand and caught her eyes.

Her stomach fluttered, and Emma got up to clear the table. She didn't need that, either. It would be hard enough already to let him leave considering how much help he'd already been. Emotionally. He was incredible emotional support.

Luckily, Patty agreed when Fillan asked if she wanted to go out on the front porch, since it allowed Emma to vacuum the dirt. She closed the window first to stifle the noise. She'd have to buy more potting soil for the plant although it was a hardy type, a pothos, the only kind she bought, and would be fine with the dirt still in there as long as it stayed watered.

When she had it clean enough, although the carpet would have to be shampooed before long, Emma went to the porch. They were on the sidewalk. Jumping over the cracks. She was holding his hand.

Patty was holding Fillan's hand and playing with him.

The sight brought tears to her eyes, both for the relief of knowing someone else would actually be able to help deal with her and the fear of knowing he would leave soon and it would be one more person to leave her. Emma couldn't imagine...

He looked over and smiled until she wiped her eyes. "Okay, Patty cake. Aunt Emma is all done. We can go back in now."

She shook her head once and kept jumping, pulling him with. Emma told him to go ahead if he wasn't getting too tired, and she sat on the top step to let her tired body rest as she watched.

~ Eighteen ~

He must have worn her out good while jumping over cracks on the sidewalk, or her thrashing about had worn her out. Not even ten o'clock and the girl was out like a light.

Emma took a deep sighing breath and went out to join Fillan on the couch, maybe too close, as she had last time, but she was so far beyond grateful ... and it was so far beyond gratitude. The image of him in the short towel with his windows and door wide open was a huge turn-on. It was just... so Fillan. So open and honest and ... bared for the world to see. So to speak.

He stroked her hair beside her face. "How is your nose?"

"My nose is not even... It's nothing compared to..."

"Everything."

"Yes."

"Your sister is not doing any better?"

"She's not going to get better. It's a waiting game at this point. She doesn't even want to get better. It's like she did this on purpose."

He was quiet for a moment. "I am sorry, Emma. I cannot imagine what you are going through."

"You have a sister, right?"

"Yes. Eugenia."

"Are you close?"

"We are, but not in age. She is fifteen years older than I am."

"Wow."

He chuckled. "I was supposed to come about thirteen years before I bothered to get around to it, so Mum says. I took the stubborn Irish trait far too seriously. They had given up long before I came. She thought she was ... well, at the end of being able and I was the quite the surprise. Genie decided I had come for her to practice on."

"And that was okay with you?"

"And why not? How many children get two mothers doting over them?"

Emma sighed. "I don't know. I didn't really have one. Helen was always the shining star, so outgoing and friendly and so smart. Really, she is. Too much, maybe. Not that Mom didn't dote on me at all, but so much of her energy was taken by trying to keep Helen out of trouble after so many years of treating her like the universe revolved around her. A waste of time, to try to keep her out of trouble. Anyway, I just kind of went my own way. Maybe I should have caused trouble now and then, right?"

Fillan stared for a moment, and then leaned over to kiss her. Hard. And long. And deep. Breathtaking. A breathtaking kiss.

"Hm." Emma pressed her lips together as his chest rose and fell fast. "Are you trying to get me to not behave myself, Fillan Reilly?"

He chuckled. "No, I... It was not the intention. Why? Are you thinking of not behaving yerself?"

With no idea how to answer, Emma moved back into him, slowly, setting a hand on his chest. Maybe. But Patty was in the house, so she backed away. "I need chocolate."

"Um..." He shrugged with his hands when she got up. "Now?"

"Yes." Emma went to the kitchen to pull out the muffins he'd put in the bag when he brought bananas and offered him one as he followed. He refused and stood against her refrigerator as she sat down. "You don't want to sit?" She stabbed the thing with a fork and took a big bite.

"I think I will stand for now."

"I have... um..."

"I donae need anything. Emma?"

"I don't know."

"You do not know what?"

"If I ... yes, I know what it is I want, but whether or not I should or can let myself is a different story."

He stood silently a while and then came over to sit next to her. "Easy enough to answer. You should not."

She met his eyes.

"With me. Since I have no choice but to leave soon. But you should..." He sighed with a shake of his head. "You should find..."

"Don't even say it." Emma set her fork down and turned toward him. "I know this has been easy with you, but it's not usually. I'm awkward with men. And don't give me that look. I mean with men I'm attracted to, not just men in general. I... Besides, who on earth is going to be flattered by the fact that I want someone to help me with my autistic niece who will soon be my daughter when I have little energy to spend other than on work and on her? How is that going to attract anyone worth attracting? I'm no idiot. I'm not enough of a catch to be worth that..."

Fillan slid a hand behind her head and gave her a soft, quick kiss. "You are enough of a catch to make me think of not going home, when, before I met you, I was more than ready to go home."

"Don't. Don't even say it."

"It is the truth."

"Fillan..." She got up, needing to move around, and paced out into the living room, away from him.

He came toward her and she paced more and he stopped, remained still, waiting... "I am going to go on back to the cabin now. Take a long, hot bath, Emma, and unwind..."

A squeal came from the back and Emma rushed to Patty's door. She was thrashing around, so Emma kept just enough distance to protect her face while she told her she was there, everything was fine, and sat next to her when she calmed, stroking her beautiful face. It took forever until she was asleep again and Emma was nearly asleep herself by then.

He likely left. She hoped he left. And she hoped he didn't. He was right, of course. She shouldn't with him, for so many reasons.

A hot bath. Maybe she would, although she had every expectation that she'd think of him in his towel, windows and door open, the breeze blowing the bottom of it away...

Getting up carefully, making sure Patty stayed asleep, she went out to put her muffin away, or finish it, and stopped when he looked up from the couch in the mostly dark living room, with the light from the kitchen glowing in on him. He looked darn near angelic with his blond curly hair glowing. Of course he was not. Fillan Reilly was nowhere near angelic and she knew it full well. She was actually surprised he hadn't taken the party girl up on her offer. It would be a much more fun summer for him.

"Is she alright?"

He hadn't left. Emma stared, thinking of the towel, of...

"Em? Should I have left?"

She walked up in front of him and slid her fingers through his beautiful hair. And soft. It was incredibly soft. When she kissed him, his thighs closed in against her legs, his hands slid under her blouse. Emma moved in closer, lowered her arms to around his shoulders as he moved back against the couch, and straddled him. He reacted so beautifully, so gently.

They didn't bother to discuss it. There was no need. Her need was too strong. He was too willing. She thought of taking him to her bed, but if Patty got up, that's always where she went first and if Emma locked the door, it would lead to a huge hissy fit and...

Fillan slipped her blouse off her shoulders and picked her up, his arms around her hips, laying her onto the couch, taking over as she wanted. He was beautiful, well built, and she told him as much before he hushed her with a kiss, rid them both of the rest of their clothes, and lowered over top of her.

That anyone would have ever doubted his masculinity was beyond her fathom. He was beautiful, beautifully masculine, and so very gentle, so attentive to her needs. Everything Mark wasn't.

She held him tight as they caught their breath and he made no attempt to pull away.

"Em." He kissed her shoulder and then her nose. "You should come to Ireland."

To Ireland. She almost laughed. "I'm sure that would be fun, getting Patty on a plane and then..."

"I could come back and go with you so you would not be doing it on your own."

He was serious. Emma again wasn't sure whether to laugh or cry. "I have to work."

"Christmas vacation? You have two weeks then, do you not?"

"Yes, but... Fillan."

"Em, this..."

"This." She shook her head. "This is a beautiful summer gift. And then you'll go on back home to your life and on to whatever you want to do, and you won't need us interfering with that."

"Em, I am serious. I can come a week before and let her get used to me again and the two of us can handle getting her there. You can stay the two weeks and I will come back with you again..."

"You realize how expensive that would be."

"If I do as my father wants and sign on with him, I could well afford it."

"You don't want to..."

"Perhaps I do. I can teach on the side."

"You don't understand. You've barely seen it yet. You don't know how it runs everything in your life. You don't even want kids or like them, from what you've said. You... This is incredible, and I will always be grateful for..."

With a roll of his eyes, he got up and got dressed.

"That's not what I meant."

"Is it not?"

"Fillan, please." Emma pulled the sheet over her, the one he'd used the night before she hadn't bothered to put away.

He went to the door and put his shoes on.

She followed him and wrapped an arm around his neck. "That's not what I meant. I mean for the help you've given me, not for..."

"The stress relief, yea?"

Emma stared. Stress relief? Is that what he thought?

"It is fine, Emma. I will at least have had that, right?" He pulled out of her grasp and opened the door.

"Please." She grabbed the back of his shirt as he stepped out onto the porch. "I don't give myself away that easily. It wasn't that."

He turned and his chest rose and fell hard. "Alright. Well, whenever you figure out if you want it or if you do not, let me know." Sliding a hand back through her hair, he gave her a deep kiss and told her good night.

Emma watched him until she couldn't see his car, until she noticed a guy sitting on his front porch across the road, staring at her. Quickly, she stepped back inside and bolted the door.

If she wanted it or not? She'd told him...

The girl back home. He was gun-shy.

Yeah, well, so was she. And she had more than herself to think about.

Heck of a way to end what had been a wonderful, breathtaking moment. With a quick check on Patty, Emma shut herself in the bathroom and turned the water hot.

Fillan got all the way home and slammed the door behind him when he realized what a stupid thing he'd just done. She had every reason to protect herself, to be wary of starting something he couldn't finish, and then he'd talked immediately of her coming home with him. It was too much too fast and... and how did he think she would bounce back and forth during vacations like a carefree bachelor when she had her niece, soon to be her daughter, to look after?

Soon. How soon? Emma avoided the conversation. She hadn't said, but it sounded like she expected a few months for Patty to adjust, to have to keep taking her to see her mom, which didn't sound like it was a good idea.

The girl had hit her in the nose. And the bruise on her arm the other day ... hit on a door, she said. Fillan expected she had help with that. Patty was too big and too strong for Emma to handle well. Maybe he could stay...

Fillan dialed her number. Four rings, five, voicemail. He hung up. What did he expect?

Unable to sit in the cabin alone, he went out onto the beach, phone in hand, and gazed up at the stars while he walked. There was no breeze and the heat penetrated him fast. Music. He heard wisps of music drifting over. The neighbor girl and her beach party, he expected. With a brief thought of walking over, Fillan turned the other direction, away from them.

At least the moon was close to full. It provided a good bit of light. Without the wind, the waves were calm, other than the pull of the moon. Good swimming time. Maybe he would. Once he got far enough away from the party for comfort, Fillan stripped down to his drawers, pondered a moment, and pulled those off, as well. He set his phone on top of his clothes, on the loudest setting, and hoped he would hear it if she called back.

The water was crisp, especially when it splashed up between his thighs, but the coolness felt good atop the heat of the night and the thoughts of his rash behavior with a girl who deserved better of him.

Emma woke with a start when her chin hit the cold water. She'd fallen asleep. In the tub. Shaken by the thought, she got out of the tub, drained it, and rubbed her cool skin dry, the fingers shriveled from being wet too long. Since she hadn't bothered to grab her robe, she wrapped the towel around her and was reminded of that girl seeing Fillan in his towel prancing around his cabin.

Grabbing her phone to take to bed with her, she noticed a missed call. He'd called. When? From the time, she guessed as soon as he got home. The cabin. It wasn't home. And that was ... two hours ago. She'd been in the tub that long?

Knowing she couldn't call him back just before one a.m., Emma thought it was just as well she didn't. He should have stayed and talked about it, let her explain, instead of running. She had no energy to deal with an overly-sensitive man on top of an autistic child and her dying sister on top of her classes of unruly kids, too many of whom hadn't been taught to listen.

Still... it had been a rather glorious twenty minutes or thereabout.

Fillan was panting hard by the time he reached shore again. It pulled him out farther than he'd realized and for a moment, he'd nearly panicked. He knew better than to panic, he did. You didn't grow up in a fishing family without knowing how to deal with rough water for a time if needed.

Still, he felt a right fool for going out there in the first place. And now he had to orient himself since he didn't see his cabin. Had he left a light on as normal? He didn't remember. He had to be west of his cabin, and a good ways from it since he no longer heard the music, unless they had turned it off. He expected they hadn't.

Walking along the beach was normally fully relaxing, whatever time of night, but given he was all exposed and unsure how far away he was, Fillan had to admit he was a wee bit nervous. He should have stayed at Emma's. His method of stress relief was far more unintelligent than hers had been.

And even if it was stress relief, what of it? He could use some of that himself about now.

By the time he was starting to feel a touch of panic return, Fillan heard it. The music. He had never been as thankful to hear bad music in all his life. And to see that he had left a light on, so by now, he could barely make out where his cabin was, which made it easier to find his clothes, and his phone. The first thing he did was to see if she called.

Nothing. As he would have expected.

Sweeping his clothes into his other hand, Fillan headed toward the light up the beach, and double-checked in case there was a message and it only didn't show. Nothing. "Come, Emma. At least call me back, love."

"You have a habit of talking to..."

He jumped at the voice. The girl at his door again. Staring. From his porch.

"Sorry. I did knock. Your light ... was on." She glanced down at him, more than only a glance.

Fillan pulled his clothes up in front of himself. "Right, and then if you are done staring at my willy, could you move out of my door so I can go in now? And no, if you are inviting me again, I think I will have to pass."

"Oh. Okay. But, you know..."

"It is an open invitation?"

"Yes." She glanced down again, at his stomach since the other part was hidden. "Don't be embarrassed. I mean, we're like, really open and all, too. You would fit right in."

Judging by the very skimpy bikini she was wearing, with only a sheer skirt over top, he could have guessed that. "Good night..."

"You forgot my name." She stepped down closer.

"I did. My apologies. It has been a very long day."

"Deb." She grinned. "So maybe you need someone to help you relax?"

"My girlfriend would not find it very much amusing, I would have to guess. Good night, Deb. And I will remember your invitation so you have no need to come and give it again." Watching the girl shrug and smile with an "I don't mind" and a toss of her hair, Fillan shook his head and went up the one step to his door.

"Hey, Fillan?" She turned back.

"Aye, Deb?"

She giggled. "Aye. That is so adorable. You're really adorable, you know that?"

"Alright, then. Good night."

"No, what I was going to say is..." She leered all the way down his body and back up. "Your girlfriend is really lucky. You should tell her I said so." With another giggle, she flipped her hair and trotted off, wagging her tail behind her like a good little lost sheep.

"Aye, what a day. I could use a real pisser about now." Locking his door behind him, although he often didn't bother, Fillan dropped his clothes into the box lined with a plastic bag that worked as a hamper, turned on the shower, and went to grab a root beer, which was as close as he could get to having an actual pisser without killing himself in the process. A fine thing that would be, and all Emma needed to have to deal with atop everything else.

His girlfriend was lucky? She didn't apparently think as much.

Downing a third of the bottle, he set it on the counter and went to wash himself good.

Emma lay in bed staring up at the dark ceiling. Would she be able to go to dance tomorrow, after everything? Or would she even be able to get away for that long? How would she face him? If she didn't go, would he call again? Maybe she'd call in the morning and ... and say what?

Anything. She had to return his call. Whatever happened from there, she had to return his call.

It was partly her own fault, the way she'd been so back and forth, saying she didn't know if she could and then coming on to him all within minutes. She deserved to have him walk out on her. The only question was whether he thought she might deserve another chance.

He had called. Of course it could have been to tell her not to bother him again, not to come back to class. Anything. But maybe it wasn't. Maybe he would realize she'd just had a very hard day and it didn't come out right, what she'd said.

You should come to Ireland.

Could be he was right. But how would she? How could she do it to Patty?

~ Nineteen ~

Dropping Patty off at school, fifteen minutes late because she wouldn't change out of her pajamas and then she wouldn't eat breakfast and Emma had to coax her all the way, she dropped back into her car and picked up her phone. Maybe he would meet her somewhere to talk since they both had the morning off.

Just before she hit his number, the phone rang. Not him. Rob. Emma tried not to sound irritated when she greeted her brother.

"Emma, you need to come over to Mom's."

"Now? I just dropped Patty off..."

"I know. I waited that long, but you need to come now."

Her breath caught. Somehow, she answered and hung up and sat for a second. *Not yet. Please not yet.*

Fillan went back and forth about a hundred times as to whether or not to try calling again. He didn't want to crowd her, but he didn't want to lose her, either. Deciding to keep it casual, he rang her number, again got her voicemail, but this time, he left a message: "Hey Em, just want to say I hope you will be in class today since we are learning the samba and I would rather have your help to show it than the old woman who keeps hitting on me, right? Would you forgive me enough to do that much?"

Hanging up, he thought maybe he shouldn't have added that last bit. Still, it would sound as though he knew he was wrong for walking out, and he expected she should know he did.

Emma forced herself back to the school to pick Patty up, and she forced herself not to cry when seeing the innocent face. How would she explain? How much did Patty already understand? She possibly understood far more than Emma had understood, that her mom was already gone and only waiting for the time to pass.

"Hi, sweetie. How was your day?"

The ABA tutor who always waited with Patty for Emma to come

asked if she was alright. Out of Patty's hearing, Emma told her the girl's mom had passed away and asked if she could please pass along the message. With her sympathies, she promised she would and said they would watch for signs of Patty needing extra attention for a while.

Extra attention. Emma had the feeling Patty would only be relieved not to be forced in to see Helen anymore. A sad thought, but she couldn't blame her niece. Part of Emma felt the same. It was hard. At least her sister was finally at peace.

Choking back the sob that had tried to come ever since Helen had slowly released Emma's fingers and stopped breathing, she held the door and made sure Patty was buckled and drove toward home. But she didn't want to go home. She wanted chocolate.

Actually, she wanted Fillan.

And she couldn't handle either right now. So she drove home, got Patty's snack out for her, an apple and a handful of pretzels, the tiny ones she liked to dip into the cheese dip Emma always had to keep on hand, and sat across from her with a warmed cup of coffee.

Their normal routine. Emma had to keep the routine as normal as possible. Inside, she wanted to scream at the top of her lungs and crumple into a ball and just shut everything out. Outside, she asked Patty about her day, knowing she wouldn't get an answer, and asked what she wanted to do and made believe everything was fine. Normal.

She wanted Fillan. Emma just wanted to see him, to hold him. Maybe it was stress relief. Maybe he was right to be angry. Hurt. Whichever he was more of, which was hard to tell. But it wasn't just that.

Choking back tears again, Emma went to find the phone she'd dropped in her handbag after Rob called her and hadn't bothered with since. She just wanted to... But he would be in class now, the class she hadn't gone to. That wasn't bound to help matters.

A missed call, and a message. Standing at the kitchen door where she could see Patty but still have a touch of almost privacy, Emma played it. The samba. He wanted to samba with her. If she could forgive him...

Shoving away the sudden tears Patty could not see, Emma paced the living room and returned to check on her. She couldn't call now. He was in class. She was missing her class. And she would miss Friday, as well, since they had scheduled the funeral for then.

The need to scream at the sky returned and Emma went to the refrigerator to pull out the ice cream and chocolate sauce. She and Patty both deserved to indulge today. They were now in this together, whatever came, the two of them.

Twenty

Emma heard the knock on her door, but she couldn't answer it, not with Patty on the verge of an episode. Apparently the chicken and vegetables Fillan left that were absolutely fine then was now absolutely taboo. The thought crossed her mind that it was Fillan Patty was missing, since they were eating what he brought and he wasn't there. A ridiculous thought. She barely knew him.

And yet maybe not ridiculous since she adjusted to him so fast, had taken his hand and jumped over sidewalk cracks with him.

It was possibly him at the door. Maybe it would help...

She cursed at the loud ring of her phone and Patty started rocking harder. Grabbing it to make it stop, Emma grimaced at Mark's voice. "Now's not a good time."

"Hello to you, too. I heard about Helen and I wanted to say I'm sorry."

"Thank you. I have to go..."

"Emma, wait. Can I come by tomorrow?"

"Why?"

"To offer my support?"

There was no way to control the snicker that forced its way out while she stroked Patty's head and told her everything was okay, then wandered into the living room so she wouldn't hear. "Support? Really, Mark? Do you even know the meaning of the word? Support? Thank you, but please don't. I have enough to deal with right now."

"Okay, fine, but will you call me if you need anything?"

"No." It came out before she realized she was saying it. "Mark, no. You understand the meaning of divorce, right? You should, since you sent me the paperwork."

"No need to get pissy. I'm trying to help."

"Then *leave me alone.*" Emma hung up and tossed her phone on the far side of the couch... The door. She wanted to check...

Patty's rocking turned into squeals, soft so far.

Fillan was about to knock again, although he considered the doorbell instead, but the *leave me alone* was too unmistakable. Did she know it was him? Was someone else bothering her?

Unsure what to do, he stood there a bit, and left. He didn't go far, though, only up to the coffee shop where they'd first sat to talk. With a hot tea in hand, Fillan found their same table, in the back corner, and made himself send a text. He hated to text. It took forever. But he thought it might be less pushy, less intrusive.

What to say, though? Since he'd made up his mind to talk about class, he did that: *Em please come to class Friday. I do not want you to give up dancing. We can be adults yes? I will behave properly and my guess is you have never behaved other than properly. You can samba with anyone else if you prefer. I am still available mornings. I will let you be now unless you call.*

Fillan considered and reread the message a couple of times before he hit send. Could be it wouldn't matter what he said. Walking out on a woman right after your first time together was likely the stupidest thing a man could ever do. Maybe not the stupidest, but up there among the stupidest.

When a return text came through, Fillan was almost afraid to look. Gritting his teeth, he opened her message:

cant friday. Im... will call when possible

She was even worse with texting than he was. When possible? What the fuck did that mean, *when possible?* Meaning when she could make herself deal with him again? Or was she that tied down with her niece?

How could she live that way?

How could he agree to do the same? Even just for the summer. He was on holiday, mostly.

Stop being such a selfish arse, Fillan. You at least get to choose. You are not the one with the right to bitch.

His temper calming, he went back to his car and started home, but decided to detour. Running by the market, he grabbed bananas and chocolate muffins, went back to Emma's, tried knocking with no answer, and tied it to the inside handle of her screen door. A peace offering.

He had to play by her rules, since they weren't hers, but Patty's, and Patty had enough struggle...

And he wanted to help. Even if for a few weeks. Wouldn't it be better than not having the help for a few weeks?

After midnight. Emma was exhausted, and yet she couldn't sleep. Her quick reply to Fillan wasn't close to what she wanted to say. She should have waited to answer until Patty was calm and she had time... But she'd already put him off so long, she was afraid not to answer at all.

She wanted to go to class Friday instead of the funeral. Helen wanted her to keep dancing; she'd understand. Her family, however, was a different story.

The rest of the week, her mornings would be tied up with funeral plans and moving Patty's things slowly from her mother's house to her own, slowly so it would be minor adjustments rather than a major change, and Emma hoped that would work.

And she had to decide what to do with Helen's things she had in storage. Much of it was from her travels, keepsakes and treasures, not furniture. Furniture would be easier. They'd sell it. But Helen's keepsakes wouldn't be easy to part with. Someone had to go through it, and already, Emma knew that was going to be left for her. When she could. Rob said he'd pay the storage fee until she could make herself do it. Nice of him, she supposed.

Unable to sleep, she got up and made herself a cup of herb tea, chamomile, the only kind she could stand, thought of Fillan as the water heated in the microwave, and took it to the living room. His sheet and pillow were still there, so Emma curled up against the end of the couch, against his pillow that now smelled like him, and pulled the sheet over top. When drowsiness kicked in, she set the cup on the coffee table and settled back in.

Twenty-one

On Wednesday morning, Emma stole out of the house into the backyard while her parents talked with their long-time friends. Taking her phone, she gave Fillan a call. She didn't want to text. She wanted his voice.

No answer. With a sigh, she thought quick about what kind of message to leave, but her brain was an exhausted jumble and she couldn't tell him over a message what was going on, so Emma said she was sorry she'd been out of touch and that, if he wanted, he could stop by around dinner time, she'd have something ready, and they could talk.

With a hard swallow to check her emotions for the hundredth or so time, Emma sat in the grass and wished she was out by the lighthouse with Fillan, or even alone. She missed her sister. By now, the finality of it was hitting hard. She had no one left to jabber about any little thing. Her few friends, which she didn't make easily, had given up on her because of Patty, because she too often had to turn them down or leave in the middle of a movie or dinner. And her sister had given up on herself, leaving her with no one left for intimate conversations.

Mark wanted to offer support? It was almost enough to make her laugh. Emma had never been able to talk to him about intimate things, even just rambling things. He did not do small talk and he did not do emotional. He'd admired her strength, he said, meaning the way she didn't have to lean on him when he didn't want to be beleaguered by a spouse who might actually need him at times.

Fillan did small talk well. He also did real talk well.

"Call me back, please." She spoke to her phone, since it was what she had available. Maybe she'd take Patty out to the beach. It was cloudy, somewhat threatening, but by the time her school was out, it could be clear enough. Of course, if it started to rain, that would be a whole other ordeal. Patty couldn't do rain. She watched it through the window, sometimes for hours on end, but heaven forbid it hit her skin.

Wrapping her hands over her head, Emma leaned down over her crossed legs. How was she going to do this alone?

Fillan checked his phone for maybe the twentieth time. Class was about to start, his step dancing class mainly with older teens and early twenties. A small class. The one after his, the hip hop dance, was full. He had stayed to watch often, intrigued by the moves, and he now and then worked on them in his cabin. He could understand the interest in the bold movements, the bold music, the rhythmic beat. It didn't do much for him, but he understood it.

The contemporary class that followed, he appreciated more. Its teacher, a young woman, asked if he wanted to join them, since male partners were hard to find, but since the students were young girls, school age still, Fillan declined. It was too intimate a dance style, as much as the Latin dances were, or more, even. He wanted no part of that, not with young girls, not even as a teacher.

And again, on Friday, he would have to teach the samba without Emma's help. Unless she changed her mind or was able to fight for that hour off, but since she hadn't answered him at all, Fillan didn't dare believe she might.

Glad Patty was quiet and relaxed during dinner for a change, Emma put the leftover casserole, brought by one of her parents' friends, away, and put *Tom and Jerry* on so she could have a little bit of space before the bath and bedtime struggle. Flipping her laptop on, Emma hoped he answered her through email instead.

There was a lot of spam but no message, so she opened the email he'd sent with the photos of him Emma had taken. Unable to help herself, she ran her fingers over the screen where his face was.

And then she snapped the thing shut.

Maybe his laptop had stopped working and he couldn't use it. He'd said it was messed up. He was supposed to bring it to her to fix. Maybe he didn't trust she could and he took it elsewhere and didn't have it back yet, or he had it back and didn't want her to know he'd taken it elsewhere.

If not for Patty, by this point, she would go to the studio to confront him as he left whatever other class he taught today. Today, Wednesday, was ... step dancing. She knew because she almost signed up for that, as well, as soon as she realized he taught it, just after he'd gone out to pull her back in to class when Cheney had nearly chased her away.

She loved him for doing that. She... She loved him ... for everything. Except his silence. That, she didn't love so much.

Needing to do something with herself while Patty was distracted, Emma put her MP3 player on with her headphones, flipped through to something that would work ... Ty Herndon, the *If You* song that had amused her so much when she heard it just after Mark had called to see if she got the paperwork and to see if she actually meant to sign it, saying he'd tear it up, withdraw the petition, if she didn't. Remembering his surprise when she told him she damned well would sign it and send it right back, Emma used the enjoyment of that moment and practiced her foxtrot steps as though Fillan was there with her.

If you... Emma sang some of it quietly as she danced, with more of an F sound than an if. There had been no *if* about whether she would. As soon as the shock of the thing wore off, she signed the stupid paperwork and took it right back to the post office to send certified, to be sure he got it.

When the song ended, she turned it to *Fighter*, but she was too emotional for that at the moment and pushed it forward to ... *Just Friends*.

At the chorus, Emma stopped dancing and closed her eyes to listen. She did not want to be only friends with him. They'd crossed that line and she did not want to backtrack.

She wanted to learn the samba. Emma very much wanted to do the samba with Fillan, not with anyone else. He'd said she could choose another partner from the group if she wanted, but she did not. Using the adrenaline that arose with the thought, she changed songs and practiced the quick step for the energy release she desperately needed.

~ Twenty-two ~

The last place Fillan wanted to be was in class. A beautiful Friday afternoon and he hadn't seen or talked to Em since Sunday. He'd kept hoping she'd change her mind, about class, or about him. Both, with the greatest luck – luck he'd never had much of and didn't expect.

By the start of class time, only about half his students were there. Had they found out what an arse he'd been and withdrawn? She wouldn't do that. Emma would not talk about their personal lives with his group. "Everyone away to the beach today, or was the samba that hard on Monday?"

"Most of them are at Emma's funeral." The always-in-the-front woman shoved a hand to her waist. "Surprised you're not."

"What?" His chest hurt. His stomach lurched. Emma's funeral?

"Her sister's. Not hers." One of the suck-up students who wouldn't miss class for a cyclone rolled her eyes. "Her sister died Monday. After a very long time of waiting for it, from what I heard. Tragic for someone so young, and with that poor kid..."

Her sister. Fillan forced breath again. "When does it start?"

"Now." The girl looked at her watch. "About ten minutes ago. I feel bad for not going, but I just can't do funerals. Can't handle it. I know that's crazy but..."

"Where? Tell me how to get there." He heard Cheney say he couldn't leave, he had class, but he paid no attention to anything except the person who could give him directions and he raced back out to his car. Her sister. Patty's mom. Patty would be with Em full time. Monday. She'd lost her on Monday and hadn't said as much?

Parking in the nearly empty funeral home lot, which he found odd if the service was there, Fillan got out and stopped. He was in dance clothes, loose shorts and a T-shirt. He couldn't go in like that. And he couldn't interrupt if it had started. So he waited. He could see the main door from where he stood leaning on the boot of the car. How long would it last? Twenty minutes already now. He had been to services that lasted no longer than that, and he'd been at those that were interminably long, which felt like torture to him and had to be worse for the families. He hoped she wouldn't have to sit through that for much longer.

Whil he waited, he tried to decide what to say to her. What could he say? Unlike Miss Suck-up at the studio, he handled funerals fine. He'd always been able to say something soothing and try to show that it wasn't the end of the world. Maybe for the body in the casket, it was. For everyone else, it was another step in the circle of life, and it happened. No use making a huge deal of it.

She had jumped him for that, as well. His ex. He was heartless, she said, after going with her to one of her distant relatives' funerals, one she hardly knew and yet still made a huge fuss about. Hypocritical, he'd said, to never bother to see the great uncle when he was alive but to throw a fit because she couldn't go see him now that he was dead even if she'd never decided to do so when she still could. Made her right furious for the longest time.

Do not make that mistake with Emma. At least convince her it matters to you that it hurts her. Wouldn't be hard to do, he expected. It did matter that she hurt. She had spent plenty of time with her sister. She'd truly loved her the way he loved his own. And he hadn't been there all week.

The large wooden doors opened and Fillan straightened. A few people drifted out into the yard. Somber-faced. Dressed in dark clothes, nice clothes, not shorts. Fillan wandered closer, to the edge of the little street, not crossing it yet to the yard where they stood. Not many. Had her sister not many friends? Not much family? Or had they not bothered?

A couple of people glanced over at him, their expressions caustic, as though he were intruding. He guessed he was since he hadn't been invited. Another small group filtered out. The dance group. One of them saw him and came to him, scanned his clothes, rambled...

But Fillan didn't hear her. Emma was there, in a dark blue straight dress, unembellished, but striking on her figure. An older couple was with her, somber but composed. Her parents, he guessed. The woman looked like her. And a man. Her age but adding a few years. With a hand on her back. Her brother? She'd mentioned... No, Fillan spotted her brother. He looked like her, as well. But harder.

The guy touching her back spoke into her ear. She didn't acknowledge him.

Fillan found himself crossing the street into the funeral home yard. Should he? The student beside him said something about his clothes, he should have dressed better, it was disrespectful...

But Emma lifted her chin at something the guy with her said and spotted him. She held Fillan's gaze. He held his position, waiting to see, from her reaction, what he should do. Stay or go? Give her a quick I'm sorry and head away? He didn't want to head away. He wanted to offer his arm, his shoulder, whatever she wanted.

The guy followed her gaze, said something to her, which she also didn't acknowledge. Emma walked away from him, away from the brother who looked to be asking where she was going, and came straight up to Fillan. She didn't speak. She stared, a curiosity mixing with her grief.

"I just now heard. Went to class..." He motioned toward his clothes. "And they told me. I am sorry, Emma. How are you doing? Where is Patty? Is she alright?"

She looked about to answer, but her eyes misted and she threw her arms over his shoulders and buried her face between her arm and his jaw. Her body heaved.

"Oh Em, I am so sorry. What can I do?" He held her close.

Her chest heaved, her breath heated his neck. Fillan stroked her head.

"Emma?" The guy who'd been touching her stood behind her. He scanned Fillan. Cocky had been far too nice a term. The guy was arrogant as all hell. Had to be the ex.

She released him, wiped her eyes, and pulled herself back to her earlier composure, but she grasped Fillan's hand and her attention stayed on him. "Thank you. For coming. I didn't expect to see you."

Was it a hint to leave? "I would have been sooner if I had known. And dressed, as well."

A light grin graced her face. "This is nice, really. All of this black... Helen would have hated it. She would be telling us to lighten up, to laugh..." A catch in her throat made her stop.

"And that is why you are in blue instead."

"Yes, but she'd still tell me I should have worn ... tie dye or ... bright yellow. Maybe I should have, but could you imagine the talk?"

"It would hardly be appropriate." The touching guy again. "Emma, they're bringing the casket out. We should go." He threw a look at Fillan and set a hand on the back of her neck. "If you'll excuse us." A possessive move.

Fillan wondered if he would excuse a punch right into his smug jaw and considered finding out until Emma stepped away from the guy and closer to him. Whatever she started to say was cut off by commotion. Patty. Her grandfather held her but she didn't want to be held. She reached out for Emma.

Emma went to Patty and the girl calmed at the touch of her head and whatever Emma said to her.

"Since she didn't introduce us..." The dark-haired guy with a hard, angular face, in a black suit with an expensive shimmer to it that also didn't seem quite appropriate, moved to block his view. "I'm Mark Turner, Emma's husband."

Husband. "Ex husband, yea?" Fillan nearly caught himself before he said it.

"Technically. At the moment. That's bound to change again as soon as she's done trying to teach me a lesson. And you are?"

"I am ... a friend of hers."

"Have a name?"

Do not box him in the jaw here, Fillan. Emma will not likely appreciate you making a scene at her sister's funeral. He considered saying, *No, I have no name. I'm invisible to English Bostonians, as I hear my ancestors were.* But he decided to play nice. For the moment. Somewhat nice. He stuck out a hand and emphasized his accent. "Fillan Reilly, from Galway. I am Emma's dance instructor and a close friend now, as well."

The guy hesitated and looked at his hand like it might be diseased, but he finally accepted. "Dance instructor?"

"Ballroom, among other things." Fillan threw his full attitude into the stare, inferring more than he'd said. "You must know already what a beautiful dancer she is, yea? It is a pleasure to help her learn. She is the absolute star of the class."

"Yes. Well." His tight grip before releasing Fillan's hand was a warning. "If you'll excuse us, we *are* having a funeral. You should leave now and let us get on with it."

Do not box him in the jaw, Fillan. Do not do it.

As he decided whether or not he should, a warm hand took his. Patty looked up into his face and tugged at him.

"Hey, Patty Cake. It is good to see you. How are you?"

"She doesn't talk. Probably doesn't understand a word you're saying." Mark Turner gave the girl a scoffing look.

"Of course she does." Emma rubbed Patty's hair. "Look who came to see you. Should we ask him to stay and sit with us? Would you like that?"

"Emma..."

"Mark, this is not your business arrangement. You aren't making the calls here. I am." Emma raised her chin and turned to Fillan. "Can you? Patty nearly yanked my arm off when I told her you were here and she saw you. It would help her deal with..." She stopped again.

"I can, but I am not dressed for..."

"I don't care. Really." Her eyes pleaded.

Her *husband* pulled his shoulders back. "Emma, I think this is inappropriate. Mr. Reilly, if you wouldn't mind..." He took Fillan's arm and tried to nudge him away.

"Take your hand off me now before y' have more trouble than you want." Fillan eyed him.

"Is that a threat?" The hand tightened.

"Release him." Emma pushed the ex. "Now."

The look the guy gave her made Fillan come within hair-splitting of actually splitting the guy's hair. *This* was her ex? Why in the hell would she do this?

"Mark, I will have you thrown out of here if you cause trouble for me today." Emma's voice was shaky, but firm. Her face showed both resolve and ... a touch of fear. Patty pulled at her, away from the ex.

"That would be a mistake, Emma."

"Don't do this today. Would you please just not do this today?" Patty pulled harder.

"I would love to sit with you and Patty." Fillan pulled her

attention back and offered his arm. "Anything I can do to help, I am glad to do."

Her eyes told him she understood his offer. If hair-splitting was needed, he was the man for the job and would do so willingly. And happily.

Before she could answer, her brother came over to interrupt, said hello with a fairly friendly nod, and moved the ex away.

Emma was exhausted. Not only from the hours of sitting with Helen as she finally gave up, and then sitting up with Patty as she tried to understand the implications of losing her mom and moving into Emma's house permanently, but more from Mark showing up at the funeral. He wasn't invited. He shouldn't have been there. Between receiving condolences at the gathering after the funeral and trying to force coffee and cut vegetables into her system to keep it functioning, she'd reflected on Mark's threat. It was a threat. He was angry with her for letting Fillan stay, for taking his side.

But he had no right. They were divorced. She could damn well do what she pleased.

And she'd been so glad to see him there, Emma could hardly contain herself. She hadn't, quite. It was a momentary weakness to cling to him the way she had. Her parents were disappointed by her lack of control. They were all about control. Don't show it. Whatever it is, don't show it. Patty's outbursts embarrassed them to no end and it only made Patty worse because she could tell. They said she didn't, but they were wrong.

And yet, their one child who was all about lack of control and seeking attention was their ... their favorite. She might as well let herself acknowledge as much.

Emma looked over at where her niece sat in a cloth looped swing with Fillan in the one beside her. The girl hadn't left his side since he arrived. Most everyone else was gone by now and she was glad for that. She wanted to go home, to take Patty and settle in... And she wanted Fillan to come, to see them home, to sit with her.

Could she ask? He'd walked out on her, after they made love. And yet he'd come when she needed him most.

"So just how friendly have you become with your *dance instructor?*"

Her heart jumped at Mark's voice behind her. Too close behind her. "Not your business."

"He's not really up to your standards, is he? A *dance* teacher? Seriously, Emma…"

She turned to the gloating face. "Actually, he's above my standards, or at least where my standards used to be. I've changed them lately."

Mark glowered behind the sarcastic grin and took her elbow. "Good attempt, my dear, but I'll let it go considering your current emotional state. Speaking of, I've talked with a full time care center willing to take the girl. It's only a couple of hours away. You can visit now and then…"

"No."

He stepped closer. "We can go back to where we were. Now that you have legal custody, it's your call. She'll be better off there, and you'll be better off with less stress in your life that you're not equipped to handle."

"No. Mark, no. She won't… I won't do it. Just because you…" A thought struck her. "Is that why you've been calling lately? You knew Helen was at the end? You were just waiting…"

"This shouldn't be your responsibility. You know that as well as I do. Just because your sister made bad choices…"

"Patty is not my responsibility."

"As I said…"

"No, I mean…" Emma looked over at the girl. Her head was slumped, as were her shoulders. But Fillan was talking to her and she at least dug her toes into the dirt enough to rock the swing back and forth. "She's not just a responsibility, Mark. She's my niece. Now… now she's my daughter. My *daughter.* Do you get that? She's mine. She stays with me. Not because she was pushed on me, because I want her. I love her and she is mine."

"You would love your own more if you'd let yourself try."

"No. Not more. And maybe someday I will. Not with you, though. That will never happen. Goodbye, Mark. You should go now. It's time for us to go home." She started away.

He gripped her elbow tighter. "I'm paying for that house you're living in. Don't forget that."

"Through the divorce settlement. You can't renege."

He grinned, a horrible sarcastic grin. "That's only valid while you're single."

"I am single."

"For our purposes, single means unattached, Emma. If I find any evidence of that ... dancer living with you, the deposits stop. No questions asked. You might remember that."

She yanked away. "He's not."

"Good. So how about I take you to dinner tonight? She can stay with your brother. He's agreed. He thinks you'd be wise to put Patty in the center I found, by the way, and go back to your own life."

"Get away from me. Just *leave*." Again wrenching away from his grip, she strode away, to Fillan. She just... She needed to be beside him.

The deposits would stop. Fine. Let them. She'd... She couldn't pay for Patty's school and the house without it. With Helen's non-existent income, she was getting help for her daughter. But Emma had a job. She had income. She wouldn't get the same help. She'd have to either take Patty out of the school that knew how to help her or move to a small apartment if Mark stopped her divorce settlement. He knew that. He knew far too much. She'd trusted him, as she thought she was supposed to. A bad move.

Or she could move her parents in with her and their social security could help pay the mortgage. There wasn't room for them all in her parents' place. It could work in hers. But then it wouldn't be hers. And she still couldn't have Fillan stay there with her.

With a deep breath, she went over to Patty and asked if she was ready to go home. The girl looked up at her and down again, tracing her tennis shoe toe in the dirt. "Come on, sweetie. It's been a really long week, hasn't it? Don't you want to come get settled?" Emma offered a hand. About the time she figured Patty wasn't going to accept it and go easily, she put her fingers in Emma's and stood, her head still ducked.

"You know you're staying with me from now on, right?" She

didn't get an answer and didn't expect one, and ran a hand over Patty's brown hair. Her grandmother had insisted it get trimmed before the funeral, so it would look nice, so the girl would "look cared for" as though wondering if she was. Emma argued, said she was upset enough and it would wait, but her mother brought a stylist in Thursday afternoon and made Rob hold Patty down so they could get the hair out of her face. The poor girl had been so shaken, Emma was up all night just to try to soothe her.

No more of that. Things were changing. If she could stand up to Mark as she had, she could stand up to her parents, as well. Helen wanted Emma to make the decisions for her daughter, and she would do that without interference. "You want to tell Fillan goodbye before we go?"

He stood next to them and caught Emma's eyes. "Can I see that you get home alright?"

"Oh." She nearly said yes, please do, but Mark was nearby. Listening, she imagined. "You don't need to. I'm glad you came. I truly appreciate it, but she needs to settle in. So do I. It's been..." She held back her emotions again, as she'd been taught. But she took his hand just for a moment. "Thank you."

~ Twenty-three ~

Fillan sat in the car and considered Turner's words. Threats. The man wanted Emma back. She was too cowed by him. And she sure as hell looked like she wanted Fillan to see her home.

She wanted him there. It was in her eyes. In the way she'd held him, cried on his shoulder. Maybe she would be alright with him dropping by so he could speak to her without Turner around watching as he had all afternoon. Resolved to try, he headed toward her place but stopped first to grab a half gallon of cookie dough ice cream, Patty's favorite, and a half gallon of peppermint chip ice cream, Emma's favorite. A bribe, he supposed. Whatever worked.

Pulling onto her street, he slowed. Another car was there. A Mercedes. Black. Pretentious. Fillan supposed he knew whose it was. With some reservation, he went on past the house. The last thing she needed was him causing trouble. Circling the block since he couldn't quite make himself leave, not convinced he shouldn't interrupt or at least check on her, he drove back to her place and stopped in front, thought again before turning off the engine, grabbed the ice cream, and strutted to the door.

Damn, he was strutting. Like some arrogant peacock trying to make a claim he had no right to make. *You are a right fool, Fillan Reilly. She will ask you to leave.* He nearly stopped himself, but couldn't quite.

It was a long time before the door opened, but he was used to waiting. She had to take care of Patty first. Still, it bothered him. Someone was with her, probably the ex...

Emma barely opened the door and gave him a curious look. "Hi, um..."

He held up the bag. "I brought something for Patty. I will not stay, unless you want..."

"Who is it?" Turner's voice came up behind her, and then a glare over top of her head. "Why are you here?"

"Mark." Emma turned to him somewhat, her chin raised, her face defiant. "This is my house. It's not your right to ask him that." When she returned her attention, her face softened. "Come in if you want. I'll understand if you don't."

He hesitated, but the look in her eyes was near begging, or so he thought, so he nodded and followed. "I have her favorite ice cream. Can I take it to her? Is she in the kitchen?" She usually was in the kitchen in the evening, at the table.

"She's in her room. I was trying to get her to come out, but..." A sly glance toward Mark told him why she wouldn't.

"Can I step back there?"

"Of course."

Turner argued, said a single male, a near stranger, should not be allowed in a young girl's room. Emma hushed him again, told Fillan to go ahead.

He heard exchanged words, quiet but heated, as he treaded back and tapped on Patty's door. She was sitting on her bed, her arms crossed in front of her chest, rocking lightly. "I brought ice cream. Want to come share it with me?"

She looked up, started to move, and heard Turner's voice. The girl froze in her tracks.

"Come, Patty. I will sit with you. It is cookie dough."

A spark in her eyes said she didn't want to resist. Just a touch more persuasion and she followed him, ducking to his other side away from Turner, her head dipped low, and beat him into the kitchen. She grabbed three bowls and three spoons. Fillan had to chuckle.

"Leave, Mark. This is my house."

"That I'm paying for." He smirked.

"Not any longer, you aren't. Go ahead. Stop the deposits."

"Oh come, Emma. I know you can't support that kid alone. Planning to move the dancer in with you? Doesn't look like he can do much for you, either. Any way around, from what I see." Another smirk.

She wanted to punch him in the jaw. "I plan to move my parents in. They can help pay the mortgage."

"Your parents? So you'll be under their thumb again?"

"Better theirs than yours."

"Is that right?" He stepped closer, lowered his head toward hers. "You didn't think so before."

"Things change. Some of us grow up."

"Grownups support themselves, Emma. Are you doing that yet?"

Heat burned throughout her body. "I support myself fine."

"Not the way I can."

"I don't care about that. I have a roof overhead and food on the table and I pay my bills. It's good enough."

"Good enough for some, my dear, not for you." He tried to touch her face but she backed away.

"Don't act like you know what I want or need. You don't know, Mark, or you don't care. I want you to leave now."

"I know you need help with that child, whether or not you'll admit it. Grownups also don't take on responsibilities they can't handle by themselves. You're not ready for this. I can help..."

"Get out. I don't want your help. I don't want anything from you any longer. I'll figure things out myself."

He laughed with an infuriating nod.

"Just go. And don't come back."

The laugh turned to a glare. "Remember that when you need someone to pull you up by your toes again."

"I won't."

"Glad you believe that."

Emma nearly slammed the door behind him but it would bother Patty, so instead, she stood leaning against it until she calmed herself. He thought Fillan couldn't do anything for her? She thought he was very wrong about that one. The only thing she didn't know was whether she could let him again.

"You alright?"

She opened her eyes to Fillan and shook her head.

"Come have ice cream with us."

Accepting his hand, she started walking and then stopped and held onto him. She only needed a minute to hold on, to focus on the warmth and strength of his body, his tenderness. It was something she'd never really had before, tenderness. If Emma allowed herself, she could easily become addicted to the feeling.

Fillan held her in close, a hand cradling her head, the other around her waist. "I am so sorry, Emma. I wish I had been here this week. I would have been if I had known."

If he'd known? "I called you."

After some silence, he tilted back to see her. "When?"

"Wednesday morning. I asked, well, suggested you could come for dinner and you didn't even..."

"I did not get any calls."

"Voicemail. I did. It was you, your message." The look on his face said he was serious, he hadn't gotten it.

"I checked it all day long nearly, every day. Em, I would have been here. I expected the bag I left would tell you as much."

"Bag?"

"Monday, after class. I stopped by but heard you say to leave you be and left again, but I dropped off bananas for Patty to be sure she had some for morning."

Her head shook.

"On the screen door handle."

"I didn't... There was nothing there. And I didn't, I wouldn't tell you to let me be. Fillan, I wouldn't... Monday?" Monday evening. "Mark. It was Mark I told to leave me alone, when he called. I told him, yelled at him, really, to leave me alone. Over the phone. Not like he took that hint well."

Fillan's chest rose and fell hard and he set a hand alongside her head. "I am so sorry. For everything the past week. For leaving Sunday night, especially. I..."

She kissed him. A quick kiss. "Can we just... It's been..." Emma bit her lip, forcing control, with her whole body wanting to scream out, or ... or to take him to bed. Emma wanted... Not for stress relief, though. She had to wait until he wouldn't think...

He returned the kiss, but slower, as his body moved up against hers.

She made herself pull back. "Patty..."

"Right." He grabbed a deep breath. "Well, then, let's go and have some ice cream. Yes?"

Fillan assured Emma he and Patty would be fine and she should go take a long bath and unwind. It took a little convincing, but finally, she touched Patty's head and told her to knock at the bathroom door if she needed her. She gave Fillan a grateful smile, somewhat of a smile, considering the grief all over her face.

At a knock on the door, he tried to decide if he should answer or let it be. If it was the ex again, Fillan was likely to knock him flat. Maybe not a bad idea. "I will be right back, Patty Cake. Look. Put the green one on the red one like this." He added to the plastic blocks tower they'd just started and went to at least see who was at the door.

Her brother and his oldest boy. Fillan figured he should let them in. The guy didn't look too surprised to see him, or bothered by it.

"Is Emma busy with Patty?"

"She is taking a bath. Patty and I are building a tower."

"Really? You mean you're building one and she's watching?"

"No, she is helping me build it." With a tilt of the head to say they should come on in, Fillan went back to sit on the floor across from her. "Look at this. How many more did you add to it?" He counted the five blocks out loud. "And in order, as well. Maybe you should be an engineer as you get older, yea?"

Rob looked astonished. The boy just smiled and said hello to his cousin. She glanced up at them and kept working as Fillan held the sides to keep it steady.

"That's um, pretty amazing."

"I told you she could, Dad. Grams and Gramps just treated her like a baby. Can I play, Patty?" Leo, as he reintroduced himself in case Fillan forgot, slowly sat on the floor between them, watching his cousin to be sure it was okay with her. She handed him blocks.

Fillan felt like a proud father. He had taught her to put them in order. They had started working at Dominoes, also, and sometimes she did a few bricks correctly and other times she took a hand and knocked them all across the room.

When Emma came out in her bathrobe, she looked at her brother and said she'd be right back, but paused again when she saw Patty stacking the blocks.

"It is our new game." Fillan watched as her eyes moistened and her head shook softly. Disbelieving. She gave him a soft grin and again told her brother she'd be back in a minute.

Emma had not expected her brother to show up. And she definitely had not wanted him to show up, not after what Mark said about him agreeing Patty should be in a full care center.

Throwing comfortable clothes on, knit shorts and a long, loose T-shirt, she breathed a sigh of something between relief, exhaustion, and frustration, and went out to see what he wanted. If he even started to bring up placing Patty somewhere, she'd literally kick him the hell out of her house.

"Did you need something?"

Rob looked over with raised eyebrows. "We came to see if you did. I was going to offer to entertain her a while so you could, well, shower and unwind. I guess I was too late for that."

"Thank you, but, yeah, she's..."

"I see. And I'm impressed. You're doing wonders with her already."

"That has nothing to do with me. I didn't even know she could, or would..." She caught Fillan's eyes. "Did you..?"

He gave her a light grin. "She seems to be willing and eager to learn when given the chance."

"Some days."

"Aye, right, well, at least there is that."

Rob glanced between them. "I tend to think it's the better stability, Em. Could be we should have moved her in with you sooner. It wouldn't have been fair to you, of course."

Emma put a finger to her mouth. "We're going to be fine, aren't we, sweetie?" Touching the girl's head, she nearly cried when Patty actually looked up and met her eyes. Only a second. But she'd responded. Directly. A huge step.

"Well." Rob stood. "Leo, let's get out of the way for tonight since everything's handled. Em, if you think she'll be okay with it, bring her over for a while tomorrow. Or let us know if we should come entertain her here for you for a couple of hours. Just ... let us know if you need us. Will you do that? I know you hate asking for help, but it's been a hard week and this will be some adjustment, so call us, even for groceries if you can't get out."

She gritted her jaw to maintain control and gave him a nod. They both told Patty and Fillan good night. Walking to the door with them, Emma gave them both hugs and her thanks.

"By the way, Em, I'm taking over her school tuition. We talked about it and it's the least we can do. I've already let the school know and it's all set. Good night, now. Try to sleep well." Her brother gave her a long hug and then walked out, his hand on Leo's back, before she could gather herself enough to say anything. Why would he take over Patty's tuition if he agreed with Mark that she should go to a full care center? Did he think it would give him more say? It wouldn't happen. Patty was legally hers, no matter how much he decided to help. It was Emma's decision. Not even her brother would change her mind.

With a deep breath, Emma returned to flop onto the couch, watching Fillan and Patty build what was looking like a castle. The better stability. Could be Rob was right, but she still thought it had something to do with Fillan, as well. Maybe she'd needed a father figure more than Emma realized. Her grandpa was her grandpa, and he was also Rob's kids' grandfather. Rob only saw her now and then, usually no more than once a week before recent events. But it could also be Fillan's calm demeanor, something Emma and Patty both needed in their lives.

After a few minutes, he came over and sat next to her, and Emma couldn't resist curling up and letting her head rest on his shoulder.

"How are ye doin', Em?"

"I don't know. Tired. Numb, I guess. It hasn't really... I just..."

He kissed the top of her head. "I was afraid Patty would be all stirred up tonight, being that she had to see her mum..."

"No, she didn't see her. I wouldn't let her go up that far. A mistake, maybe, as Mom said it was, but she already knows... She's known for a long time. I think she's..."

"Relieved, to an extent?"

"Yes. And in some ways, so am I. It was so hard to see Helen that way, hurting, so at least she's not now. But I miss her. Already."

"I will not pretend to know how ye feel, Emma, but I am sorry. You have had too much loss in a short time, aye? Your husband and your sister and what freedom ye did have nearly all together."

"Fillan?"

"What can I do?"

She slid a hand up to his face as she shifted. "Let me have this for the summer. You and me. I know the more used to you being here we get, the harder it'll be later, but I don't care. You... You being here has really been ... some kind of a Godsend. More than you can understand."

He leaned in slowly, gently, and met her lips, only for a moment. "I am yours for the summer. And after summer, we will keep in touch still, yes? It is easy enough these days with video messaging and such. You can have what ye need of me this summer if I can hold onto your friendship after then."

"Yes. Of course." Emma smoothed her fingers down along his face, checked to see that Patty was still immersed in her building, and gave him a longer, deeper kiss.

Emma curled into him, her face ducked into his chest as he lay half propped against a pillow against the arm of the couch. She wanted him for the summer. Fillan nearly told her she would have to accept more than the summer, that she should move to Ireland with him and... He couldn't ask her.

Not yet. He had things he had to sort out first, and she needed time to get past her mourning, to gather herself and get Patty on her new routine. After she did so, she very well could not need him so much.

"I know you're wondering." Her voice was muffled against his skin as she played with the few hairs that had actually bothered to grow on his chest.

"What is it ye think I am wondering?"

"Mark. Why I married him."

"Aye, I did have to wonder, but you do not have to explain yerself to me, Emma. Past is past, yes?"

"Yes and no. I'm sorry he was so rude to you. There's no call for it."

"Doesnae matter to me in the slightest."

She raised her face to see his. "No?"

"And why would it? I care nothing of his opinion. The way he walked out on you when you needed him, and the way he was acting the maggot at your sister's funeral, nonetheless, tells me what he thinks matters less than a wee snake in a field of wild boars."

"Um, what?"

Fillan realized he'd allowed his accent to strengthen, as always happened when he got too emotional. Turner mattered only for what he had done to Emma. He was a wee snake, as far as Fillan was concerned, and though he had done nothing to him personally, Fillan would gladly stomp him against the ground in protection of Emma, and Patty.

"He was acting what?"

"Ah, acting the maggot. It means acting a fool, making an arse of himself."

She chuckled. "And what do you know about snakes? I thought there were no snakes in Ireland. Didn't St. Patrick drive them out?"

"And now ye are only being cheeky. To answer, there are some by now due to eejits buying the things to show off and then releasing them due to not wanting to care for them, but they are few and here and there. Otherwise, no, Ireland was far too cold for the evil things back when it was still connected to the mainland. We managed to get out away before they made it that far over."

"The splitting of Pangea."

"Aye, and you know of it?"

"I'm a teacher, Fillan." She teased.

"Right. I tend to forget since you are not like any of the teachers I had way back in the day. Sadly." He stroked her hair when she chuckled. "Technically, no, there are no snakes in Ireland; none are native, which is fine with me."

"You don't like snakes."

"I do not, as most of us do not. Due to our reverence to St. Patrick, you might say, and his use of them to mean something evil.

Although, I tend to think it is innate to human nature to not trust a creature that slithers and skulks in the grass looking for prey and sneaks up on you unaware."

"A protective instinct. I would guess you're right. Most of us don't like them, either."

He kissed her head. He loved the way she could lie naked in his arms having just made love with him and talk normally about normal things. He had never had such before. It was always *good on ye and time to sleep, or leave, now, thank ye very much.* He much preferred to be able to talk, to feel like it was more than a physical release. "I think we have gotten off the track a wee bit."

"Oh, not really. We are still talking about snakes, right? Because ... Mark was pretty much that, a smooth talker just waiting..." She sighed. "We were college sweethearts and it went too far one night. I didn't mean for it to, but it did and ... well, that was that, really. It was expected that I would stay with him. So I did. I made him wait a while before I accepted, as though I wasn't sure I would, but of course I knew I would. He made sure everyone knew I ... well, that he'd made me his and I just... I was young and stupid. I took his interest in me as love and it wasn't. Not really."

"No, not love, not that I could see. It is possession. He wanted to own you. Still does."

"Yes. It was always that. By the time I woke up from my dreamy new love haze to see him for who he really was, it was too late. And then he had the nerve to leave me. Now he thinks I'll put Patty in a full care center and go back to him and..."

"You would not?" Fillan felt himself tense at the thought.

"No. I'll pick up a second job first. I'll take care of things myself. He can go straight to hell for all I care. Seriously. I mean that, even if I shouldn't."

"I will agree with you on that one." He caressed her face, her forehead, eyebrows, nose, mouth. She wrapped her arms around his neck and held tight. He enveloped her in his arms, sheltered her as though he could erase her pain. He could not, and he knew as much. Perhaps, though, he could help her release it. He could see her pushing it back, forcing herself shut. As her parents did. And her brother. They were all closed tight. He thought it might be natural for them, but it was not for her.

"The worst is over now, yes? You have been waiting for this and dreading it and now you can pull yourself up again. I will be here a few weeks yet and I will help you as I can. You will be well, Emma. More than well. You and Patty will be wonderfully happy together. I guarantee you will."

Emma nodded against his shoulder and he took to kissing any skin he could find, shifting them both on the couch, under the sheet, to find more skin, until she sat up, pulled her long T-shirt over her body, and stood, offering a hand.

He sat up and pulled her between his legs, barely covered by the sheet. "You want me to leave before she wakes?"

"No. I want you to come to bed with me."

"Will it be safe? She will not walk in?"

"I can't guarantee she won't, so we'll have to stay covered. But... I can't ask you to keep staying and..."

"Keep staying?"

"Well, whenever you want. I figure that might happen more if I don't make you stay on the couch."

He grinned and stood up in front of her, with a quick kiss. "Emma, my love, I do not care where we are if ye are at my side."

"Come to bed, Fillan Reilly. You have given yourself to me for the next few weeks, and I plan to take full advantage of that while I can." She led him to her room, closed the door, and lay next to him again, sliding one bare leg between his.

~ Twenty-four ~

Fillan sat quietly and let his sister rail on him for being out of touch for so long. When she took a breath, he told her his laptop had been out of commission and Emma had fixed it for him, which led to what he'd been doing the past week. In all truth, he told Eugenia he'd spent every minute not working with Em and Patty. He told her of Emma losing her sister, of her autistic niece becoming her legal daughter, of how he was trying to help them regroup, and that he was working on finding a way to help them when he had to go home.

Eugenia grew quiet herself, a rare thing indeed. He had managed to stun her, he supposed. Finally, she raised a large mug to her lips, eyeing him over top. He knew without asking it was mint tea with a touch of anise. Revolting drink, Fillan always told her. Good for the body, she said. He guessed she was right, as strong and hearty as she was for a female. He'd heard endless times, even once he was full grown, how easily his big sister could take him if she wanted, that he had better be good to her.

It wasn't true, to be honest, not for many years, since Fillan was far stronger than he looked. But it was nigh inconceivable that he would be anything but good to Genie, as she was the one he respected most in the world. Genie had uncommonly good common sense. He often expected she got his share of it as well as her own.

"It sounds as if ye are staying at her place more than in yours. Is it right?"

"The past week I have, yea."

"And then you are going to pack up and leave them at the end of summer?"

"Little choice I have."

She took a long sip of the tea again. "You could invite them to come with you."

"Right, Genie. Come and stay in my little shack in a country you do not know if ye will like in a little village with no proper setup to help Patty. I am sure she will take a huge shine to that idea."

"Sounds like you have thought the idea through already."

"I have. How could I not? But it would be unfair to ask. I have hinted of it and she brushed away the thought as if there was no merit t'it. She has her work here. She does not want to leave all she has built, and why should she?"

"And it will be fair to leave them so abruptly after you have invaded their lives as you have? I hope you are taking precautions well, in the least, so as not to leave her with more on her hands than she has already."

"We are both taking precautions. Emma has no plan to have wee ones atop of Patty and her needs. It is enough for her already, she says." He felt his body heave a sigh.

Genie tilted her head with squinted eyes. "Fillan Reilly, why did you sound so glum when you said as much? You would not be lying to me?"

"I have never lied to you, even when I should have."

She snorted. "Yea and you should have at times. I would worry about you less." With a roll of her eyes, she set her mug down and leaned closer to the screen, to the web camera. "What has she said about it? About you leaving her and the child?"

"Hardly a thing. Last she said was she was glad to have me while she could have me. Nothing more. She seems alright enough with it. And yet..."

"Ye are not alright with it."

"I would like to bring her back with me, both her and Patty. To be full honest."

"Ask her. Do not hint, Fillan. You ask her outright if she will."

"Genie, how can I? I cannot expect it of her."

"No, you cannot expect it. You have to know she will in all likelihood turn you down and prepare yerself for that. At least it is her choice, then. You are not simply packing up and saying thanks for the ride, lass, see ya maybe sometime in the future. She will feel better knowing you want it, even if she says no, as she will, I would think."

"Right and then I will have to know she turned me down. It would be easier not to offer than to be rejected."

"Fillan, you pushed this with this girl knowing full well she had a complicated life already and knowing you were coming home. You do the right thing and think of her first for a change. If you care about her as you seem, you will put her first. Be the gentleman I kept trying to teach you to be or I will box your ears first thing you step foot back here."

Fillan sighed. Of course she was right. As she always was. "I will see how things go as the time comes."

"As the time comes? Your plane ticket is set for six weeks from t'morra. Do you not think you should give her what time you can?"

"If she is going to say no anyway, why does it matter, Genie?"

"You want it to look like you are only asking out of courtesy?"

He shoved a hand through his hair. "Alright. Alright."

"Then do not ask her, you eejit. You do not care enough or I wouldnae have to push you to do the right thing. So enjoy the next few weeks and then say gotta go, nice havin' you, and get on the plane and do not look back. What does it matter? You are having your fun."

"Do not be an arse."

"That is what I'm telling you. In the least, tell the girl I said you should ask her to come so she knows it is not the whole family as a lot who is so full of ourselves and our own needs to the extent of others."

"I will yea." Fillan rolled his eyes. "I have to go now. She is waiting. I said I would be a few moments only."

"Fillan." Her voice softened. "I can see you care well for the girl. I am only looking out for you, right? And I am glad you have put that other li'l dosser out of your mind. I am grateful to your Emma for having done that for you."

"All good and well, Genie, but do ye think it will be at all likely I will be able to find anyone who can stand up to what Emma is to me by now? She turns me down and I will be a life bachelor. Is that what you want?"

"That is what you have always had in mind, is it not, Fillan?"

Catching himself, he had to think about that a moment. It was. He'd told Emma right off first it was, he had no intentions of ever marrying. When had that changed? "It is what I have said, sure enough. I suppose I am not sure about that anymore."

"If you feel that way, love, you might have to make some kind of adjustment of your own, rather than leaving it to her. And with that said, I am signing off here now. Go on and spend the time you can with your lovely Emma. Let me know if your plans change at all, without waiting until the last wee moment to do so, if you would."

An adjustment of his own. Was she telling him he should stay? Fillan supposed it would be easier for him to change homes than it would be for her, all considered, except he did not want to be away from home long-term.

Self-centered eejit. You are a fine one, Fillan. You find this great girl and you are still thinking of yourself first. You are about to ask her to do what you are not willing. How could he?

Either way, he'd left her on her own long enough. It was time to make a decision, as Genie had said.

Walking along the edge of the water, completely on her own, or nearly, since he was up in his little beach shack talking to his sister, was heavenly. Emma heard nothing but the waves rolling against the shore and some birds here and there. The heat of the day had waned enough to be warm and comfortable without sweating, and she pulled the swim wrap off her shoulders to tie it around her waist instead.

She was glad Patty had gone to Rob's without a fuss and hadn't thrown a fit when Emma said she was leaving for a while. Leo jumped right in to distract and entertain her, along with his younger brother and sister, and Patty went with them to the family room. The slight wave she gave Emma and Fillan said she was fine there.

Finally. For the first time since the funeral, a day over a week, Emma had the ability to fully unwind and let her thoughts wander.

Could be she wasn't quite ready for that, though. Too much thinking time only made it harder to not cry for her sister, or rather, for herself, her own loss. She hadn't yet, not really. Patty was doing well and Emma did not want to change that.

As she headed back toward the shack just a little way, enough to be able to sit on the sand without getting wet again, Emma wondered if Fillan mentioned her to his sister, and if so, what he'd said or was saying. Would she convince him not to get too hooked, that he belonged back in Ireland and that his family expected him to come home? Maybe not to get entangled with someone already so entangled? He was a year younger than Emma, twenty-five, barely, so a year and a half. Never married. No children. Why should he take on something that was very much not his responsibility? Especially given the fact he didn't particularly want children.

How he was so good with Patty when he wasn't a fan of kids overall, she didn't understand. His sister didn't have kids, either. Maybe something in their raising? He'd hardly spoken of his parents at all, other than being fifteen years younger than Eugenia and "quite the surprise" for his mother who'd been forty-two at the time. That would make her sixty-seven. Emma's mother was fifty-nine, having had her, the youngest of the three, at thirty-three. She looked much older, though. Too many years of worry with Helen took their toll.

Helen, the brightest star of the household, always so upbeat, always smiling. Helen's smile had always lit up a room. It was her best feature. What had been so wrong in her life that she had to do this to herself? So it was hard to deal with Patty. It was. Still, the love Emma had for the child from the beginning was enough to overcome the difficulties of the struggle. Helen had to feel so much more love for her own daughter, for the infant she cried over as the doctors warned there could be issues with her health because of Helen's state when she was conceived, and for the first few weeks she hadn't known she was expecting.

Emma had done her best to tell Helen it would be fine before Patty was born, and after the diagnosis, to assure Helen autism just happened and it likely had nothing to do with anything Helen had done. No one knew why. There was no reason to sit around and blame herself when perfectly healthy women who did everything right, by the book, still had children with autism or otherwise. It wasn't a punishment. It wasn't a bad thing. Patty was a gift just exactly as she was, and Emma constantly said as much.

Still, Helen never stopped blaming herself. The self-blame and guilt did worse things than anything else Helen had done. That's what actually killed her sister. The drugs were only a symptom.

A deep breath surged through her soul. Emma couldn't make the same mistake. She had to let Helen go and forgive herself for not being able to save her sister. Patty needed her to be happy.

"Em?" Fillan walked up behind her and lowered to her side.

"Hey. You didn't talk long."

"No, I only wanted to check in. She is very grateful to you for fixing the ghastly machine, she wants you to know."

She gave him a grin and took his hand.

"What is wrong, Emma?"

"No, nothing. I..." She shook her head. It was too soon to talk about it.

"Ye are thinking of Helen."

"Yes. I guess I'm still wondering if I could have done more."

"Em." Fillan shifted to face her, pushing one leg underneath her bent knees, and crossing the other in front of him, between them, up against her hip. "You are taking good care of her daughter and loving her as your own. What more could you do for her? The rest was up to her, not to anyone else in the world."

She nodded.

"You know..." He slid an arm over her knee. "Since you have missed the past two weeks of class, I think I should teach you the samba privately."

She had the feeling that wasn't what he was going to say, but the thought of learning the samba with him, privately, was hard to refuse. He stood and offered a hand to help her up, then took her in his arms. "The samba is counted in 8 beats: 1-a-2, 3-a-4, 5-a-6, 7-a-8, with the even numbers getting a full count. The first two split a beat. One-a..." He demonstrated his part and then turned to show her part, and took her in his arms again.

"This would be easier with music. On not on sand."

"We will do both in a bit. First learn the steps. Come." Fillan led her down to the edge of the water where the sand was packed harder. The water washed up over their feet as they took the moves slowly, from as much distance as possible while staying in hold, and then he sped the count and closed in. "Ball-flat, ball, ball-flat, and bounce. Samba is much about the bounce of the knees. Right. Good. And now the whisk, the same steps, only move the right foot behind the left and only touch the ball with it."

Emma nearly stopped dancing when he started humming a song, a soft slow song, music only, and he sang the beat counts with it as though she'd forgotten. She gave him a soft grin and focused on her steps, and on his voice, his touch, the warmish breeze off the ocean, and the water brushing at their feet.

"You are a beautiful dancer." He returned the grin and went back to humming.

"And you have a nice voice. What is that?"

"Hinder. *Lips of an Angel.* Whisk left, ball-flat, right ball, left ball-flat. Nice."

"You know the words?"

"Yes. Whisk right."

"Sing them."

"Ah. I am not sure it is the right music for now. Music, yes, words, no." He hummed to keep the rhythm.

"I don't care."

"Do not say I didn't warn you."

Emma closed her eyes as he sang, so softly, so close to her ear, in the dusk in the water... He sang the first verse and the chorus and went back to humming. Until he stopped.

"What?"

"Are you going to sleep?"

"No. Just enjoying you. This... I would do this with you every night, if I could."

He stared, holding her, his eyes locked on, questioning.

Emma kissed him and released his hand to slide her arms around his shoulders.

"Em." Fillan weaved his fingers through her hair and held her close into his body, skin on skin, since he hadn't put his shirt back on after they went for a swim earlier. "You could come to Ireland with me, you and Patty. You can teach there. I do not know what the requirements would be, but I can find out well enough..."

She pulled back somewhat. "I... It's much too soon to even... We're just trying to find a routine, you know, and I want to get my master's. I can't just..."

"Alright. I am not pushing you. It is … an offer."

He was getting defensive, as he had the night after they first made love and he walked out. "Thank you." She ran fingers alongside his face. "Maybe … in the future, after... Maybe. I can't answer right now, but thank you. If I was still unencumbered and free to just run off, I would probably be jumping all over that. As things are..."

"I understand, Emma. I only want you to know this is not... I know we had intended to only hang out this summer, but..."

"I know."

He nodded. "So, back to where we were..." Fillan claimed her hand, set his other on her waist, and led her back into the dance, humming a different song this time.

Until a shrill voice called his name from up the beach. Emma turned to see who it belonged to and Fillan groaned quietly.

"Wow, look at you." The girl, in a ridiculously skimpy bikini, gripped a guy's hand, a tall hunky guy with slicked back dark hair and skimpy trunks, pulling him along. "You didn't tell me you could dance, too. Hi." She looked at Emma. "I'm Deb. You must be the girlfriend he mentioned. I wondered if he just said he had one to blow me off, you know, but wow, you two are so cute dancing like that. You should show us how." Introducing the guy who promptly said he was not dancing, she started talking again, about the invitation still being open and they should both come join the party.

"Thank you, but no. We are headed in for the night." Fillan set a hand on Emma's back and started toward the cabin.

"Oh, but we have lots of fun." The bouncy girl jumped up around in front of them, walking backward now.

"And we have only a wee bit of time when it is only the two of us, so..."

"Oh, I get it. Maybe tomorrow, then? We're out there most nights."

"Good night, Deb." Fillan moved to Emma's other side, between her and the hunky guy.

Back at the cabin, in the glow of its light, Fillan took a deep breath and lowered to the bottom step of his small porch. "Sorry about that."

She sat next to him. "The neighbor girl who caught you in a towel, I'm guessing?"

"Aye, well, she caught me in less than that a few days back."

Listening to Fillan talk about going for a swim late at night and getting farther away than he expected, in the nip (naked, he had to explain), and running into the neighbor girl that way, Emma laughed. The image of it, along with his attitude she could hear in his voice and imagine easily, and then the girl looking back to tell him his girlfriend was lucky, so she thought, and he should tell her so, was all too much, and she couldn't help laughing.

"Ye think it is funny, do ye, another girl staring at me in the all-in-all? I did not just find it so funny when her tag-along was doing it to you even as barely dressed as ye are."

He was jealous. Somehow, it made her laugh harder.

"Thank you greatly, Emma. I am offended, I think."

"No, you're not." She barely got it out, and her stomach was starting to hurt from laughing.

"Am I not? And why would I not be? Ye could be only a wee bit possessive in return, could ye?"

"Oh, trust me, if I was worried about her, I wouldn't find it so funny."

"But you are not? She is a looker, yes?"

"She's an airhead. Not your type."

"And ye know that much of me already?"

"Yes." Emma gasped breaths as her laughter calmed. But it started again as the image flooded back.

"Aye, great." Fillan picked her up with an arm around her back and lay her in the sand, leaning his body over top, stroking her hair. "It is good to hear ye laugh, even at my expense."

She calmed with his skin against hers, his eyes studying her, and the laughter turned to tears, every bit as uncontrollable. Go to Ireland with him? Emma wanted to say yes, please take me with you, away from everything. Please. But she'd never leave Patty and ... and everything was too much at once. She missed her sister. She missed the ability to just be Patty's aunt and to be able to consider a family of her own, to be able to run off with Fillan. She hated how much Helen was going to miss of Patty's life. She hated the grief she saw in her parents. She hated the thought of never again laughing with her big sister. She wanted to say yes and run off with him, away from everything, and she couldn't.

He kissed her forehead and stroked her hair.

"Sorry. I'm..." She gasped it out.

"No, you are fine. Go on, Emma. Let it out. It is better."

Clinging to him, she didn't have much choice. She couldn't stop it. Her body took over, eventually calming as she held him, as he kissed her head, her face, wiped thumbs over her eyes to clear the moisture away. Her body gasped short, fast breaths, trying to recover, to stabilize.

"It is better to let it out, yes?"

"I wish I could say yes to you and just go. I really wish I could. I want you to know that."

He met her lips softly, briefly. "Someday, maybe you will. You are right. It is too early. But as the airhead girl said, it is an open invitation."

She laughed again. Emma knew darn well what kind of invitation the girl was offering. "Don't you take her up on that."

"Not very likely, unless you go with me. That is the second or third mate I have seen her with since I have been here."

"Good for her, I guess."

"Is it? You would like to meet up with some of her friends?"

"No. I mean... Helen used to be much the same, always out partying with different people, different guys. She said it was nothing, just some flirting. I never really believed she was happy, though. I think she was chasing happiness in ways that would never bring it to her. I mean I think that girl might believe now she's having plenty of fun, but..."

Fillan kissed her hard and deep, moving in closer. And then he shifted, raised to his knees, picked her up, and carried her into the cabin, to the little bathroom with its small shower, and set her down. "You go first. Remember, the water only gets lukewarm."

When he started to move away, she grasped his hand. "Stay, Fillan. You can wash my back."

Twenty-five

Emma took a deep breath and hoped this was a good idea. How she let Fillan talk her into taking Patty to dance with her after she picked her up from school, Emma wasn't sure. Actually, she did know. She wanted to go and it was her only option.

Patty had done well at Rob's Saturday afternoon through Sunday evening, allowing Emma not only the luxury of Fillan at his cabin Saturday, all night, but a lazy Sunday morning with him. They got up late and showered again and went in for brunch, lingering over coffee. He dropped her off at her house and ran errands while she went to pick Patty up. There were a few minor incidents, Rob said, when the younger two boys got loud, but nothing to worry about.

This, though... It would be too much commotion.

"Okay, sweetie. I tell you what..." She turned to Patty before she opened a door, giving her time to look around and see where they were. "We're going to try this. Okay? If you don't want to be here, just let me know and we'll leave. You don't have to stay. Where are you going?"

The girl suddenly unbuckled her belt and jumped out of the car, leaving Emma scrambling to catch up.

Fillan gave her a big smile and Patty... She hugged him. Emma stood staring. Her niece, her daughter, wouldn't even hug her. Anyone. Ever. His grin was sweet, not gloating, only ... happy. He was honestly happy the girl was giving him a hug. "Nice to see you, too, Patty cake. Did ye have a good day at school?"

Emma couldn't do anything but watch. Patty's head was raised to look at him, not at his feet. At least she looked at or close to his face.

A couple of women from class who always rode together stopped to tell Emma they were glad she was back and looked curiously at their teacher with a girl hanging on him.

"My ... daughter. She's taken a shine to Fillan."

One of them started toward Patty, asking her name, but Emma stepped in front. "Please. She's... Her name is Patty, and she's autistic.

She hates to be touched or to have anyone too close. Usually. This is...” Emma didn't even know how to finish the thought. That look was on their faces, the pity look that Emma hated to see, but what else could they do? It was a shame for Patty to have to live so cut off from normal activities, from people who wouldn't try to understand and wouldn't give her the space she needed.

“How about you come in and dance with us today, Patty cake? Want to try?”

“Oh. Fillan...” Emma's head shook. “If I'm lucky, she'll sit and let me do class, but...”

“We will see.” He threw a grin at Emma, said hello to the women, and took Patty's hand to lead her into the building.

Emma braced herself for when the doors shut behind her. Outside was almost always better than inside. And it was loud, with students gathering for class and talking, laughing. She saw Patty tense, but Fillan talked to her, told her names of those he knew, told her where they were heading...

A natural. He was a natural, understanding how to deal with her symptoms so easily instead of spending hour upon hour of research as Emma had done to try to find anything to help her understand and know what to do, what not to do.

Figured she'd find a man like that who was going back to effing Ireland in a few weeks' time.

Emma settled Patty in a chair close to where she would be, touched Fillan's arm before he left to get the class started, and stayed close when the music began. The girl was tucked into herself by now and Emma knew it was only a matter of minutes before she'd have to take her out. Still, it was worth a try.

“We are starting the rumba today.” Fillan called attention to himself with a nice little hip movement. “It is a basic box step like the waltz, but while the samba is all about the knees and bounce, the rumba is all about the hips and smooth movements.” He showed off with his graceful box step and sliding hips. Such a mix of elegance and sensuality. She loved to see him waltz and foxtrot, but the Latin dances were absolutely made for him.

Ten minutes into class, as she kept an eye on Patty, Emma was stunned again. Patty was watching, mainly her focus was at feet level, but watching and unwrapping herself, sitting up almost straight. Fillan gave Emma a smile when he noticed, also.

"Emma."

She looked over at him, at the way he said her name. A couple of glances around her said they noticed it, also.

"Will ye help me teach the underarm turn?"

With a glance at Patty to be sure she was still fine, she gave him a light nod and moved to the front of the group. He'd already taught her, out there on the beach at his cabin, and she was sure it would show that he had, but she couldn't bother to be concerned about what they knew or assumed. He was hers for the summer.

She set her right hand in his and her left hand on his shoulder. They started with a couple of box steps and as he released her right hand, she stepped toward him and then out around in a half circle and rejoined him to finish the box step.

"Beautiful." He gave her a grin and they repeated it a couple of times with his instruction to the rest of the group.

During the rest of class, Emma vacillated between watching Fillan and helping him show moves he'd already taught her and keeping an eye on Patty. The girl was watching them dance together, her and Fillan. She was calm and still and Emma nearly cried thinking about it, wondering if it was Fillan or the music or the dance. Emma always had to keep her music soft when she could play it at all around her niece. Her daughter. She still had trouble figuring out how to think of her now. She was both, technically. Which took priority?

After class, they heard all kinds of comments about how nicely they danced together, how "cute" they were, and so on. And those not at the funeral told her how sorry they were about her sister. With Fillan at her side, she withstood the sympathies fine.

It was Fillan. For both Patty and for herself. He was so very calming. Everything was just easier to take when he was there.

Emma broke from the conversation and went to sit beside Patty to ask what she thought about class. Patty raised her eyes to meet hers, only for a second, with a light smile, and stood, grasping Emma's hand, taking her over to Fillan and grabbing his hand, as well, looking at the door.

"She's ready to go."

He nodded. "You were wonderful, too, Patty cake. Thank you for allowing your aunt to help me out today. How about I take you two beautiful girls for ice cream now?"

They took their separate cars and Emma told Patty the whole way there that Fillan was meeting them in only a few minutes. Her heart sank at the thought of her baby getting so hooked to him. She had every idea that it would be harder on Patty for Fillan to leave than it was to lose her mom, since really, she still had a mom and Emma had been that for her for a long time, most of her life to some extent.

Outside the ice cream shop, Patty stopped suddenly when she saw a group of young teens laughing and blaring their music, some loud hip hop type beat. She starting rocking herself with her arms crossed in front of her stomach.

"It's alright. It's just music, sweetie. I know some of the kids. It's fine. We're going inside away from them. Okay?" She rocked harder and when Fillan came up in front of them, Emma shook her head to tell him they couldn't stay.

"It will be fine." He took Patty's hand. "Look. Just do this. Hear the beat?" Breaking into moves Emma had seen here and there from area kids and on television, Fillan talked to Patty and the kids looked over at him, laughing to start with and then moving closer as he showed his expertise.

Emma had to laugh. Her elegant Irish ballroom pro doing whatever those moves were called, getting admiration from young teens out there on the sidewalk was too funny not to laugh. Patty looked at her a moment and then back at Fillan, mostly at his feet, and started rocking again. No, not rocking. Moving, with the beat. Dancing? Pre-dancing?

She exchanged looks with Fillan and he smiled and encouraged the girl, then told Emma to try it with him. Shaking her head since she had no idea how to do that, Emma gave in as Patty relaxed. She knew full well how silly she had to look out there in her sun dress and sandals trying to imitate hip hop moves, but Patty laughed.

Emma stopped and stared. She'd laughed.

Fillan smiled again and tried to get Patty to follow his feet. She was not having any part of that, but she laughed again, at Emma. At that moment, Emma thought there was nothing at all better in the world than to be laughed at for looking so silly. She didn't even care if some of the kids were former students. Patty was laughing. In public. With too much noise. And too many people around her.

Fillan wasn't sure whether to be flattered or to feel guilty when Patty went to his car instead of Emma's and wouldn't budge when Emma asked her to go with her. "It is alright with me, Em. I am a safe driver."

"I wasn't worried. I just... You don't have to..."

He touched her face. "It is fine. We will meet you at the house, if you are okay with it."

"I have to go to the store. I'll just run in and out and go back while she's in school tomorrow, but..."

"Go ahead then. Patty and I will jump over the sidewalk cracks and try not to step on the ants until you get home." He could see the fight inside her as to whether to trust he could handle the girl. "Emma, I have your number if I need it. We will be fine."

"I won't be long."

"I am not worried." He gave her a soft kiss and asked if he could let Patty sit up front with him since she was big enough.

"No. She plays with stuff. I've kept her in the back ever since she threw my gear shift into park in the middle of the road. Scared the heck out of me. We nearly got bashed in the rear, not to mention my car didn't like it."

"Alright, then, the back it is." Fillan opened the door, assured Emma the vehicle had child safety locks so Patty couldn't open it while the car was moving, and touched her face again. "Relax, Emma. I will take good care of her."

With a light nod, she told Patty to behave and she'd be there in a few minutes. When she gave Fillan a key to her house so he could take her inside, he told her it wasn't necessary, but she closed his hand over it and gave him a light kiss.

Fillan talked with the girl on the way back to Emma's, or anyway, he talked to her. She was listening, he could tell, and he did not want her to change her mind about being away from Emma and so he talked about dance and the things they saw from the windows, and he mentioned Ireland as a way to start working into the fact that his home was away and he would have to go back. He would not say as much when he had her away from Emma. No need rocking the boat that much.

Pulling up to her house, Fillan saw the black car there again. He pondered whether to drive away and wait for Emma to come, but his ire flared too fast, so he pulled in front of the house, leaving the space in the drive for Emma. The guy was sitting in his car, just waiting. Creepy as all hell.

"Wait here, Patty cake." Fillan left his door part open so he could hear her and went to Turner's car window. "She is not home. Did you need something I can help you with?"

Turner glanced at him up and down. "You're living here now?"

"No, I do not live here. I am meeting her here. What does it matter to you?"

Shoving the door open, hitting Fillan in the hip in process, Turner got out, his shoulders back, chin forward, like a bull waiting to charge or trying to intimidate with his extra height. "It's no concern of yours why I wish to speak with my wife."

"Ex. Not wife. And as I am her friend, it is my concern."

"Friend?" He snickered. "I'm no idiot. I know you're staying here. Where is Emma, since you seem to know?"

"She will be here shortly." Fillan saw Patty get out of the car.

Turner looked at the girl and looked at him. "Why's she with you?"

Fillan didn't bother to answer. He went to Patty when the girl saw Turner and stopped, her arms crossed in front, her eyes on the grass. "It is all fine. Wait in the car until your Aunt Emma comes. Yes?" She didn't move, but Turner came over and she started rocking. "Patty cake, it is fine. Come. We will jump over the cracks. Remember?"

"Maybe I should call the cops and let them ask what you're doing with a minor child not related to you."

Fillan eyed him. "Call if you like. It will only make you look foolish when Emma comes 'round and tells them why she is with me." The girl rocked harder. "Move away. You are bothering her."

"Don't even try to give me orders on the property I'm paying for. She did tell you I'm still supporting her?"

"Her financial business is not mine. It is her house, and you are upsetting her niece." He stroked Patty's head. "It is all fine. Come. We will sit on the porch to wait. Right?" Fillan kept his voice calm and friendly. He wanted to take her inside, but he didn't want this guy to know Emma gave him a key if it would cause trouble for her.

Patty started that direction with his prompting, walking around him to get farther away from Turner, but the asshole moved in front of them, blocking the steps.

"What is your fucking problem?" Fillan put himself between Turner and the girl. "You were fool enough to let Emma go, to tell her to go. It is not your business who chooses to see. She has told you to leave her alone. You should have enough respect for her to do so."

"She only signed it out of trying to prove something, so don't think whatever you're doing with her is going to last. I can forgive her little summer conquest as part of trying to prove herself, but it's only that. Our split is temporary, as I knew it would be or I would never have agreed to help pay for this falling down piece of garbage she picked out. She tends to do that, you realize, take in strays no one else wants."

Fillan only kept himself from pounding the guy because Patty was behind him, now clinging to the back of his shirt and pulling at him. "What you think of me doesnae mean more than a rat's piece of crap, so you know. Come, Patty cake." He backed up, eyeing Turner to watch for the need to defend himself and watching that he wouldn't step on her toes, meaning to get her farther away, back in the car if possible.

"Such lovely language in front of the child. It only goes to show Emma is not good at parenting decisions, to entrust her in your care. That girl needs to be somewhere they know what to do with her instead of Emma treating her like a little puppy dog she strokes for her own ego or sense of justice or for whatever reason she's doing this."

"Mind what you say in front of her."

A sarcastic grin accompanied two steps closer to Fillan so the guy was right up in his face, looking down at him. "You dare warn me after your vulgarity?"

"I am talking about you, not about her. She understands what you are saying. She understands I am protecting her. And she understands you are an obnoxious bully, which is why she does not like you."

"She understands nothing more than an animal does, if that much."

Do not punch him in the jaw, Fillan. Think of the girl. Do not do it. His whole body was tense from restraining himself and Patty pulled harder on his shirt, trying to pull him away. Protecting him? Either way, Fillan was not letting the asshole win. "Contrary to what you said, you are the possibly the biggest idiot I have ever met. She does understand. And I understand that you are trying to get me to throw the first punch because you think it would be an easy way to remove me from Emma's life. I am not near the idiot you are and it is not going to work. Do not think I have any fear of you. I do not."

He snickered. "If you say so."

"Come 'round again when the girl is not here and get in my face if you want to find out."

"Is that a threat?"

"It is absolutely nowhere near a threat. I never throw the first punch. I am good at throwing the last one, though." Fillan went through the scenario in his head, waiting for it to come, thinking about how he could keep Patty out of the way.

"*Mark.* Back *away* from him. *Why* are you here?" Emma made a beeline across the grass and wrapped her niece in her arms. "Baby, it's okay." She looked at Fillan. "What's going on?"

"He was here when we pulled in. She was fine until she saw him."

"I'm sure she was." She glared at her ex. "*Why* are you here?"

Turner crept away from Fillan toward Emma. "Are you in the habit of leaving the girl, a defenseless girl at that, in the care of strange men? That could easily be neglect at best, and a good reason to put her in someone else's care. I bet your brother would love to hear that you did."

"Fillan is not a stranger and you know it. She's fine with him and it was her idea to ride home with him instead of with me." Emma pulled her phone out and sent a quick text to someone, then stuck it back in her pocket. "Leave, Mark. I don't want you here."

He snickered. "I'm sure you don't. You expected no one would find out you're letting a retarded girl, a minor, choose to get in a car with a man she barely knows?"

Emma's back straightened. "She is not retarded. She is autistic. She's also very smart and she understands what you're saying, so knock it off."

"Whatever you want to call it. Fact is it's a bad parenting choice, Emma. I suppose it's good we haven't had children yet so I know to keep watch over what you're doing with them when we do have."

"You are insane, Mark. Truly. That's never going to happen. Get off of my property."

"As I told you, Emma, if you want me to keep paying for this excuse for a house, you can't have your dancer friend living here. It's a breach of contract."

"And as I told you, stop the payments if you wish. I will not live under your thumb any longer. Now leave. Shh, Patty, it's alright, sweetie. Why don't you go on inside with Fillan now?" She glared at Turner who was still blocking her path. "Move out of my way."

"Is this dancer going to be able to afford the kind of rent I'm giving you to live here?"

"He's not living here and he has his own place to take care of, not that it's your business. I can manage fine. Go. And get out of the way so I can get her inside and calmed down."

Patty was rocking in Emma's arms. Fillan had to wonder if Emma realized yet that the girl had allowed herself to be hugged, to let Emma shelter her physically. He turned enough that Turner wouldn't see him hand her the house key. "Go on in, Emma. She needs to stay with you until she calms. I will see him out and away."

"No." She gave it back to him, purposely letting the guy see what she was doing. "You could have just gone inside. That's why I gave it to you. Mark, move out of their way."

"So much for not living here."

"Not your business. Move before I call the police and have them move you."

"I will stop the checks, Emma."

"Go ahead. Just move. Patty, go inside with Fillan. Okay?"

Inside? "I am not leaving you here alone with him." Whatever she said, that wasn't going to happen.

"I'm fine. Really. Please, take her in and away from this. She's getting too upset. Patty, it's fine. Everything's okay. He's leaving."

"I'm not, actually. Whether or not I send more checks, I have paid for this property so far. Tell your *boyfriend* to leave and we can go inside and talk."

"This is *my* house, and you're *not* coming in."

He grasped Emma's arm, tight, and Fillan was about to take him down, but she released Patty to him and twisted her arm back around to get it out of his grasp, then punched him right in the stomach.

Pulling Patty around behind him in case he had to jump in, Fillan had to try hard not to laugh.

"Now *go*. And *don't* touch me again."

Turner stared a moment, then snickered. "Trying to show off for your summer fling? You'd hardly hurt a fly that way, Emma, dear. But good for show, I guess."

"Take her for a walk, please." Emma pleaded with her eyes.

Fillan couldn't do it. He couldn't go farther than where he could watch. First, he eyed Turner and spoke quietly. "You touch her again and I will be all over your arse no matter who is around. Also not a threat. Come, Patty cake. Let's find some music, right?"

Taking her over to his car, Fillan turned the ignition enough to get the radio going and tuned it to something upbeat. Keeping an eye on Emma, he kept Patty turned away so she wouldn't see them arguing, turned the radio high enough she wouldn't hear too much of it, and showed her some dance moves. It worked well enough to unwind her, just enough, but not enough he could walk away and over to Turner to force him to leave. He could do it, despite the size difference. Could be Emma didn't believe he could, and Fillan would hardly fault her for thinking so, but he could.

As he pondered trying to get Patty in the car to stay safely out of the way, another car pulled in, behind Emma's. Her brother got out, looked over at Fillan and Patty, and strode straight to his sister.

Emma felt the relief flow through her system as Rob took her side.

"What's up, Em?" He set a hand on her back, facing Mark.

"One question. And I needed to ask you in front of him. Are you working with him to get me to put Patty in a full care center?"

Rob's expression answered for him. "What?"

"He says you are, that you don't think I can do this."

"And you believed him?"

"I don't know what to believe anymore, but I'm telling you both it's not going to happen. Patty is my daughter now. I've always been there for her. I'm always the one who made the sacrifices for her when everyone else was too busy. And she's making huge improvements only in the last couple of weeks. She's going nowhere, so you might as well..."

"Emma." Rob turned and lowered his hand to take hers. "I don't know what this lout has been telling you, but I would never try to take her from you. You're right. This is where she belongs."

"You're not siding with him anymore? Because you used to."

"I haven't sided with him about anything since he walked out on you." When Mark tried to interfere, Rob threw him a warning glance. "And I'm sorry I ever did. I think he conned us both. Patty is ... making unbelievable progress. I'm amazed. You're a wonderful mom. Don't listen to anyone who says otherwise."

Getting too choked up, which she didn't want to do in front of her ex, Emma swallowed hard. "Thank you. Would you please tell him to leave since I've done that at least ten times now and he won't go?"

Rob's shoulders straightened and he took a step toward Mark. "Leave, as she said. Stay off my sister's property and do not bother her again, or we will file a harassment charge. I'm sure your employers would not want to see that come across their desk."

"*I* am paying for this property."

"As per your divorce agreement. Because you have to. And I

guarantee if you try to renege on what you owe her, because you do owe her for everything she gave up for you, we will take you to court."

"The agreement also says if she moves someone in here, the contract is null and void. Considering that dancer has a key to the place..."

"Mark." Rob's voice lowered, a sign he was getting angry. "I suggest you read it again. It says if she gets remarried. She can very well move Fillan in here if she so chooses and you still get to pay her what you owe her. If she marries ... anyone, then you're off the hook. Personally, if I were her, I would be vengeful enough to just live with him for the three years of the contract and get what she can back out of you, and then marry him, if she chooses."

"Rob..." Emma did not want Fillan to hear marriage talk.

"I know." He set the hand on her back again. "You aren't that vengeful, sadly. But don't let him intimidate you out of what he owes you. That's what he's trying to do. You would have had your masters before now if he hadn't stopped you. He owes you, Em. Don't let him out of it."

"I owe her? She's the one who put someone else above her marriage, above her vows. She owes me."

"I did not." Emma saw Fillan come closer, trying to decide whether to join them. Patty was sitting in the grass playing with something and listening to music from Fillan's car. She reached a hand toward him and moved in to take his hand, for the support he was quietly offering.

"Mark, you put yourself above us, always, and before me. All I did was try to help my dying sister and her baby girl and you were so freaking selfish it drove you crazy. I won't go into all the things you said to me, but I did not break my vows. You did. Respect is part of the vows, too, you know. You walked out on us, not me. I didn't even realize what real respect was until..." She swallowed hard and looked at Fillan. "Until my dancer, as you call him, came along. By now, I'm more glad than I can tell you that you served those papers. I feel free for the first time in my life. I will never go back to you. Never. Leave now, and stay the hell away from me."

Emma watched until he got in his car and pulled away, and then wrapped herself into her dancer.

"Beautiful, Emma. You handled him beautifully. Are you alright?"

She nodded, touched his face, and turned to Rob. "Thank you for coming."

"I could have dealt with him, Em." Fillan tilted his head toward her. "I only did not want to do it in front of her. I would have if needed."

"I'm sure you could have, but I don't want you to. It's not your fight. I knew darn well he'd never risk touching Rob. I wasn't sure, though..."

"I handle myself well."

She grinned and squeezed his fingers. "I have no doubt of that at all. But I don't trust what he would do if you did and I don't want you getting kicked out of here before you have to go."

"It was a good call." Rob looked between them. "No offense, and I'm sure you could have, Fillan, but I know the legalities of her decree and I needed to know what he was up to. I'm glad you called me, Emma. And don't ever think I would side with any man over you. Before... I thought I was helping you. He made it sound like that's what he was doing, and it's the only reason I ever listened to him. All right? You've got to talk to me better. It's pretty much just us now, with Mom and Dad in failing health, and I suspect that will worsen now with Helen gone. Be ready for that, all right?"

She nodded. She knew it every bit as much as he did.

"Here." He handed Fillan his card. "In case you ever need to reach me. And in all honesty..." Rob looked over at where Patty was playing, stacking CDs on top of each other, Emma now realized. "I meant what I said. It's a relief to me to know you're around so much, especially at nights. I worry about them alone."

"Rob..."

"I know you handle yourself fine, but a big brother can't help but worry over his little sister and niece being by themselves when the neighbors all know you are and you hardly know them." He set a hand on Fillan's shoulder. "So, as far as I'm concerned, you could move in and not bother me at all."

"He's only here for the summer, Rob. I told you…"

"Well. At least there's that. Maybe don't tell your neighbors as much and they won't know, at least for a while, whether or not he's here. On that note, I'm headed home. Call anytime you need. And if Mark comes back, call the cops first and me second and we'll file a harassment charge. I'll back you on it." With a kiss to Emma's head, he went to talk to Patty a moment.

"You know she's playing with your CDs."

Fillan grinned. "It was the only thing I had. I asked her not to open them."

"She doesn't always listen that well."

"It is fine." He slid fingers up along her face and alongside her head. "You realize I plan to come back to visit. I think I am going to have to make it a habit to come and visit, until you get sick of me, anyway."

"Don't make promises you won't keep." She set her hands on his hips.

"No, I never do." He wiped moisture from her eyes. "Let me turn off the radio and we will go tell your brother how Patty laughed at you today." Instead of turning it off, Fillan scanned stations and found a similar beat to that at the ice cream shop.

With a smile and with Patty and Rob both watching, he slid up next to Emma and pulled her into the rhythm, with hip sways and a low dip…

"This is really not my style, you know."

"But you look nice doing it."

"Okay." Her eyes rolled.

"How about this, then?" He reached back in to stick a CD into the slot. Something old, from the Seventies, Emma suspected. She only somewhat recognized the song. He took her in his arms and moved them into a rumba, making it as close and sultry as he could.

Emma noticed a couple of her neighbors watching, but she didn't stop him. His expression seemed to be daring her, so she let him take it to the next level, teaching her hip twists with a figure eight movement, going around behind her to help get the motion right, guiding her hips with his hands, and then he moved back to her front to take her hands and move her in close as they did it together.

"You are a beautiful dancer." He smiled and watched her hips.

"You're a good teacher."

With a slight nod of thanks, he moved her into a turn and dipped her low. When Patty clapped, Fillan chuckled and turned off the music.

"Very nice, Emma." Rob gave her a sweet grin. "You've always had a natural grace, unlike any of the rest of us. I'm glad you decided to do this. If you're here next summer, I may have to bring my wife in for classes. Just don't expect us to look like that." He offered Fillan a hand, told Patty goodbye, and left for home.

As he pulled out, Patty handed Fillan a few CDs, asking for music, he guessed. "Let's take them inside. Yes? We can dance more in there." The girl headed straight to the house and they had to catch up. Excited, about music, and dance.

Maybe he could find a way to keep helping her progress.

~ Twenty-six ~

"I have something for you." Glad Patty agreed so easily to stay with Rob's family after much of a day of sight-seeing and hiking around the cape so he could have time to sit and talk with Emma alone, Fillan reached behind him and pulled the plastic bag from the table behind the couch. "It is nothing perverted. Do not worry." He gave her a grin.

"I almost wish it was." With a quick return grin that affected him more than he wanted to let it, she reached in and pulled out the DVD. "Movement therapy?"

"As close as I could find to a dance therapy video. I have been researching in my spare time, mainly at night when I wish you had been here with me. It says it can sometimes work well with autism, because of the repetitive motion that appears to calm her and because it is a means of expression which is particularly good for non-verbal children. With the way she enjoyed watching class, I expect it might not hurt to try. I can do it with her, if you like. I have been looking at good ways to approach it..."

Emma slipped a hand around his head and pulled him in. Her mouth overtook his, her tongue deepening the kiss, turning it quickly passionate. Obviously, she'd set the video down since both hands were on him, the second on his stomach, sliding around...

"Em..." He nearly gasped for breath. "I cannot guarantee it will help and she maybe will not even try it..."

"I know. Thank you." She teased his lips.

"I have watched it and it looks to be a good possible start. If it is not, we can try something else. And I only mean to help her..."

"I know." She kissed him harder, insistent.

He found his hand sliding up underneath her skirt, the soft flowing skirt that barely hit her knees in front and fell down around the back of her legs. He caressed her thigh and she pulled farther into him. "Hm, now I have to wonder how you would have reacted if it had been something perverted instead."

She chuckled and moved back to stand up, reaching for his hand. "Guess you'll have to try that if you want to know. Come dance with me."

Glad to oblige, Fillan turned on his stereo and took her in his arms. "Did you want to learn another dance? Cha cha?"

"Not tonight." She moved her body up against his, swaying with the soft melody, and backed up to remove the draped sheer top covering a stretchy low-cut camisole. In return, he pulled his shirt over his head.

Rain began. He could hear it through his open windows over the soft music, instrumental rock guitar. Emma looked toward the nearest window as it grew heavier, gave him a grin, and took his hand to lead him outside. In the hard rain.

"You like the rain?"

"I do. And wind, as I told you." She opened her arms wide, her face up, eyes closed. "I'm always tempted to do this at home, but my neighbors would probably have me committed."

"Em." Fillan moved in and cupped a hand around her head, bringing her eyes to his in the fading glow of the lowering sun. "Promise me you willnae find another mate while I am away. I will come back as I can. I promise I will. And I know I should not ask you, since I have no right, but the closer it gets, the more it shoots pain through my heart to think of you in another man's arms."

With a soft grin, she gave him that look that said he was being ridiculous. "Make love to me, Fillan. Right here."

"In the rain?"

"Yes."

"You will get cold." He kissed her neck as he grasped her skirt and slid it slowly up her legs.

"I don't get cold easily."

"Emma. Tell me you will not find another man."

"Shh." She took over, leading him to where she wanted him.

Fillan thought about reminding her of his neighbor who dropped by as she pleased, but since it was raining, he figured it was unlikely. And hell, she'd already seen him not in action and cold from the ocean water. At least he would redeem himself if she walked over while he was in Emma's complete control.

She held him tight as she lay on top of him, her breath heavy, as heavy as his, her arms around his neck. The long, hot shower after their rain rendezvous had stirred them both again and he took her straight to his bed. "Fillan." She whispered next to his ear. "I won't find anyone else. I'll wait for you as long as there's still any chance of you coming back. I love you far too much to want anyone else."

He pulled away enough to find her eyes. "Yeah?"

"Yes. And now I know how it's supposed to be, how much I sold myself out with Mark just to..."

"I love you, too, Em. And so did I. The hell with them, right? They donae matter now."

"Right. They don't." Cuddling down in against his side, Emma kissed his shoulder and closed her eyes.

He didn't speak and she was glad for it. She just wanted to lie there and hold him, enjoy the moment, their sweat mingled, their breath easing together, their heartbeats meshing in different rhythms while rain fell on the roof and in the sand, breathing its soft fresh scent in through the window.

She wanted this, and she would wait for him all the rest of the year until next summer if needed. Even if it was only a summer fling every year, Emma wanted this.

Twenty-seven

Later. Emma gripped his shirt and considered his words from three days earlier. *Come later.* Move to Ireland, he meant. How could she? Patty needed her school, her cousins, her routine. She needed ... Fillan. She loved him. Patty loved him.

And so did Emma. But move to Ireland? Would her teaching degree transfer? She rather doubted it would and she had no interest in starting again. Still, spending only summers together already seemed somewhat impossible to think of.

They walked along rock-strewn Balston Beach in South Truro and she told Fillan of how the Pilgrims hadn't first landed in Plymouth, as many thought. They anchored in Provincetown Harbor, had come to shore in Truro and exchanged some fire with the Pamet Indians with no casualties, and then moved along up to Plymouth. The Cape wasn't suitable for settling, they'd decided. And by this time, it was over settled, at least as far as Emma was concerned. At least during the summer with the tons of tourists that made it hard for her to take Patty out and about. She loved the Cape, but she loved it most during every other part of the year than tourist season.

Two weeks left and then he'd leave. As much as Fillan talked of coming back next summer, Emma couldn't let herself count on it. She pretended not to be thinking about it as Patty stopped to gather rounded flat rocks and stacked them atop each other. Emma took the chance to sit in the warm sand. Her feet were tired after wandering the other side of Truro, Pamet River and Corn Hill where the Pilgrims had found and snatched a supply of corn the Indians had gathered, and Edward Hopper's house since Fillan showed interest in it. They still planned to go to Highland Lighthouse, the first on Cape Cod and an old haunt of Henry David Thoreau's, but he wanted to be there at sunset. A poet, her Fillan was. He talked of what he saw in such a beautiful way and he often stopped and simply took in his surroundings. He had a ton of photos, he said, far more than he'd planned to take.

Patty was content with her rocks and so Fillan lowered beside Emma, rubbing a hand over her back. "Have you thought more of coming with me?"

"Where?" She grimaced when a rather tall rock pile fell over, but Patty just started again, changing the rocks around.

"Ireland, Em. Coming with me. Or coming later once you have things settled here. Are you even considering it?"

"I can't." She heard it come out before she even thought. "Look at her. She's finally settling in well. She's more content than I've seen ... ever. How can I disrupt her whole world again? I think... I think I will ask Jodi, the girl from class looking for a roommate, if she's interested in moving in. Patty likes her. She can help with her dance videos..."

He picked up a rock and tossed it out into the water. "She would be alright. It is being with you helping her most. You would be there and so she would be alright."

"And you. She loves you, you know."

"And you, Emma? You said you did, as well. We could..."

"Don't. Fillan..." Emma brushed fingers through his hair. "I'm not ready for such a big step. I'm finally settling, also. I think, now that I don't have someone holding me back, I'll go for my master's degree and then I can make more and everything will work fine. It's time to be a grown up and part of that is..." She heard Mark's voice in that statement and cringed inwardly. "Facing reality. The reality is that I'm not ready for that kind of a step. If you decide to come back next summer, you can stay with us."

"If you do not have someone new by then."

Emma nearly laughed at his sulk, his slumped shoulders, his head turned in avoidance. "I won't have." She pulled his face back to hers. "I won't have. We'll still talk through messenger like you do with your sister. We can still have part of this. For right now, that's all I can do."

His chest rose hard and fell softly. "Alright, Em. That was our agreement. I haven't the right to expect anything more." He stood and brushed sand off his legs beneath the long baggy shorts. "Come, Patty. Ready to go up in the lighthouse?"

Emma wasn't sure she would once they got to it, and she had to let her take a handful of rocks with her, but she strode easily at Fillan's side toward the car.

He could return for the Christmas holiday. Looking out over the Atlantic Ocean from atop Highland Lighthouse, Fillan was glad to be going home soon. Part of him was. Too much of him wanted to stay. He could return. He could take the job his father wanted him to take and move his teaching to part time on evenings and weekends, which would fill his time, and save money to come back in December. And then again next summer. A nice arrangement, he tried to tell himself. Free much of the year and two beautiful companions here and there as he could. And maybe they could come and visit once she got her head wrapped 'round the idea she could.

She would have Easter break in spring. She could come then for the week. Would Patty do alright with flying? That, he didn't know. He knew it concerned Emma to try.

At least Patty had no negative reaction to his contact with Emma. Taking advantage of the mood they'd given him wandering the Cape in the gorgeous heat of the summer sun, Fillan pulled Emma into his arms as the sun set over the ocean. Patty still didn't object, so he kissed her, his Emma. And he hoped like hell she was right that she would not find anyone new.

"We should get home. I'm starving. Aren't you?" Emma stroked fingers down his shoulder.

"I'll take you to dinner since we are out."

"Oh, Fillan, you've done enough."

He skimmed her lips. "I will be thrifty again when I go back home. We havenae gone to The Moors yet."

"It's too crowded. She won't like it."

"What do y' think, Patty?" He kept a hand on Emma's back as he leaned around her to see the girl staring out at the sunset. "Can we take Emma to her favorite restaurant tonight? Will you be alright with that?"

Patty glanced between them, stuck the two rocks she'd been juggling in one hand in her pockets, one on each side, and took his hand, and then Emma's hand.

"I would say she is willing to give it a try." Fillan shrugged. "If it does not work, we will leave. Good enough?"

Emma slipped out to her backyard and sat cross-legged on the damp grass to look up at the twinkling stars. Did they look the same in Ireland? She supposed they would. She swatted at buzzing mosquitoes and then wiped the remains of one off her palm into the grass.

So much for a normal dinner. Too crowded. Too noisy. Not for her, but for Patty. She'd known better. She let Fillan talk her into trying against her better judgment and of course it hadn't worked. They'd left just after they sat down, as she apologized to the server who'd brought water and silverware and would have to clean it up for the next patrons with nothing to show for her trouble. Emma would normally leave a small tip just because, but she was too flustered to think of it. She'd felt guilty all the way home.

Luckily Patty was tired from their long day out and settled right into bed when it was time.

She looked up at Fillan when he wandered out beside her and stroked fingers over her head.

"You alright?"

"Yes. Sorry. I should have just said it wouldn't work..."

"You did say as much. I still think it was worth the try. You should have your brother help you try with her now and then, get her used to it. I think it will work eventually, as nothing happens."

"You're very sweet, you know. It'll be a lucky girl who winds up with you. I want you to remember that."

Fillan lowered to the grass and wrapped around her from behind. "Ye are one of the very few people on earth who would call me that. I am not, in general. I am pig-headed and set on my own path and even my own sister tells me oft enough I am far too full of myself. So if you see me as sweet, it is something you have brought out. I am grateful to you for it."

She leaned back against him with a deep sigh, wrapping her arms over his.

"Are ye going to be alright, Em? On your own with Patty. Will you be offended if I say the idea of it bothers me?"

"I'll be fine. We'll be fine. Rob is around if we need him."

Fillan snuggled closer and kissed her head. "And you will not go back to Turner?"

"Never." Her body tensed at the thought. "I'll be fine. Really. This summer... This time with you has shown me more of who I am, what I can do and what I really want. Thank you for that."

"I did nothing except..."

"More than you know." She turned to face him better and touched his face. "You will always matter to me, Fillan. You will always be a part of me. I'm grateful for whatever made you come for the summer." Meeting his lips to stop whatever he was about to say, Emma slid her hand down his chest and up inside his shirt. "Come inside. She should sleep well tonight."

If the girl thought she was going to be rid of him that easily, only because a wee ocean would be between them, she would have to think again.

Fillan led her to her stereo and put one of the CDs Patty had pulled from his car into her player. As Van Morrison came quietly through the speakers, Fillan advanced it to *Moondance* and pulled her in for a Viennese Waltz. With so little space to work with, it was harder to pull off. He would love to get her out on an open dance floor and show her off. Someday, maybe she would do so with him. In the meantime, he would take what he could get.

"Emma." He leaned her back into a perfect hold. "I am not going to go find another girl. You should know as much."

"You think so now. But..."

He swirled her back up and around in a natural turn to a fleck roll, moving them into the kitchen to go around the table, pausing with another hold. "And I am holding you to what you said before, that you will not find another man."

"I won't. But Fillan..."

Another quick roll and a change of direction, and Fillan took her into a running weave, smiling as she kept up with him with little trouble, back out to the living room. "Someday, love, you and I are going to be out on a large ballroom floor showing off what a good teacher I am. Just so you are aware."

She grinned. "Is that right?"

Switching abruptly from the waltz to a simple slow dance, Fillan released her hand and ran fingers through her hair, his body against hers, her arms sliding around his neck. "I love you, Emma. The end of the summer will not be the end of this. I will not allow it. There is no point in arguing the fact, since you know as well as I do it could not be possible to find such a right partnership. You need me as well as I need you."

Emma stopped moving. "You need me? The other part of that I won't argue, but..."

"You think I do not?"

"I think you do not." She stroked fingertips along the back of his neck. "I'm glad you think you want me, though, at least for now."

With a shake of his head, Fillan went to move the track up. As *Crazy Love* started, he reclaimed his love and led her into a rumba, singing it to her. Halfway through the song, she broke from the dance and wrapped around him. Her fingers caressed the hair at his nape and she kissed his neck.

"Emma, my love, you are wrong. I do need you. You have made me so much more than I have ever been."

"Hm, I think that was Patty more than me."

He pulled back to catch her eyes. "It was both. I wouldnae have bothered to try with her if not for you. Tell me again you willnae find another mate while I am away."

"I won't find another mate." It was a gentle whisper beside his ear. "I will wait, in case you find you want us enough to come all the way back over here. And don't tell me again now that you will. We'll see, right?"

Fillan knew there wasn't a thing more he could say to make her believe it, so she would have to wait and see, then. He would prove it to her.

Twenty-eight

While Emma called Rob to check on Patty, Fillan lit torches around the front of his cabin. He would miss the place, as little of it as there was, and with as little time as he'd spent there. In the morning, he would fly home. Back to his Ireland, to Galway, to the job his father wanted him to take. Dock supervisor. On the fishing dock he worked every summer as he was growing, under his father's supervision. Not a bad job. It was outdoors and active. It had been good for his muscle strength and would be again, beyond his dance training. His father had been manager back then and now he owned it. Fillan was unsure how well that would work, but he would give it a try. It was good pay. No further need to count every penny would be a good thing. Saving for plane tickets much faster would be an even better thing. Unless she changed her mind, he meant to come back to see her as often as possible.

She didn't believe he would and he guessed it was fair.

But he would.

Ambling back up the beach from where she'd wandered, Emma hung up with a sigh and came to him, her bare feet digging into the sand, her swim wrap swaying with her soft stride.

"Everything alright?" He slid a hand up her thigh under the mesh wrap.

"She's unsettled, but okay, Rob said. He said it like he didn't really mean it, though."

"He will handle her well." Fillan raised his hand higher, to her waist. "I have not taught you the tango yet, as I promised. I would say it is time." Scanning her curves and near naked skin as he backed away, Fillan stepped inside the open door just long enough to turn the music on.

Starting with a song only to tease her about saying she liked it the other day when some kid drove past blaring it out her car window, he put on Luke Bryan's *Shake It For Me*. She gave him that look, the one that said she was trying to convince him he wasn't funny, but he gripped her around the waist and moved them together in a samba roll. She'd learned samba rolls quickly and did them well.

"That's not the tango."

He chuckled and went to change the music to Hinder.

"Alright, then. For the tango, you have to be in close hold. Wrap your left arm around the outside of mine." Fillan positioned her left hand and caught their free hands together, held out away from their bodies. "Simple steps, right foot back. Slow, slow, quick, quick, slow." Taking it slowly until she had the movements down, they brought it up to speed with the music, their eyes often locked, and he added the reverse embrace, cross walk, and promenade, and then the more sensual pasada, cuatro, and leg caresses.

"Nice, Em. I could have you doing competitions with me before you know it."

"I like this one. You should have taught it to me sooner." Her eyes caught his in a tease as her leg caressed his.

"We will work on it more next time we are together. Let's try it with the right music." He backed away gently and went to put on Gavin Rossdale's *Future World*. And she was right; he should have taught her the tango much sooner.

As the song ended, she met his lips, slid her hands along his bare sides, and pressed a bare leg up between his, with her leg wrapping around his.

"You are supposed to do that from the outside of my leg."

"Am I?" She moved away, slowly, grabbed her towel from the chair, and spread it over the sand. Lowering onto it, she untied her mesh wrap up and tossed it to the chair.

Under the dark sky and the small torches flickering with the salty ocean breeze, Fillan took to her side and lowered her to the towel. They were alone other than the blue heron calling from the shore line and waves splashing over the rocks. And he had to leave her in the morning. The tightening of his heart told him it was wrong to leave her and he covered his thoughts by running his lips down her body, slowly, leaving her with as nice a memory as he could manage.

Emma opened her eyes to the herons calling in the distance and cuddled closer to Fillan as they lay naked other than the light blanket. In his bed. She badly wanted to stay right there in the little beach shack with him for ... for as long as he would allow.

And she couldn't. He was leaving.

With a sigh and brushed-away moisture from her eyes that she wouldn't let him see, Emma kissed his chest and then his neck. "Fillan." He stirred and she kissed him again, his neck, then his lips. "We have to get up." She checked her watch. "Soon."

With a sound she wasn't sure was a groan or her name, he rolled over and pressed her onto her back. "Morning, love. It is nice to wake up to you this way." He slid a hand along her body.

Returning the favor, Emma found him ready for her and urged him closer.

"Again?" He threw that charming grin she loved.

"Once more. Before I send you home."

"And I thought this part of things did not matter so much to ye."

"It didn't. Before."

"Right, then, Fillan, make it matter to the girl before ye have to head back across the ocean." He rolled his eyes with a grin. "'Twas a good plan, to be sure."

She chuckled and kissed his chest. "Don't worry, my Irish leprechaun. It only matters with you. And it's still far from the most important thing."

"Lucky for me, yea?" He turned her onto her back and moved over top of her.

Much faster than the night before, he was still as fully passionate and Emma could hardly make herself get up after they were both spent to run through the lukewarm shower. He'd said it was never better than lukewarm. In the summer, she supposed that was good enough. In the summer, a lot of things could happen that wouldn't normally and it was fine. Before real life returned and left only the memories of the incredible warmth and the freedom of bare feet, bare shoulders, long swims through cool water, and bare naked passion on the beach. Or in a beach shack.

~ Twenty-nine ~

Fillan trekked over the slippery rocks in the light rain, carefully, making his way to the lighthouse. He had heard the main story of how it was built for the owner to be able to get his supplies from the Galway ferry, but he liked the other story better, that the owner's wife had it built as a beacon to draw her pub-crawling husband home safe again each night.

Either way, there was something Fillan loved about Ballycurrin Lighthouse. Against his better judgment, he climbed the narrow stone steps curling around the outside of the 20-some foot stone tower and sat at the top, hands clenching the metal rail at his head, feet dangling down over the rocks. Looking out over Lough Corrib, he spotted two small fishing boats anchored at the edge and thought of Emma's stories of Pilgrims and the early Long Point fishermen who floated their houses across the bay from Provincetown as they left the little arm peninsula the Mayflower had sailed around to dock.

Three weeks he had been home and he was entrenched in his job as crew manager for his father's fishing company. He liked it better than he'd expected. Of course he was in charge this time instead of being a peon following anyone's orders who decided to give him orders. It always made a difference. He had done his time through the years. It was only right he was able to give orders these days, although it wasn't an easy thing for him.

In his free time, Fillan continued his research on anything that might help Patty, on new dance movements he could put on a video and send along to Emma. He had yet to do as much, but he thought of doing it. So far, he found it hard enough to talk with her across the ocean through a computer rather than in person. It hurt him physically to see her face and not be able to touch her skin.

Sniffing it aside and telling himself it was the cold and the rain, he scratched at the stubble on his chin that was only allowed on weekends when he did not have to work. His father was a tyrant about being neat and clean and punctual. Not that Fillan found a thing wrong with that. At least these days, he found not a thing wrong with it. He had to fit the part of the new job. And he did well enough.

Even if his heart and soul were back in Provincetown, across the Atlantic, with Emma and Patty.

Get a hold on yourself, mate. Ye cannot leave here for good and you know it.

Looking out over the lough, Fillan thought of how he'd asked her to do the same, to leave her home and move with him. A right fool he was to think she would. She had more of a career than he had, at least at the time he had asked, and she had a child who needed to stay on her regular schedule. How could he have asked it of her?

He sat up there until the rain grew heavier, colder, and then made his way back down, across the rocks, down the little road alongside the estate. He could ask her to come stay over the winter holiday. Rent the little two bedroom cottage at the estate. Show her one of his favorite lighthouses as a returned favor and kiss her at the top. If she would dare climb out over the rocks to get to it. She was easily smarter than he was himself and likely would not, as they were not nearly as smooth as the breakwater they had treaded to get to her favorite lighthouse.

And it would be frigid in December. But then there was the Jacuzzi in the main bath of the cottage to warm up in again. He knew only because a relative had come to stay, to visit without being too close, and his kin of some sort had asked him in. A rough several days that came to, with his head ringing and thumping and swirling all at once on top of the nausea and the hives covering his body from the alcohol he knew he could not touch, due to the allergy. A rare thing, to be allergic to it, but they had ruled out everything otherwise. It had been the last time he had made the mistake of ignoring it. He did learn. Not always fast enough, but he did learn.

If he were to ever marry, they would have to toast with sparkling wine instead of the real thing. Some Irishman he was when he couldn't drink even a spot without getting hives.

Ah well, there were worse things to have to avoid. Such as the girl. Who had come back. And who was offering herself far too easily and far too openly. She was proud of him for taking his father's offered job. She could stay with him if he was finally going to be a "real man" as she had said. He hadn't given in. His memories of Emma were far too fresh.

And he wanted only her.

Closing the door of his old but trusty auto against the rain and turning the heater to high, Fillan dropped his head to the steering wheel. He only wanted Em.

"Mark, stop calling me. I mean it." Emma pulled into the staff parking lot and rolled her eyes at the same old *you need me* speech. "Look. You call again and I'll change my number to unlisted. Are we understood yet?"

"I know where you live and where you work."

"I know how to file a harassment complaint, too. Don't think I won't. Goodbye, Mark." Hanging up, Emma shook her head. The first two weeks of the school year was hard enough with the kids still wound up from summer freedom, and Emma was still coping with Patty watching out the window for Fillan to come and banging on the laptop to say she wanted to talk to him. Not to mention how much she missed him already herself. The last thing she needed was to be badgered by her ex.

He knew where she worked. It sounded like a threat. The more she thought about it, the more it bothered her, so Emma went first to the main office to tell them not to let his calls through if he tried and that he was no longer to be on her visitor list. Then she called Patty's school and warned them that her ex was not to have any access to Patty whatsoever.

Just in case.

Emma expected it was all unnecessary, but it made her feel better. As she also expected, her class was wired and jittery and trying to teach them math first thing on a Friday morning was not working. She should just move with Fillan as he wanted. No more Mark calls. No more pouting from Patty, at least no extra pouting, anyway. No more lying in bed at night, alone, thinking about him and wondering how he was doing with the job he didn't particularly want. No more trying to teach students who did not want to be there.

Except she loved to teach. She just had to find a way to make it work better. Like Fillan did for Patty.

Like Fillan did...

With a sudden brainstorm, Emma closed her book and walked around to the front of her desk. "Okay, let's put our books away." They all stared at her and at each other and looked at the clock. Confused. "I know, you weren't ready for summer to be over. To be honest, neither was I. Okay? So, how about we try something new? Close your books and move your desks to the edge of the room. Go ahead. Work in pairs and pick them up. Don't drag them."

Emma supervised getting the desks lined up out of the way. "Good job. Now line yourselves up, arms out, leave enough space you're not touching, in neat rows, please." As they were lining themselves up, Emma nearly laughed at a groan from a student about doing calisthenics like he had to at home when he wouldn't pay attention. "No calisthenics, although I like that idea, too."

She put on the instrumental music she often used during free study time since it helped them work rather than talk. "In order to work out some of the *I don't want to be here* jitters, we're going to start learning some dances." Emma waited through laughter and shuffling about and her biggest talker showing off his dance moves. "Very nice, but we'll be learning ballroom dance, starting with the waltz."

Groans filled the room.

"Either that or get your math books back out. Your choice." As she suspected, even the tough boys decided they'd rather dance than do math.

Satisfied about her plan working and getting a productive day out of the eleven- and twelve-year-olds, and then about Patty having a better day at school according to her main ABA tutor, Emma decided they should treat themselves with ice cream, which they hadn't done since Fillan left three weeks ago.

They barely pulled in before her phone rang again. Ready to tell her ex off, she breathed a sigh of relief at her brother's number instead.

"Hey, Em. Just checking in since it's been a few days. What are you guys up to?"

"We're about to get ice cream because we both had good days and decided to celebrate."

"Glad to hear it. Can Leo and I come join you? We're on our own for the evening since it's soccer night."

"Of course." Telling him where they were, Emma let Patty know Leo was coming and grinned when the girl bounced her excitement. Leo had done a nice job filling in, playing blocks with her, jumping over sidewalk cracks with her, and even playing catch with a large cushioned softball.

Patty pointed at a different ice cream flavor than she usually got, and Emma debated staying with the other one, but she figured it was worth a try. Nearly following her niece's lead, she looked at different options, but for now, she wanted the same one she usually bought, the kind Fillan had picked up for her. Paying and thanking the girl behind the counter, she found a table back out of the way of main traffic and faced Patty away from the door.

No sooner than they got settled, a large group of kids came in, noisy kids with a couple of parents or chaperones, ones she recognized. The adults gave her a nod and Emma returned it, but the noise was already affecting Patty. She shoved her hands against her ears, her shoulders hunching up.

"Hey, it's okay." Emma reached over to touch her head but she pulled away. "All right, sweetie. Let's go sit outside." She stood, motioning for Patty to get up with her. Instead, the girl started rocking. She wasn't moving until it calmed.

Knowing the response she'd likely get, Emma had to try. "Can you guys quiet down some, please?"

Some of them looked at each other. One of them said they weren't in school and didn't have to obey the teacher outside of school.

"Please. Just for a minute. We're leaving." She touched Patty's head, but the obnoxious ones of the group got louder, stomping to the beat of the music that was plenty quiet by itself, which was why Emma always chose the place. "Come on, sweetie. Let's take our ice cream outside. Patty, come with me." By now, she was rocking, her arms in front of her chest, her head ducked.

"All right girls. Enough." One of the women stepped in, with a look at Patty. "Is she okay? Do you need help?"

Quietly, Emma told the woman she was autistic and she couldn't handle the noise. They might as well understand...

"I'm so sorry. Your daughter? We didn't know..."

"Yes, it's fine, just..." She looked over at the noisiest girl.

"Of course." With a hushed voice, as though the woman was sharing news of a plague or something, she walked through the girls, quieting them down, which brought stares instead.

"See, sweetie? It's all fine now. Let's take this outside."

"Em?" Rob took her side, surprising her. "What happened?"

"Noise. Hi Leo, how about asking her if she'll go outside with you? She's shut me out by now." Bracing for a scene, Emma took a deep breath of relief when Patty responded to her cousin. She grabbed the bowls of ice cream, gave the helpful woman a grateful nod, and followed out to a table where, beside her cousin, Patty acted like nothing ever happened.

She explained briefly, away from where the girl could hear her, and told Rob Mark had called again.

"Report him, Emma. You asked him to leave you alone."

"Maybe. I can't think about it right now."

"Rough day?"

"Rough three weeks."

He studied her a moment. "You miss him a hell of a lot more than you're trying to show."

Choking back sudden emotions, Emma shrugged and offered to go get the two of them ice cream, her treat. Rob told her to sit and enjoy hers and he went to get it himself.

More than she was trying to show? What was she supposed to do? It wouldn't help anything to act like the world ended, even if part of it kind of had. First with Helen, then with Fillan.

Listening to Leo joke and talk with Patty, and watching her slight grin in return, Emma put it aside and focused on what was right, Patty's progress, her brother and nephew's help, the woman inside who meant well although she didn't really understand. And peppermint ice cream covered with almond shavings.

Thirty

Stepping out the school's front door, Emma shivered at a gust of wind and pulled her jacket tighter. The end of September already. Nearly six weeks since she'd seen Fillan and nearly a week since she'd been able to video message him. She'd expected it. He'd gone on back to his life as Emma had known he would. She was okay with it in general. He'd given her something so precious, she couldn't ever be too melancholy that he wasn't there. She enjoyed remembering their days together, his eyes smiling into hers, his gentleness, and his passion for her. And for Patty. He'd done so much for Patty. The girl grabbed her dance video every day the moment they walked in the door.

Emma was often too tired for it. She blamed the beginning of the school year, which was always the hardest time of the year, even worse than the end of school and the days before winter break, while her students still remembered their summer freedom and had trouble settling in to the routine again. She agreed with them. At least this year she did. She also blamed trying to grade homework at ten o'clock at night, or later, after Patty finally fell asleep.

She knew better. It was her longing for Fillan that kept her so unusually fatigued. And missing her sister. A bit of depression. Nothing more. It would pass.

Still, as tired as Emma was, she couldn't turn Patty down. The movements were calming to her, as well. Late at night when Patty was asleep and her work was done, Emma often turned her own music on low and practiced the dances Fillan taught her, in class, and alone. Most often these days, she used music from the Irish band he'd introduced her to, The Script, starting with their *Superheroes* song. On the days when she wanted to dwell in her pouting, she put on Van Morrison instead, remembering Fillan in her arms, his voice instructing, praising. Always upbeat. Never critical.

Such a beautiful man.

She heard some student yell a goodbye and waved in that

direction with the learned smile. But her thoughts remained on him. She wanted to ask how his job was going, how it was working with his father. Mostly, she wanted to know if that girl had come home, if he was back with her. Anyway she thought she wanted to know. She supposed that could be why he was never available when she checked to see if he was online. There was rarely a day without at least a quick message, although it had been a couple of days since he'd even done that.

Emma hadn't had the chance to tell him the school made her stop the in-class dance lessons since they weren't part of the curriculum, even though it was doing wonders for her more energetic students. She supposed a couple of them didn't like it and complained. Why else would anyone care? Her lesson plans were still getting done. She wanted to talk to him about it in person, or at least face to face, not through a message.

If he was back with the girl, though, Emma knew it was likely they wouldn't talk face to face again, depending on how jealous the girl was. And if he was with her, Emma hoped the girl would be worth the second chance and that he would be happy. A little bitty tiny part of her wanted to punch the girl in the jaw and tell her to stay away, but most of her just wanted Fillan to be happy.

She jolted back when she realized she'd walked right into someone while her thoughts were distracted. "I'm sorry..." A man. Familiar scent. She looked up ... at Mark's smirking smile.

"Must have been deep in thought."

"Yes, I... What are you doing here?"

"Asking you to dinner. Had enough time to get over your Irish dancer yet?"

"Go away, Mark." She swerved around him but he blocked the door to her car.

"Come, Emma. You know it's for the best." He reached out to touch her hair.

She stepped back. "Move."

"Look, I know what it's like to need something ... different from time to time and I can't hold that against you, now, can I? Considering everything. At some point, though, you have to realize when it's time to throw your hands up. Go to dinner with me, Emma. Let's talk."

"No. Move away from my car."

He closed in. "Just one uninterrupted talk. I'm willing to give in on keeping the girl with you, since you seem intent to do it. Let's go talk about it, and if you don't change your mind..." He put a hand on her thigh. "Then... I'll leave it alone."

"No, Mark. No. It's not going to happen, so just leave me alone now, as I asked you."

"Emma." He pressed closer.

She pushed him back.

"Everything okay?"

She looked over at the woman's voice on the sidewalk. From the dance class. The one who warned Fillan that she wasn't very nice. "It's fine. Thank you. I was just leaving."

Mark backed away enough to be decent and it gave her just enough room to turn and unlock her door as the woman asked about Patty and kept talking until Emma threw a rushed goodbye, slipped inside, and closed the door, locking it immediately.

She started the car and rolled her window down only half an inch. "Don't bother me again." Shoving the gear in reverse, she wasn't sure she'd care if she ran over his feet. He was at least smart enough to stay back far enough she didn't.

Are you over your Irish dancer? The nerve of the man. *Couldn't hold it against her.* Jerk. Of course he couldn't. They were divorced. She at least hadn't had *something different* while she was still married, as Emma had suspected he had. She hadn't been sure until now.

It was time to change her name, back to her maiden name so it would be the same as Patty's. That should give him enough of a hint that she meant no as in never.

By the time she stopped to pick up her daughter, Emma was shaking with fury. How dare he? And why was he in Provincetown again, which he said he hated? He would *give in* about keeping Patty? Like it was his choice? As a compromise, she expected; he would graciously allow her to keep her daughter if she would move to Boston and quit working. Stupid man.

She calmed easily when Patty gave her a big smile and trotted over to meet her. Patty smiled far more than she had before. Emma was afraid that would stop when Fillan left since she loved him so. The girl had pouted for a couple of weeks, heavily, but she perked up again when they talked over the computer. Whenever she slapped her hand on Emma's laptop asking for Fillan, Emma tried, so Patty would know she was trying. And every time, she would brace herself for the meltdown she expected when he wasn't available. It hadn't come yet.

"How about ice cream today?" She rubbed a hand down Patty's hair. Emma been trying to take Patty for ice cream ever since the day those kids were so loud, but she wouldn't go, wouldn't get out of the car. "What do you think?"

"No. Noisy."

Emma froze at Patty's voice. Her *voice*. Emma hadn't heard her voice since she was very little, other than in squeals. She had to try to hide her surprise, to act like it was normal. "Okay. Then we can get some to take home if you want? Can we stop at the store?"

She nodded.

Helen had told Emma she could. She'd said over and over the girl talked well when she chose to but she just chose not to.

Emma had to turn away as she closed the door behind her daughter to wipe moisture from her eyes. She nearly called her brother, but Emma wanted to tell Fillan first, even if she had to do it through a message. Maybe it was unfair, since Rob was still around helping and she was his niece, but still...

The phone rang as she got to the store. Rob. Pulling into the nearest free spot, Emma answered as she told Patty to wait just a minute.

"Hey, Em, what are you guys up to?"

Telling him quickly, Emma made herself not say anything about Patty's *no*. He asked if they could come over to the house in twenty minutes or so, and although it was odd for Rob to come on a weekday, she said it was fine. Maybe Patty had said something in school, too, and they'd let him know? Possible, Emma supposed, since he was paying her tuition, but why wouldn't he have called her?

Her phone rang again inside the store, but she saw Mark's

number and hung up on him. Along with changing her name, it was time to change her number. Emma would tell Rob when she saw him. Both. About Mark showing up at the school and about changing her name and number. And about Patty's *no*. It was only right. Fillan was pulling away. She couldn't put him first when he'd stopped putting them first. Never again would she do that.

"No, sweetie. You don't want that." Emma tried to take the package of spicy chips from her hands. "Here. You can get these." Trying to substitute regular chips they would both eat for the spicy ones neither of them wanted, Emma sighed when Patty refused. "You won't eat them. They'll just sit there and..." It was the kind Fillan bought. "Oh, Patty. I know you miss him, but we have to let go. Okay?"

The girl grabbed it away.

"Fine. Get it." Maybe Rob's boys would want them. "Let's go now. Uncle Rob is coming over."

"Leo?"

Her frustration waned. She'd asked for her cousin. Glad as hell it was Leo she asked for and not Fillan, Emma set a hand on her head. "I don't know, sweetie. He didn't say. Maybe. Let's go home and see." Emma hoped Leo would be there and she could leave Patty in their care long enough to take a breather. Mark had her too flustered. It had to stop. She didn't want to file a complaint and her ex would know she didn't want to, but she was about one phone call away from doing it. The problem was mainly that she was unsure it would help. Even if they picked him up, they'd let him go, and as long as she was still on her own, he wouldn't give up.

Maybe she would move, but she liked her house.

Seeing a car in her driveway, Emma took a deep breath. Rob was there already. She pulled in on the other side of him and Patty nearly jumped out before she stopped.

"Hey, Patty." Rob smiled as he accepted a hug.

"So, guess what we did today?" Emma grabbed her briefcase and slung it over her arm.

"Leo here?"

Rob's jaw dropped at Patty's voice.

"Um, yeah. That." Emma smiled.

"She asked for Leo?"

"No. She said no to getting ice cream because it's too loud, which came out 'No. Noisy.' But... Patty, wait for me, okay?" Emma headed around Rob's car to keep up with her. "Next thing she said was to ask if Leo was..."

Patty screeched, bouncing up and down. Jumping, not bouncing, with a screech, a happy screech. "Leo?"

"No, I brought you a visitor." He nodded his head as a sign she should go on around the little shrub between the driveway and the porch.

Visitor? Who would..? She stepped into view of her front porch in time to see Patty tackle him. Fillan. He laughed and hugged her.

Emma's heart nearly stopped. His hair was shorter. He looked more weather-roughened. But he was there. Feeling moisture flooding her eyes, Emma gritted her teeth, forcing herself not to look as ecstatic as Patty was acting, and held her ground. A visitor. Just visiting. She hadn't expected him so soon, if at all, but still, he was visiting and she had to tell herself as much.

Fillan caught her eyes, gave her a grin, said something to Patty, and freed himself. He ambled over and, with his hand caught still, he stopped a couple of feet away. "Thought I would surprise you."

"You did." Her heart raced. Her stomach twisted. On the outside, though, she stayed calm.

"Is it alright?" His eyes twinkled and his jaw twitched as though fighting as hard to stay in control as she was.

"Of course. I thought maybe you'd ... moved on to other things by now, since I haven't heard from you much."

"I am sorry about that, Em. I was making plans and working extra to make up for being away, gettin' the boy taking over for me ready for the job."

She had to wonder if he meant... Temporarily. He of course had someone taking over while he visited.

"So I heard her askin' for Leo just now." He tilted his head at Patty. "I hope it is alright that it is only me instead."

"I think she's okay with that."

"Yea?" He peered into Emma's eyes. "And how about her mum? Is she okay with that, as well?"

Her head nodded of its own accord.

"Ye are sure now? It is a long flight, and so..."

"You didn't go back to your ex."

"No, Emma. She did try. She tried hard, to be honest. But I do not want her." He took a couple of steps closer.

"You deserve better." It came out a whisper.

"Yes, and I found far better. The longer I was there, spending my days fishing, the more I wondered what the hell I thought I was trying to prove anyway. I know well what I want, and so I came back after it."

The moisture returned to her eyes and this time Emma couldn't stop it. Rob pulled Patty just far enough from Fillan to free him and he stepped up closer, his head tilted, watching her. "Tell me I did not waste my time coming back for you."

For her. He came back for her. Trying to answer, to say anything, Emma realized it wasn't going to happen with so many emotions in her way, so much chaos in her head, so she threw her arms over his shoulders and kissed him.

Fillan wrapped an arm around Emma's shoulders when she joined him on the couch. It was late already. Patty's excitement kept her up far too long, but he'd loved hearing her voice, even if only a couple of words. Her first day of deciding to talk, and he'd barely gotten back for it. She was doing well. Emma told him they did the music therapy videos most every day.

She also told him that her school had made her stop teaching dance in her class, which he found unbelievable and a shame. Dance was wonderful for kids, all kids. She said she didn't force any of them. There were a few who didn't want to and she let them do other things instead. But he was proud of her for trying and told her as much.

She also told him about Turner's continued advances. Truth be told, she'd hardly stopped talking since Rob left, which was right after they got Patty inside and calmed to enough extent. That was going to stop. Fillan would help her make him stop.

"So should I ask how long you're staying?" Emma set a hand on his chest.

"In a hurry to get me out again?"

"No. I just want to prepare myself."

"A good idea, to be sure, since it may not be what you are looking for or expecting." He raised her face back to his when she turned away. "My father and I had a good long talk the other night. Much of it was about you. He is intent on meeting you, I should let you know. And since he could see how much I was distracted and how serious I was about getting back to you, he decided to be content enough to have my help during the summer months. At least he became content with that when I told him I was looking into the Massachusetts Maritime School to learn a steady trade with a decent income that can support a family. I have a job here in the meantime, with your brother's help. He agreed to sponsor me for a green card rather than only a work visa, and I have checked into getting certified in movement therapy. Patty's school is willing to let me start working with them as I learn..."

"Wait." Emma stared up at him. "Here? You're studying and working here?"

"Sure and I cannot sponge off you if I am staying, now, can I? I will have to hold my own weight so I am not a burden..."

"Staying?"

"If ye allow. I would like you to come and spend summers with me in Ireland. My father needs the most help then and you have said you like it least here while it is so crowded. I will have to go back myself during summers even if you cannot since deserting my family that long is something I am not willing to do, but I will give you the rest of my time if you want it, Emma. If you cannot do full summers, then maybe you could come for part of the summer and for Christmas holidays? If it will work with Patty. I understand if it will not, but I thought we could try it once, go on a short trip and see how she does..."

"Yes." Emma shifted and wrapped her arms around his neck. "I would love to spend summers with you in Ireland. And Christmas, too. Patty will be fine there for a couple of months a year. With you, she will be. Yes. Of course. That way I can still work and ... and I love that you plan to do movement therapy. It's wonderful, Fillan, truly. I'm impressed."

"Big plans for only a dance teacher, right?"

"Only? I already found that impressive. It's a beautiful thing, you know. It really is."

Unable to resist, Fillan pressed his mouth against hers. They could talk more later. He wanted her fully in his arms.

Yes. Of course. He'd expected hesitation, reasons it wouldn't work, or might not work, or that she'd need time to think about it. He did not expect *of course yes* right away.

"So." He kissed in front of her ear and enjoyed the scent of her, which he had also missed terribly. "Should I be looking for a place to stay? The beach cabin might still be open and..."

"No."

"No?"

"Stay with me." She kissed his neck.

"What about Turner and his threat..?"

"I don't care."

"You are sure?"

"Yes. Please. Stay with me."

He closed his eyes and felt his body both unwind and tense at the same time. "Em."

"Hm?" She teased his lips.

"It has been a long day by now. Can we..."

She stood, grasped his hand, and tugged it gently, taking him into her room. Emma closed the door and slid her arms back over his shoulders. "So where are we taking Patty for this short trip you're talking about?"

"I would love to go in west a bit, the heartland, it is called, yes?"

"The Midwest?"

"Right. Is there anywhere you can suggest, or would like to visit and have not yet?"

"Lots of places."

"Choose one and we will go."

"There's a big water park that sits on a big lake in Iowa that a friend, or ex friend, used to visit now and then. Her family is there, I think. Her uncle is an artist of some kind. Anyway, it seems…"

"When will you next get a few days off?"

"I'll take a few days off. You came all this way back, that's the least I can do, right?"

"Em."

"Hm?"

"Damn, I have missed you."

"Me, too. And I need a quick shower. Come wash my back."

"You will have trouble getting up for work in the morning as it is."

"I think I might need a personal day tomorrow. About time I actually used one."

Thirty-one

Terribly thankful to her brother for offering to pick Patty up and take her to school since he'd assumed Emma wouldn't be going to work, she lowered onto her couch with a cup of coffee and enjoyed a deep, relaxing breath.

After the chaos of the day before, the lows and highs that were more exhausting than her recently normal numb-like low of always missing him but otherwise just routine days, Emma needed the day off. She reflected on the way she'd talked Fillan's ear off all evening until she fell asleep, after being rendered speechless by his sudden presence. By this morning, the last thing she wanted was to talk. She wanted quiet. She wanted time to let the chaos unravel.

Is that why Patty didn't talk? Getting through each day was hard for the girl with its overwhelming noise and constant activity. At her grandparents' house, the TV was always on, and always loud due to her father's bad hearing, and her mother was a talker. Maybe it wasn't Emma's presence that helped, but the relative quiet at her house. Other than her music that she kept low when Patty was there, there wasn't much extraneous noise. If a neighbor started a lawn mower during warm months, she closed the windows until it stopped. The small television was rarely on. After the noise of the school day, Emma wanted ... needed ... quiet in order to unwind.

Maybe Patty always needed quiet to...

"What do ye want to do today?" Fillan came out from the back in his sweat pants and nothing more, his hair wet and mussed from his quick shower. The man tended to shower morning and night, so she learned. In and out showers. A bit of a clean freak, he admitted.

"There's hot tea on the stove."

"Ye are drinking tea?"

"No, I have coffee. I made the tea for you. Help yourself. You'll have to make yourself at home if you're staying here."

He gave her a charming grin. "Happy to do so." Disappearing into the kitchen, he returned with a steaming mug and lowered beside her. His hand slipped underneath her robe to her leg and rested just below her thigh. "So then, how about a walk along the shore today?"

"Okay. Later. When do you start work? You said you had the job already?"

"Monday after this coming. Gave myself time to get settled somewhere if it had been needed."

"You weren't sure I'd want you to stay?"

"I was not going to presume." He leaned in to kiss her head.

"You are actually staying." Emma felt her emotions try to creep back in and overwhelm her, and pushed it away.

"You donae believe I will?"

"I'm just..." She couldn't even describe her mix of happiness and wariness. She'd learned long ago to keep things on an even keel, to not expect too much.

Fillan set his mug on the coffee table and took hers to do the same. Grasping her hands, he turned to face her more. "Do you know the biggest reason the girl back home gave up on me?"

"I don't..."

"I need y' to know, Em." He raised her fingers to his lips and sighed. "She thought there was something wrong with me, deeply wrong with me, down inside, because ... because I have never been able to settle on one thing too long, because I always knew there was something more somewhere else and I could not help wanting to know what it might be. It is why I came here. To see more. To get away far enough to convince myself I wanted to stay where I was and keep doing what I was. I thought being away from it would draw me closer to it. And more than that, she left because I admitted to her that I never wanted anything to do with children. There are more opportunities for dance classes with children but I could not do it because, to be fully honest, I have never liked them much. Even when I was a child, I did not."

"But you're so good with Patty..."

"Patty ... has shown me ... something I do not understand, and yet she has changed my mind. To an extent. I am still not a fan of the way too many act as though their parents are servants to them, or of the horse play and general unconcern about how they are annoying others, or when they are doing anything but what they are supposed to be doing. I am not one to talk, so my father has always said, since he used to see my dancing as the same, as a way to get out of things that mattered. By now, he sees it differently and he was proud of the way I worked on the boat and at the dock. He says I have grown a fair bit over the summer. It is because of you and Patty."

"She did the same for me." Emma brushed fingers through his damp hair. "If not for her, I never would have walked out on Mark, and he's right. He did serve the papers, but I'd already walked away from him, for her, because she needed me."

"Good for her."

"Yes."

"And we are going to have to get him to let you alone."

"Well, I think once he sees that you're here for good, he'll know there's no point. Anyway, I think that's true."

Fillan gave her a soft kiss. "We will take care of it. Because that girl was wrong, Em. It was not me. It is not that I cannot settle. It was only not the right person and not the right place. And it is not all children I dislike. Patty, yea she is not a young child, but in ways she is and ... I do love her, Em. As I love you. And I mean, not the same, of course, but I see children differently now, the struggle it takes to try to live in an adult world when ye are not wired to do so..."

Emma slid her arms over his shoulders and met his lips. "Fillan." She spoke next to his ear. "I love you as you are, and you don't have to worry. I won't push you about kids the way Mark pushed me. I don't think anyone should have them if they don't really want them."

"And you do not?"

"I'm... Between Patty and my job, it's just not a need for me. Some would say there's something wrong with me for thinking that way, I suppose, but it's worse to let yourself be pushed into something because others think you should want it. By now, I think she'll get stable enough I wouldn't refuse, with the right person, but it's not a need, either."

"Right. It is what I am trying to tell you, as well. I would not refuse, with you, but if you do not..."

She kissed him again. Emma didn't want to talk anymore. She

wanted... She wanted the sweet, intense passion that came from her Irish dancer. He responded quickly, pushing her robe off her shoulders, kissing her neck...

The doorbell made her jump. Who would ring the doorbell? She had a sign to knock instead, because of Patty. Patty... Emma pulled the robe back over her shoulders and rushed to the door, afraid something happened.

Mark. At her door. An amused grin covered his face as he scanned her open robe revealing part of her nightgown.

Emma pulled it closed. "Why are you here?"

"You weren't at work today. You don't look sick."

"How do you know I'm not at work?"

He gave her a shrug and scanned her again as he pulled the screen door open. "Can I come in?"

"No." She put a foot against the inside of the main door. "What do you want?"

"To talk, Emma, as I keep telling you..." He stopped and the grin fell from his face as Fillan came up behind her.

"Obviously, there's no point." Emma moved into Fillan as he slid an arm around her back. "And he's moved in, so he will be here every night, and every morning."

"Moved in?" His face went dark.

"Goodbye, Mark."

"You can't be serious."

"Do ye want me to make him leave, Em? I would be happy to do so, since Patty is not here to see it."

"Not necessary." She slid a hand up his bare chest and leaned in to kiss him while she shoved the door closed and locked it. Then she took his hand and led him back to her room.

Thirty-two

On his last weekday before he started work, Fillan kissed his girls goodbye as they were getting ready for their school days and jumped into the old car he'd picked up for his own running around.

It was early, and Emma shook her head when he got up at five a.m. to go out and walk a new trail, but he was an early riser, driven into him from his boyhood days. Sun up to sun down. It was good enough for nature; it was good enough for him, his father had always said. *Nature will tell ye what is best for ye if ye will listen t'it, Fillan.* It was natural to sleep less during warm months when there was more work to be done outdoors. As he and his father were fishing and working the land in any weather that happened to come, his mum and sister were working extra to put away food for the cold months, healthy food with plenty of warm month vitamins to help endure the long length of cold. *Workin' in the rain will not hurt ye, lad. It is good for the plants and it is good for a man's strength.* A strong man, his father. Function first. Take care of the mundane before you stop to think of anything else.

Mundane had never worked well for Fillan. The unusual and unexpected were far more entertaining. His mundane needs were basic. He often shrugged many of them off to get to the more entertaining things in life: sitting in a field watching the birds – other than seagulls and pigeons, he liked birds; sitting at a pub's outdoor table watching women with his mates; standing on the shore or up on hill watching boats, sailboats in particular, scoot in and out and back and forth, bobbing with the tides and wakes; and dance of course. His salvation, dance was. His mum was a near genius to have harnessed his energy by putting him into dance classes. She had fought terrible hard with his father for it.

By now, his father understood how it was a necessary part of Fillan's life, and what good he could do with it. They had talked of Emma, but also of Patty. *"Tis good ye found something outside your own self, Fillan, to put your heart into."*

"Yea, Dad, but you know I cannot ask them to move here with their lives so rooted back in the States."

"Right enough, ye are. Ye will have to make the bigger sacrifice for the good of the child, if ye want it enough."

"And you and Mum will be alright with my choice, then, if I were to move across the ocean?"

His father had been silent for some time until he moved in to give Fillan a rare hug. "We are right proud of you, Fillan. Do what ye need to do and come and see us as oft' as ye can. We will be glad to help ye do it, if ye need, since it will be for our own benefit, and more so yet if your young woman changes your mind about wanting offspring of your own. Your mother would not mind as much." With a wink, he'd returned to his stalwart self. "Now off with ye, then, and get to work. I amnae paying ye to dally."

"Yea, Dad. I will take care of the girls well and do my best to make ye proud." He spoke into the early morning light as he pulled onto Doane Road to find the big glacial rock he had heard of.

Hanging his hiking bag over his back and his camera over his shoulder, Fillan grabbed a lung full of fresh, crisp Atlantic air, stretched his legs out, and headed first to the rock. He laughed when he got to it, so the sign said. A big rock, to be sure, compared to the sandy beach land, but only a rock. Wanting to check the view from the top of the thing, Fillan tucked his camera into his bag so it wouldn't sway and found footholds. An easy climb, he would have to bring the girls back and let Patty climb it with him. It did not afford much of a view considering the surrounding trees were so tall. Still, he pulled his camera out to get what he could, to include a shot looking straight down from where he stood that turned out well enough to keep.

Being the end of September with the kids in school and a chilly breeze warning of the cold to come, Fillan had the place to himself, and so he settled on top of the rock to enjoy the silence.

Their five day trip out west, somewhat west but not the west, except to easterners, had gone well enough. The airport was stressful to Patty, but they were prepared with earphones playing soft music to drown out the commotion. The officials would not allow her through security with them on, but they got by with Fillan going through first and waiting on the other side for her. Her eyes were down, her shoulders hunched most of the time, until the plane took off and her eyes got wide.

Emma was nervous as could be, but Patty pointed and talked about the clouds until she grew tired and slept for much of the flight. Getting her back off the plane and into the baggage claim area was nearly a disaster, but they held back and waited until everyone else grabbed their bags and left and Fillan told her to come look at the moving sidewalk. She was fascinated by the thing and they rode up and down it far longer than he and Emma wanted.

In Storm Lake, they walked along the lake and through the tree museum labeled with where each had come from. Patty's favorite part was touching the hand-carved tree trunks in the park. She would not, through any kind of coercion, go into the water park.

Still, it was a good test and Emma expected Patty would be okay flying to Ireland, especially if she would sleep.

Climbing back down the rock, Fillan headed down the trail toward the beach. He loved that Emma had no concern letting him go off on his own as he was used to doing, but also expressed interest in sometimes going with him. She did not find it anywhere near boring. She listened to him talk of the wildlife he saw and she had printed some of the photos he'd taken around Ireland to show her class, repeating some of the stories he'd told her.

Fillan very much couldn't wait to take her there so she could see it herself.

During lunch break, Emma gave him a quick call. He was out at the Coast Guard beach wandering around thinking of her. Or so he said. She knew he was nervous about starting his new job in the morning, but she also knew he would be wonderful at it and the school would love him. She wasn't at all sure whether he would enjoy working with kids all day most every day, but maybe since they were autistic kids like Patty, he would be fine with it.

She couldn't help be grateful he would be right there close to Patty, sometimes with her. It would make Emma's days easier knowing she wouldn't have to worry.

Telling him she loved him and to have fun, Emma hung up and turned around to nearly run into another teacher, one she hadn't talked to much. "Sorry."

"No, it was my fault. Do you have a minute to talk?"

"Sure." A touch wary, Emma grabbed her lunch and sat with the older teacher, one of the most respected in the school. She'd already heard rumors going around, about the man she was *living with* – horror of horrors. Why it mattered, she didn't know, especially in Provincetown where most anything was acceptable. She kept it to herself at work, without talking about him as others did about their spouses. He was plenty well of age, even though a year younger than she was. And Emma was single. She was doing nothing that should bother anyone.

"So, there's ... I'm not supposed to say anything because her parents are touchy about it, but one of my students has a lot of signs of ... well, possible autism. I'm not an expert on that, of course, and I may be wrong, but I didn't know if you could guide me? If I could ask you about what I'm seeing and get your thoughts?"

"Of course."

"Yes? Thank you. I'm not sure what I can do, anyway, but doesn't she need special guidance if she is? She does talk, but barely, and they say she's only shy..."

"That's common. I mean for parents and professionals to accept a girl's unwillingness or inability to talk as only shyness. They're so often not diagnosed because it's different with girls, usually. Most of the focus has been on boys since they tend to be more disruptive."

"Your ... niece... She is your niece, right?"

"My niece and my daughter now. Yes."

"I'm sorry about your sister, by the way. But how did you know? What were the signs?"

Emma talked about Patty, how she was rather atypical for an autistic girl, since she had more pronounced symptoms, about things Emma had figured out worked and didn't work to help control the outbursts. From the signs of the eight-year-old girl, Emma agreed she should be evaluated and that it would be tricky to get the parents to understand how it could help without insulting them, since too many saw it as their own failure somehow. At the end of lunch hour, she agreed to help as she could and to talk with the parents if they wanted. It was a fine line, though, since Emma wasn't a counselor and couldn't make a diagnosis. Instead, she would share research and her own experience and leave it in their hands.

The conversation stressed her enough to be ready to go home to her Irish dancer who calmed her so easily. Still, Emma was glad if she could help at all, glad to know that maybe everything she was dealing with, that Patty was dealing with, might help another child, and the child's parents.

During the conversation, there was a suggestion of having a support group of sorts for teachers who wanted to know more about what to watch for in students. Emma agreed, but she insisted someone trained and certified had to be there. And then there was the question as to why Emma didn't get trained. She'd blown it off at the time, but the thought followed her throughout the day.

Fillan went to greet them as they pulled in. Emma always let Patty hug him first, and when the girl went on inside to find the yogurt topped with blueberries he had her eating as an after school snack, Emma held him close.

"Mm, you smell like the ocean." She kissed his neck.

"And you smell of old lady cologne."

She chuckled. "Had a talk with one of the other teachers today. Something I want to run by you later."

"A good talk?"

"Yes. Did you have a good day out there? Take any nice photos?"

"I did. You may laugh, since most are of little bitty ones that were out there with a couple of young girls, mothers, I would guess. They kept telling the wee ones to stay out of the water and of course they did not listen. I caught one right at the moment of splashing in on his behind as the water came up to hit his back, right before he started to bellow like he had been thrown in."

"Be careful about taking photos of other peoples' kids, Fillan. Some parents get jumpy about that."

"Right, well, I went to show them and offered to delete them if they had rather I do so, which would have made me a fair bit annoyed since they were good shots."

"What did they say?"

"They gave me an email address and asked if I would send them. Even offered money for it, which I did not take."

Emma shook her head. "It's because you're so charming, you know. You'd probably get away with most anything."

"Is that right? And what are you going to let me get away with, Emma, my love?"

"Most anything, probably."

He groaned lightly and set a hand to his heart to signal a fake heart attack from her flirting. The girl was determined to drive him crazy, he believed.

She threw a grin and took his hand to take him inside. "Mm, something smells good."

"Being out by the ocean put me in the mood for a good fish fry, and so I have dinner almost ready. Sweet potatoes are in the oven and we have plums for dessert." He pulled out a chair next to where Patty had her snack nearly done. "I have coffee made, as well. Sit and I will get it for you."

Instead of sitting, she wrapped her arms around him. "I could get used to coming home and having dinner waiting. Be careful."

"Or what?" He caressed fingers along her face.

"Or I might have to do everything I can to convince you that you can't live without me anymore than I want to live without you."

"It is too late for that, since I already know I cannot. Sit, Em."

"I need to change and I'm likely not to want to get back up if I sit down. It's easier to stay up."

He studied her eyes. "Ye are tired tonight."

"I am."

"Well, then..." Fillan swept her up into his arms. "Stay right there, Patty cake. We will be back in a minute." He took her to their room and set her on the bed, laying her down gently with a soft kiss, then removed her shoes.

"What are you doing?"

"Helping you change."

She laughed and sat up. "Thanks, anyway. I'll be out in a minute." Getting up, she pulled out of her work clothes and into clingy soft sweats and a soft flannel shirt.

He stayed while she did, with an ear on Patty in case he needed to go check on her. Emma fussed at him, in teasing, then came to him and set her hands on his chest. He gave her another soft kiss and picked her back up into his arms.

"Okay, I'm not all that tired. I can walk." She kissed his jaw.

"Yeah, but if I keep you from getting more tired, chances are better you will dance with me tonight."

"Hm, and how do you mean that? Because I'm never real sure anymore."

He laughed as he took her to the kitchen and swung her in a circle. "However you want me to mean it, love."

"My turn, Fillan. My turn." Patty jumped out of her chair.

Emma looked at him and shrugged. "Argue with that."

"I cannot possibly." He set Emma in her chair, poured coffee to set in front of her, and scooped the girl into his arms. Her laughter was the second best thing in the world. Emma would always be the first. Whatever came of the future, Emma deserved to be first to him, always.

"It's beautiful, Fillan."

Looking out over Lough Corrib past Ballycurrin Light at the blue-gray water tousled with wind and fringed by gray-white ice against the imposing boulders, he gave her a soft shrug, despite how much he agreed. "It does not stand out as your Cape lighthouses do, but it is easier to climb to the top and you do not have to feel entombed to do so." Even not especially bothered by closed in spaces, Fillan couldn't help being claustrophobic inside Cape Cod's tall, thin lighthouses. "When we are back for the summer, I will take you around to see those on the coast."

"But this one ... it's really charming. Like you." Emma touched his cheek with her cold fingers.

"Like me, yea. Short and stout and not all too impressive."

"No, like you as in sturdy and sweet and strong and different than the rest, which, to me, is a very good thing. A hidden treasure, you are, Fillan Reilly."

With a deep contented sigh, he pulled her in against him, his arm slipping under her coat to the warm skin. "You know you have won my family over and above how I expected you would, right?"

"They're being nice because I'm company."

He laughed. "Which only goes to show you do not know them well yet. No, Emma, it is the same reason you have me working with children, as well as becoming, or ... thinking of becoming..." He caught himself, but not soon enough.

Her eyebrows raised. "Becoming what?"

"You realize I do hate to have to introduce you as Emma Turner."

She swept her hair back out of her face and held it in one hand against the cold wind's aggressiveness. "Because it reminds you I was married to Mark. I plan to change it, as I said."

"To your maiden name." Fillan backed up a step and took her hand with a nod out at the little short but sturdy abandoned lighthouse out on the rocks. "What would you say about going up to the top? The only hard part is climbing the rocks to get out to it. Are you willing at all? Or does it look too treacherous?"

"You remember I teach fifth graders, right? And I brought Patty to Ireland in an airplane to meet your family. You think those rocks scare me?"

"Come, then, but watch for ice. It is bound to be slippery."

More than once, Fillan nearly lost his own footing while he worried about hers and while she badgered him to answer what he meant about becoming... what he couldn't say quite yet.

She made it easily past the rocks and up the small slick stone steps, her strong feminine hand and long fingers gripped bravely on the metal railing. At the top, she cuddled in against him, for the warmth, he figured, at least partly, and again said it was beautiful, that she loved Ireland and looked forward to seeing more.

His mum had argued his idea to take Emma out to the water in the cold December wind, but Em wanted to go. She wanted to let him show off his favorite place before they went back to the States, to her students. Genie and Patty got on right well, from the moment they met, to Emma's surprise, and to his own, he had to admit, and the girl was alright with staying at the house without Emma for a bit of time.

It was nearly dusk Christmas Eve and they couldn't stay long.

"Okay." Emma stroked fingers down his chest over his sweater, under his jacket. "Becoming what, Fillan? A father? If that's what you meant, you can say it. You are, of course. Patty feels as though you are. I'm fine with making that official."

He gazed into the hazy blue-green of the lake and the liquid blue-gray sky. Nearly the same hue in different tones, with the little expanse of land in the distance breaking the boundary and darkish clouds echoing the color of the icy white water edges. "If I want more than that, Emma?"

She was silent and still. Far too long. Dark gray-black petrels circled in the air watching for a meal. He admired how the rough weather didn't bother them at all. And he admired how it didn't bother Em. She liked cold, she said. She liked misty gray days when the dampness of the air moistened her skin. She liked quiet and open and solitude.

She loved his little house and garden.

"Em. I think you should wait to change your name."

Her face turned to his, but still, she stayed silent.

"I think I would like to be a father, more than an adoptive father t' Patty, which I would gladly agree to. I am sorry for my family trying to assume we would and have asked them to stop. And, as I said earlier, if you do not want it, I will not press the issue. If you agree, I will hear plenty about it from my family and closest friends who know I have not been children friendly, but I am enjoying working with them now that Patty has shown me how to look at things differently and..."

"Yes."

He met her eyes, her moist round gorgeous brown eyes. "Yes? And which are you saying yes to?"

"Well, I have to assume you're proposing because you know I won't purposely have children any other way and I would love to have them with you. At least one. Maybe only one, though, depending. We'll have to see how things go and think about it from there. I also would insist you accept me forever if you want to be Patty's legal father, which you also know. So yes, I accept."

He felt a chuckle come from deep in his chest, from his very soul. "You will feel silly now if I say I was not proposing, will you not?"

Emma took his face in her chilly fingers and warm palms and brought her lips to his. "Fillan." She teased his mouth, then nearly whispered. "Maybe I'm not waiting any longer for you to propose. I've given you time. So let's get this settled already. Marry me. And then I'll change my name to yours and go forward instead of backward."

He kissed the side of her head as his eyes clenched. "You think marrying me will move you forward?"

"Yes. Because you truly love me, and Patty. How could it not?"

"I do love you, Em. Truly. And it would only be fair if I inch you forward since you have truly shoved me further that direction than I could have imagined."

"Is that a yes?"

"You are an impatient girl, to be sure."

"Not usually. Usually, I wait and just go with the flow of things. But sometimes you can't do that, right? Sometimes you have to grab onto what you really want." She slid her hands down to his stomach and gripped his sweater in her fists. "And I really want this. You; most of all, I want you. And summers in Ireland. A father for Patty, someone who *wants* to be her father. Someone ... someone who treats me like this and looks at me that way. *This*, Fillan. I want all of this. And the dancing, too."

With a light nod, he reached down into his coat pocket and pulled out the little box. "I am proposing, Em. Or I am accepting. However you wish to look at it."

"Mutual agreement." A grin flickered across her face and she offered her hand.

"Seems the best way to fit things together." He teased by holding her hand but waiting with the ring. "And when you get to know my family better, you will still want to come here for the summer and put up with a visit from the whole caboodle of them at times, in the States, where they will expect to stay with us?"

"Yes. We can rent cots if needed."

"I am teasing, Em."

"I know, but I'd be willing."

"So you are not impatient, but you are desperate?"

"I am far from desperate, as you well know. I am getting cold. And it is getting late and we need to get back. So stop your dawdling and put that ring on my finger already. You know I can put up with you just fine."

With the grin he knew she liked, Fillan lowered to one knee, kissed her fingers, and put the diamond in place. As far as he was concerned, it was crafted so carefully by the earth just to be where it was right now.

And so was he.

~~ ~~ ~~

EllaMKaye.com

Acknowledgements

Autism Awareness.

Everyone is aware, but as Fillan points out in the story, no matter how aware we are of its existence, most of us don't understand what it's like to deal with the day-to-day of having a child or other loved one on the spectrum, in particular, high on the spectrum when what's a regular daily schedule for most is a huge struggle just to cope. Even little things such as putting shoes on can be a test of wills.

One of the things that struck me while hearing an acquaintance talk about her son's autism years ago was how she could never have music playing in her house when he was there. He could not deal with it. As a music lover, I couldn't imagine how even that one thing would govern and disrupt a music lover's life. How many other things that the rest of us never bother to think about are major events in a family dealing with autism? To those who are, I applaud your patience, even when you seem to have none, and your daily efforts that go so unnoticed.

In recent years, my daughter became an ABA tutor working with a young autistic boy. As she told me while proofing the story, the terms low or high functioning are not officially used anymore. However, while doing research, I found them widely used and so I included it since Emma would have found the same research.

Thank you to Liz for answering questions beyond my research and for sharing your knowledge. Thank you, also, for being the kind of person who willingly steps in to try to help parents and autistic children understand each other better in order to elevate functioning. Nothing you do in this world matters more than assisting children and helping them live better lives. <3

Thank you, also, to those who read this story when it was still a novella and left praise and suggestions. When I went back to prepare it for print, I found too much left unsaid. Therefore, the full novel.

Caveat. Every mental disorder affects every individual differently, and this book is not meant to be a catch-all of symptoms, or of help/advice. It is fiction, and the characters are inspired by a mix of personal stories and research, but they are not representative of anyone in particular.

Music Mentioned in this Story

(I do not own any rights to any song/album/artist listed. All are used fairly under US copyright law. Permission for use of artist and titles is not required nor implied.)

Bob Seger: *Against the Wind*
Van Morrison: *Moondance, Crazy Love, Into the Mystic*
Gavin Rossdale: *Future World*
Ty Herndon: *If You, Fighter, Just Friends*
Hinder: *Lips of an Angel*
Luke Bryan: *Shake it for me*
The Script: *Superheroes*

About The Author

Ella M. Kaye uses her art and psychology background to create contemporary love stories with mental health issues set around the creative arts. Each of her novels and novellas fall under one of three series: Dancers & Lighthouses, Artists & Cottages, and Songwriters & Cities. Kaye has been writing romantically inclined literary fiction that branches into straight mainstream in both novel and short story form under the name LK Hunsaker for more than two decades. After many moves as a military spouse, she is settled in western Pennsylvania where she enjoys the abundant foliage and recreational lakes along with the hilly vistas.

Pieces of Light is the third book in the Dancers & Lighthouses series which can be read in any order.

www.ellamkaye.com
www.lkhunsaker.com

(For previews of each book, see EllaMKaye.com)

Pier Lights (2013)
Dancers & Lighthouses Series

Caroline was a relevé away from becoming prima ballerina when, partly due to her own actions, she was injured enough to end her ballet career. With a strong determination, along with some help and hindrance from her antisocial tendencies, Caroline returns to her beloved Folly Beach, finds a grittier dancing job, and makes up her mind to land on top.

Due to a disfiguring facial scar, Dio hides away on his South Carolina farm during the day, where keeping watch over his aging and mentally failing mother strains his time and energy. Venturing into Charleston only for his night job in a strip club allows him to keep needed contact with others while maintaining distance.

When the two collide amid the glow of the lights from the pier, their personal scars push them away, and pull them in, like the ebb and flow of the Atlantic.

~~

Shadowed Lights (2014)
Dancers & Lighthouses Series

Delaney Griffin welcomed her sister's large family into her small home when they were displaced by Hurricane Sandy. With five noisy kids and an overbearing brother-in-law threatening her sanity, Delaney spends much of her free time cleaning up the wildlife refuge and helping at the local food bank. Still, the lack of privacy, along with having no space to dance, her only passionate release, causes her debilitating social anxiety to escalate.

Eli Forrester has come from small town Indiana to Barnegat, New Jersey with his company to help restore the coast. A high-rise worker who loves new people and new places, he fears nothing, except water. When he accidentally kicks one of the sea critters Delaney is trying to help rescue, Eli is drawn to the quiet New Jersey girl. Unwilling to take her cues to leave her alone, he is alternately put off and turned on by her odd behavior.

Under shadow of devastation, fear, and forced separation, Delaney and Eli search for their own rescue light.

~~

Shadows of Greens & Memories (2015)
Artists & Cottages Series

Francis Barrett returns to her hometown of Storm Lake, Iowa to take care of the family holdings, such as they are, after her father passes. While turning his garden shed into a small but livable cottage, she runs into an old flame she admired from afar but never dared speak with during their high school days. Using her secret passion of oil painting to unwind from long days of clearing out the mess, Francis finds her father also had a secret passion and left behind a tale of a man she didn't truly know.

George Frederick McKenry never left the Midwest town where he was born other than brief travels with his four children, who he now has custody of since his ex moved into a condo with her new boyfriend. Running into the one girl from school who rebuffed him when he asked her out, G.F. can't help checking on her and making sure she's getting along alright. False assumptions and past resentments fade as Fran and G.F. let down their guards in order to create new memories.

~~

Shadows of Blues & Echoes (2016)
Artists & Cottages Series

Gillian Hart has big ambitions while working as a reporter for a small circulation paper in Denver, Colorado. When her editor and friend assigns a story about some rich businessman who chucks it all to live in the woods alone outside Durango, she does her best to fight it. With no choice but to give in, Gillian determines to use it as a stepping stone.

Hank Dennison wants nothing but solitude while he recovers from a life-changing devastation he has managed to hide from the public. The last thing he wants is another nosy journalist badgering him, especially one who knows nothing about survival in the wilderness and taxes his waning strength. Noticing the darkness of depression that weighs her down, despite her attempt to hide it, Hank determines to keep her off the path that led him to his own illness.

~~

Shadows of Rust & Reels (2017)
Artists & Cottages Series

By day, Holli Jacoby is a jewelry artist in her hometown of Williamstown, West Virginia. Abandoned by her family, Holli mainly stays to herself, preferring her potter's wheel to the risk of letting others see, and take advantage of, the uncontrollable effects of her bipolar disorder.

Isaac Bradshaw is a welder who spends much of his off time assisting his parents due to his father's declining health. While playing pool, he notices a fiery brunette eye him as though she knows him. He soon learns "fiery" is an understatement, and his buddy warns him against the girl, but something keeps him drawn to her.

Despite their earlier crossed paths and a shared love of adventure, Holli's roller coaster life might be more than Isaac is willing to handle. When the bottom falls out beneath her, their relationship hits a critical test.

~~

A Melody in the Dark (2017)
Singers & Songwriters series (a prequel novella)
published by Fire Star Press as part of the *Music of the Heart* anthology

Meladee Lerner is a single mom and struggling songwriter who moved to Pittsburgh to escape a marriage she didn't want. It's 1979, just after the big snow storm that paralyzed the city, when they run into Niall Dillon, a hard-working young Pittsburgher with strong Irish roots. Niall is making plans to travel the US on his own, but one eventful night gives him second thoughts.

~~ ~~ ~~

Watch for more books from both series, as well as from the new Singers & Songwriters series, coming 2019.